Cynthia Hickey

WORTHY

The Pretty Must Die, the complete story

By Cynthia Hickey

ISBN-10:1-944203-43-5

ISBN-13:978-1-944203-43-6

DEDICATION

To God for all the ideas, to my husband for his support, and to the best readers in the world…mine!

PROLOGUE

Twenty-five years earlier

"I'm not interested in going to a frat party." Maureen Monroe opened her beloved copy of *Gone With the Wind* and settled in for a night with her favorite southern belle.

"Stop being a party pooper." Allison lifted her bangs, sprayed them with hairspray, and then attacked the strands with a hair dryer.

Maureen peered over the top of the book. "Why do you want to go anywhere looking like a rooster?"

"It's the style." She grinned. "Blake will be there."

"Still not interested."

"Come on." She faced Maureen. "He's a fox, and definitely interested in you."

"You aren't going to leave me alone, are you?" Maureen sighed and closed her book. "I'm not into the whole college party scene."

"You should have some fun before you graduate and start hunting down the bad guys."

She groaned and got off her twin bed and headed for the closet. The night was warm, perfect for the new sundress she'd bought from a nearby thrift store. She changed her clothes and pushed Allison away from the mirror. A quick brush of her red hair and a smattering of lipgloss was good enough for her. "I'm ready."

"That's it?" Allison pouted. "I hate how pretty you are with so little effort."

"Good genes." Maureen slipped her feet into a pair of flat sandals. "Hurry up before I change my mind." Allison slung a strappy purse over her shoulder and headed out the door, leaving Maureen to follow.

They traipsed across campus to a field on the outskirts where music blared from boom boxes, laughter filled the air, and already drunk frat boys flirted with anything in a skirt. Maureen plastered a smile on her face and headed to the punch bowl.

One sniff told her it was already spiked. She grabbed a glass of water instead and turned to survey the crowd.

"Hey, gorgeous!" Blake slung an arm around her shoulders. "Smile for the camera."

Someone snapped their picture.

"Come dance with me."

"You're drunk." Whiskey fumes stung her nostrils.

"Not very." He grabbed her hand and dragged her to a patch of packed down dirt. A slow song started on the radio, and he plastered her against him, leaning heavily on her shoulders.

"Seriously, Blake, I'm not in the mood."

His eyes narrowed. "I'm the envy of every man here."

"So?" She shrugged out of his arms. "There are plenty of pretty girls here dying to dance with you."

"I don't want them." He pouted like a little boy who'd had his favorite toy taken away. "I want you."

"I need to go to the bathroom." She headed for a port-a-potty.

He jogged after her.

As she reached for the handle on the plastic door, he grabbed her hand and dragged her into the bushes. "Blake!"

"I know what will get you in the mood." He nuzzled her neck.

"What have I ever done to give you the impression I'm this type of girl?" She shoved against his chest.

"Plenty," he growled, pushing her farther into the trees.

Before she could scream, she found herself flat on her back in the leaves, something sharp poking her in the thigh. "What's in your pocket?"

"My knife. I don't go anywhere without it," he muttered against her lips. "Relax."

"I'll scream."

He clapped a hand over her mouth. "You can't tease a man the way you do and not expect repercussions."

She bucked under him. Her heart hammered against her chest, her breathing rapid.

He fumbled with the zipper on his jeans, then thrust her dress over her head, shoving part of it into her mouth as a gag.

Whimpering, she continued to fight, struggling to reach the knife in his pocket. Anything to keep him from doing what he planned. She screamed behind the gag as he succeeded, then closed her eyes against the attack. When he collapsed on top of her, she grabbed the knife and slashed, thrusting her dress out of her face.

The knife dug deep into the side of his face.

He howled.

She screamed and rolled him off her, his blood splashing onto her bare arms and chest.

"Hey!" Three college students barged onto the scene.

Blake cupped his torn face. "I'll kill you." He pulled up his pants and fled.

Maureen rolled into a ball and sobbed. One of the other men scooped her into his arms. She closed her eyes and gave into the darkness.

1

"Why are you doing this to me?" The beautiful brunette stared up at him with tear-filled eyes.

He tightened the zip tie. "The pretty must die."

"What? Why?" She sobbed. "What are you going to do to me?"

Hadn't his response to her first question told her what was on his mind? Stupidity was one of the reasons he had to kill her...and those like her. The world was filled with people who thought their good looks allowed them to trod over those less attractive and more intelligent. No more! He would rid the world of pretty people, starting with those in Clear Springs, Arkansas.

She kicked at him before he could tie her feet. One of her stilettos clipped his chin, cutting the skin. She struggled to her feet and tottered into the bushes.

He shook his head and swiped the back of his hand across the bleeding cut. She could try to run, but he would catch her. Then, she would pay for all the pain he had experienced in his life.

With a sigh, he pushed to his feet and headed after the woman, grabbing the high heel that had clipped him from the dirt. If she lost the other one, the chase would be more challenging. His heart rate accelerated in anticipation. The victims always ran. His mother had run, then screamed, until he silenced her forever. The only one who hadn't was Maureen. Dear, stupid, teasing Maureen.

His victim's red dress flashed through the trees. She tripped and fell. He lunged forward, grabbing her hair. With one slash of his razor-sharp knife, he rid the world of one more pretty person who thought most people didn't matter. His spirit soared with a hawk circling above the forest.

~

Cassidy Monroe slid her police issued Glock 19 into its holster and rushed out the police department front door. A homicide call warranted quick action before bumbling sightseers ruined the crime scene. "Detective Monroe is headed to the site," she radioed the one and only other officer in Clear Springs: a new man she had yet to meet since he was assigned to their small office that morning after Cassidy's former partner took a job in Little Rock. Before that, she'd worked solo for almost a year. Something she had preferred.

"I'm already here. The body is by the creek. Take the road right past mile marker 59." His deep voice—was that a Scottish accent?—rippled over the airwaves.

She shook her head and slid behind the wheel of her older model jeep. While she was glad not to be the only officer in their small town, she didn't like being one-upped by the new guy. She set a flashing light in the front window of her vehicle and sped toward the woods. Why did she have to have a partner? In a town as small as Clear Springs, Arkansas, it was quite manageable to work separately.

Twenty minutes later, her jeep bounced down a rutted path barely recognizable as a road. She stopped next to a brand new Ford pickup and cut the ignition. Grabbing her camera and aluminum forensic case, she slid from the jeep and jogged through the trees.

A tall, dark-haired man with eyes the color of a summer sky and a smile that would melt butter, turned to greet her. For the first time in as long as she could remember, she regretted wearing faded jeans and a tee shirt with a small hole under the arm.

"You must be my partner, Cassidy Monroe." He thrust out his hand, his brogue shooting straight to her heart and sending fire through her limbs.

"Yes, and, uh, you are Colin MacKenzie?" She yanked her gaze from his and focused on the body next to the creek. Since when did her smart mouth get tongue-tied?

"Sorry we haven't met before now." Colin squatted next to her. "The call came through before I made it to the office."

"That's fine." Cassidy was at work early every morning and always had her cell phone on for calls that came through during the night.

The body, throat cut, blood soaking into the moss under the victim, was clothed in a scarlet dress. A matching stiletto was placed on a nearby log. Even in death the woman's beauty was easy to see.

"Do we have an ID?" Cassidy snapped a photo, then moved to take one from another angle.

"Yes." Colin motioned to a sequined clutch next to the log. "Amber Wilson, a model from Los Angeles who is here visiting relatives. There are signs of a struggle and evidence to show that she ran from her pursuer. There's something over here that you should see."

Cassidy joined him at the water's edge. Written in the dirt were the words, "The pretty must die."

"That doesn't sound as if our killer will stop with Amber." Her blood chilled.

The only deaths they'd had to deal with in their town prior to this were accidental shootings and car accidents. She wasn't equipped to deal with a serial killer, if this is what they had. She shook her head to clear it. One poor dead woman didn't mean they had a sicko on their hands. It could just as easily have been an angry boyfriend that killed her. "Where's the other shoe?"

"Haven't located it yet."

The sound of voices pulled her from her thoughts. Sarah Robertson, local reporter and all around gossip, teetered toward them on high heels. "Keep her back," Cassidy ordered Colin. "She has no sense around a crime scene."

His brow furrowed, no doubt unhappy that she had told him to keep the woman back, but until Cassidy knew what kind of a cop he was, she was remaining in control. Handsome men, in her experience, were most often more worried about how they looked than working hard. Cassidy prided herself on her no-nonsense approach to fashion. Comfortable clothes, gym shoes, and hair pulled back into a ponytail was her daily uniform.

She finished processing the scene as the EMTs arrived. She stood and glanced around to make sure she didn't miss anything important. The area was clean. No footprints. Broken branches that showed the path the victim had fled. No torn fabric or strands of hair on low-hanging branches. Finding the culprit was going to be a challenge.

Colin flirted and kept Sarah occupied, his laugh rumbling across the clearing. Cassidy sighed. She leaned against a tree and waited while the EMTs bagged the body and loaded it onto a portable gurney. Since they knew the victim's identity, the next stop would be to her family. A job Cassidy hated. Their grief always sent her heart spiraling to the pit of her stomach and resulted in her shedding tears into her pillow at night.

"Come on, Don Juan." She motioned for Colin to follow her. "We have work to do."

"Could I get a statement, Detective?" Sarah trotted next to her.

"Didn't Detective MacKenzie tell you anything?" She glanced at Colin.

"No. The man is as handsome as Adonis and as tight-lipped as a clam."

"I can't tell you anything until we notify the family." Cassidy headed for her jeep. "Call me this afternoon."

"Thanks, Cassidy. Bye, Colin," she said in a singsong voice. "You owe me a drink."

Cassidy groaned and climbed into her jeep. "Meet me at the station," she said before closing her door. They might as well ride together from then on out.

~

Working with Cassidy wasn't going to be a hardship. Colin noticed right away that she was thorough and good at her job, not to mention beautiful, despite the plain Jane way she dressed.

He opened the passenger door of her jeep and slid inside. "Would you like me to break the news to the family?"

"I can do it." Her hands trembled as she placed them on the steering wheel.

"I don't mind. I have a degree in psychology."

"Really?" She cast him a surprised look.

"And dual citizenship, not to mention I speak French and Spanish." He grinned. "I'm more than a pretty face."

She rolled her eyes and drove from the parking lot. "Spare me. I'm more interested in your mind and how well you can do your job. It doesn't matter to me what you look like."

He laughed. "You're going to be more fun than my old partner. He was past retirement age, overweight, and more interested in doing paperwork than chasing the bad guys."

"He probably just wanted to live long enough to receive his pension." She glanced at the navigator in her jeep. "You can do the talking with the family."

He nodded and stared out the window, remembering how her amazing green eyes had shadowed over when the subject of visiting the family was broached. It was low on his list of pleasant things to do, but perhaps his offer would soften his new partner's heart toward him. He'd like to be friends with her. He had so few in the States, having left his family behind in Scotland, and turning down a job with Scotland Yard. Killing an innocent young woman would do that to a person.

Funny how life worked. He'd accepted the job in a small Arkansas town to take things easy and found his first case to be a murder. He rubbed his chin, noting he'd forgotten to shave. Life had a strange way of putting a person right smack dab in the middle of something they had no desire to be in.

They stopped in front of a white ranch style house on the outskirts of town. Colin took a deep breath and shoved open his door. What he and Cassidy had to do was nothing compared to what the family would feel.

Taking a deep breath, he rang the doorbell. A middle-aged woman, looking like an older model of the victim, greeted them with a smile.

Colin showed his badge. "May we come in?"

She grabbed her throat, eyes wide, and nodded. "Mark, the police are here."

A thin man, well over six feet tall, a cup of coffee in his hand, joined them in the foyer. "What's my girl done now?"

"Is there somewhere we can sit and talk?" Cassidy asked, stepping next to the wife.

Mrs. Wilson nodded. "This isn't good, is it?"

"No, ma'am." Cassidy took her by the arm and steered her into a modern styled living room.

Once the parents were seated, Colin perched on the sofa next to them. "We'll need a positive identification, but we believe we found Amber's body in the woods. Her identification was close by."

"Drugs?" Mr. Wilson asked, his words shaky.

"No, sir." Colin kept his eyes fixed on the man's, willing

strength into him. "She was murdered. I'm so sorry. When was the last time you saw your daughter?"

"Last night. She said she was going to a party," he said. His chin quivered.

"We hated those parties," Mrs. Wilson sobbed. "Once she moved to California to pursue modeling, she got involved in all kinds of things no decent girl should be involved in. Now, she's gone and there is no way she can change her path." She covered her face with her hands.

"Could the things she was involved in have caused someone to kill her?" Colin laid a hand over Mr. Wilson's.

"Here in Clear Springs? I don't see how. The friends she left here are good kids, for the most part."

"But your first statement upon hearing she was dead was to ask if drugs were involved." Colin glanced at Cassidy.

"Some pot. That's all we've ever found her to use here, but out there...in that...place, well, she spent some time in rehab for harder stuff." The pain in the man's eyes was almost Colin's undoing.

He fished a business card from his pocket. "If you think of anything else, anything at all, don't hesitate to call. We'll be back tomorrow to look through her things. Maybe we'll find a clue as to who wanted to harm her. Also, if you could get us a list of her friends here in town, that might help."

Mrs. Wilson nodded. "We'll head to the morgue right away. My poor baby.

Back outside, Cassidy faced Colin. "We should check her room now."

"Let them grieve. We'll be back in the morning."

"What if something is disturbed?" She crossed her arms. "What if they know her murderer and hide evidence?"

"I can sense things about people." He opened the car door for her. "They are nothing more than grieving parents. Let them be. Besides," he grinned, "we have her cell phone. You can spend the next few hours going through her phone log. Come on. We have a killer to catch."

2

"For a pretty girl, she didn't get many calls." Cassidy nursed a cup of coffee while Colin scanned printouts of Amber's phone log.

"How long ago did she leave here?" He peered over the papers. "Maybe she cut her ties so badly no one wanted to remain friends."

Cassidy shrugged. "Maybe." In her experience, the beautiful, popular people were usually surrounded by not-so-true friends. Other than a couple of calls to her modeling agency in California over two weeks ago, Amber's phone was disturbingly empty. "We'll send it to the forensic analyst in Little Rock. They might be able to retrieve something."

"Hmm." Colin leaned back in his chair. "It's possible the killer deleted most of the messages. The question is why?"

"Do you think she was a random target?" Cassidy didn't think so. Instinct told her she knew her killer, at least for a short while before her death. Who in Clear Springs would want the beautiful dead? Someone tormented by them?

"I don't think so, and I don't think she met that person while she was wearing that red gown, either. I'm still puzzled as to why she had only one shoe. Do you think her killer took the other as a souvenir?" Colin stared out the small office window. "Are there any modeling agencies around here?"

Cassidy shook her head and reached for yesterday's newspaper. "Find someone to get us a copy of every paper printed this week. Maybe our killer placed an advertisement that Amber couldn't resist."

She watched him leave the room. Colin was the epitome of tall, dark, and handsome, towering over her five foot three frame by a foot. His eyes, a starburst of dark and light blue, oh, yes, she had noticed, pierced through to her soul while having the ability to soften and console grieving parents.

What was God thinking to make such a man her partner? Cassidy needed to focus on her job. She glanced at the framed photo of her mother, murdered in cold blood ten years before. She needed to bring her mother's killer to justice. Her case had been cold for too long. Cassidy sighed. She was no closer to solving the death today then she was on her first day as a cop.

"A very distraught mother brought this in." Laura, the overworked receptionist of the tiny police office set a sheet of lined paper on Cassidy's desk. "She said you were waiting for it."

"Thank you." Cassidy scanned the paper. On it was five names. Written across the top was the heading "Amber's friends". *Thank you, Mrs. Wilson.* At least now they had a place to start.

"Here are the newspapers." Colin dropped them on her desk and leaned over her shoulder.

Her senses went into overdrive at his musky cologne. "Ah, the friends."

"Yes." She handed him the list and reached for a paper, flipping to the classifieds.

On the third paper, Wednesday's edition, she found the first clue to help them solve Amber's murder. "Colin, listen… Needed. A beautiful woman to act as model for evening gown advertisement. Audition in person at …" She read off the address. "That's a warehouse by the river. Let's go." She grabbed her holster from the back of her chair and dashed from the building, followed closely by Colin.

He snatched the keys from her hand, flashing her a wide smile. "I'll drive."

She rolled her eyes and changed direction to the front passenger seat. It was her jeep. She should be the one driving. "Don't do that again," she said, fastening her seatbelt.

"I don't like being the passenger."

"Neither do I." She glared to show him she meant business, then stared out the window as he drove from the parking lot.

"Don't pout."

She whipped back to face him. "I don't pout."

"Yes, you do."

"Whatever." Having him as her partner was going to be a job in itself. She needed to get him trained, and soon. Her last partner had been more than happy to let her call the shots.

"It looks deserted." Colin cut the ignition.

"It's most likely a dead end, but we have to check it out." Cassidy unholstered her weapon and pushed open her door.

"I'll enter first." Colin held out his hand. "Please."

She stared into his face, noting a shadow of pain flicker across his eyes. Chivalry, and something else, was alive and well in Arkansas.

Guns held at the ready, they approached a metal door to the side of a larger rolling door. Cassidy gave Colin a nod as he turned the door handle. The door swung open with a groan.

Colin took a deep breath and stepped in. Cassidy followed, then moved to his side.

As suspected, the warehouse was devoid of life. Their footsteps echoed in the cavernous room. In a far corner draped a curtain. A tripod lay on its side. The type of lights used by photographers were placed around the photography area. Footprints marred the dust.

Cassidy squinted, making out something pinned to the backdrop. She moved closer. A photo of a smiling, posing Amber wearing the dress they'd found her in was taped there. The killer had lured the girl here, then taken her to the woods and murdered her. "I doubt he'll use this place again."

"You think he plans on killing again?" Colin slid his gun into its holster.

"I know he will." She reached a trembling hand toward the photo. "I've seen his setup before."

He narrowed his eyes. "Explain."

"This is the same man that murdered my mother."

In the case files were crime scene photos of this exact scene, but in a different location. Always beautiful, Cassidy's mother had gone undercover as a model to catch a man who preyed on women who loved the camera. He'd never been caught.

~

"I'll get your bag out of the car. We need to process the scene." Colin jogged outside, giving Cassidy a few minutes to compose herself. He had a lot of questions that needed answers, but they would wait. He pulled her aluminum case from the trunk. By the time he joined her, she stood ramrod straight, her features composed.

She took the case from him and got to work. Colin was perceptive if nothing else. She still needed time. He was fine with it.

While she snapped pictures of the scene, he squatted next to the footprints. They weren't looking for a small man. The prints were as large as the ones Colin left, putting the unsub at six feet tall, at least. He'd read Cassidy's file. He was familiar with her mother's case. How had the murderer escaped capture for so many years?

He straightened. "Do you think that perhaps the unsub doesn't live in Clear Springs? Maybe he returns for an anniversary of some kind."

Cassidy glanced his way. "Since my mother, we haven't had anything like this happen again until now. That was ten years ago."

"There has to be a trigger. A killer doesn't stay dormant for ten years, then kill again unless something pulled him out." He stared at Cassidy. "You just had a birthday."

"Yeah, so?" She slid her camera back in her case, then jerked upright. "I'm the same age my mother was when she died. You think I'm the trigger? The target?"

He scanned the loose pants and baggy blouse she wore. "You're beautiful enough, but other than that, you don't fit the profile of his victims. That's why you downplay your looks. Because your mother was killed for hers."

"How I dress is no concern of yours." She headed for the door.

"I'm right, aren't I?" He moved in front of her.

"Move." She shoved past him. Her actions were answer enough.

Colin strung crime scene tape across the warehouse entrances before joining Cassidy at the jeep. He wanted to press for information; make her see he was right. And, if he was, she was in grave danger. The killer could be coming after her.

She slid behind the steering wheel and gave him a defiant look. Fine, he'd let her drive, but they were not finished with their discussion.

"Let's grab something to eat before visiting the people on the friends list."

"A burger okay?"

"Sounds great." He settled in and kept his mouth shut for the next fifteen minutes. They would be spending a lot of time together. He'd get the answers he wanted…in time.

"Bill's has the best burgers." Cassidy stopped in front of a barn-like building.

Colin's stomach rumbled. Dives usually had the best food, and he'd skipped breakfast. He slid from the jeep and held the diner door open. Once Cassidy was relaxed with good food, he'd grill her for more information. If she remained tight-lipped, he'd spend some more time immersed in her mother's cold case.

A waitress led them to a booth in front of a large plate-glass window. Colin waited until Cassidy was seated, then slid across from her. He pretended to peruse the menu when he actually studied her.

The vibrant red hair, dark green eyes, straight nose and full lips. Even without makeup and her hair sloppily piled on top of her head, she was stunning. If she were the target, why had the unsub killed Amber? Why not go after Cassidy years ago after killing her mother?

"You know the unsub." He dropped the menu on the table.

She sighed. "I've thought so, too, but can't think of a single person who wanted my mother dead." She shook her head. "She went undercover to find the person killng models. That's where she met him. I don't think he's a family friend."

"Did you meet anyone new while she was undercover?"

"I don't think so. I was fifteen years old." She raised cold eyes to him. "I have no idea whether my mother brought her work home with her. There wasn't a parade of men coming through our home."

He held up his hands in defense. "I'm sorry. That's not what I meant at all."

"I didn't take unnecessary offense." She stiffened. "Mom never brought anyone home. She said all she needed was me and her job. I don't think I've met the killer."

The waitress arrived to take their orders, thus giving him a few moments to rethink his direction of questioning. After they both ordered cheeseburger meals, he rested his arms on the table and kept his gaze locked on Cassidy's face. His best intense stare usually worked on those he questioned.

Cassidy rolled her eyes. "Cut it out. I can give that look with the best of them."

He laughed and straightened. "I'm only trying to help you. It's quite possible that, by solving Amber's murder, we also solve your mother's."

"That would be convenient."

"You're a prickly gal, aren't you? I'm not the enemy, you know."

She sighed. "I'm sorry. I spent three years of my life in foster care. I don't trust easily."

"And I come across a bit strong."

"A bit." Her eyes softened, the corners of her mouth easing into a smile. "I'll try and think harder about who I might know. That's all I can promise."

"That's all I ask. That you don't discount the possibility that your mother angered someone badly enough that they would resurface, and possibly be coming after you."

~

He stared at the ten faces in front of him and smiled. Not one of them could be considered good-looking. One or two mildly attractive, maybe. All had responded to his post on a hard-to-find chat room and a personal ad in the newspaper about being mistreated by those whom society looked upon favorably. After a period of testing, he would find his worthy followers. Outcasts willing to help him in his quest.

"All of those who have ridiculed us, beaten us down, bullied us because they deem themselves better than us based upon our looks must be dealt with." He ran a finger down the scar that ran from his right eye to his mouth. "They must pay for their crimes against us. If you do not have the stomach for revenge, you are free to go. Now."

One man, slight in build, stood. "I thought this was a support group. Sorry, but this isn't for me." He glanced around the room. "May God have mercy on all of you." He spun and almost ran from the room.

Draco, the name he had given himself, the name for Dragon, laughed. The man had made his choice and would be dealt with later. The dragon left no witnesses. Made no excuses for his plans. He definitely didn't call upon a God who had cursed him in love.

"Is there anyone else who feels that my quest is unjust? Is there anyone else willing to remain in the shadow of conceit and be stomped upon? If so, leave now. Once you begin your training, the only way out is through the fire of my wrath. I have designed special coats with colors of protection once you have proven yourselves worthy." He motioned to leather jackets hanging on the wall. "There is a gold bowl on the stand in front of me. Write on slips of paper all those who have wronged you and they will be dealt with. Everything you need to start over afterward is in the packet under your seat."

The remaining nine, seven men and two women, stayed seated, their faces a mixture of hope and the desire for revenge. Once Draco finished with them, they would all want those who had tormented them to die, and he would help them. They would love him. He would become their hero.

3

Cassidy poured coffee from the pitcher into a mug and handed it to Colin. If they started pursuing the track of the unsub being the same person who murdered her mother, they might miss a clue leading to who killed Amber. She couldn't risk that. The poor girl deserved justice. Still, the lure of finding her mother's killer...

"I can practically see the wheels turning in your head." Colin leaned back in his chair and propped his feet on the desk. "Want to talk about it?"

"No." Cassidy took her seat and rifled through the few envelopes on her desk. With her and Colin as the only two police officers in town, some days the mail piled up. She'd once tried to have the receptionist wade through it, but some of the darker "fan" mail they received sent the poor woman into fits.

She spotted a plain white envelope with the address being glued on letters from a magazine. "Got something."

After pulling on a pair of rubber gloves, she slit the envelope with a letter opener. "It's a poem" The yellowed page signified the sender had ripped it from an old book.

She Walks in Beauty
By Lord Byron

She walks in beauty, like the night
Of cloudless climes and starry skies;
And all that's best of dark and bright
Meet in her aspect and her eyes:
Thus mellow'd to that tender light
Which heaven to gaudy day denies.

One shade the more, one ray the less,
Had half impaired the nameless grace
Which waves in every raven tress,
Or softly lightens o'er her face;
Where thoughts serenely sweet express
How pure, how dear their dwelling-place.

And on that cheek, and o'er that brow,
So soft, so calm, yet eloquent,
The smiles that win, the tints that glow,
But tell of days in goodness spent,
A mind at peace with all below,
A heart whose love is innocent!

Colin peered over her shoulder. "He has seen through your attempts to hide how attractive you are."

"I'm not hiding anything." She slid the page into a bag and yanked off her gloves. "I simply find it easier to wear comfortable clothes and have a non-fussy hairstyle."

"No, you're definitely hiding." He perched on the corner of her desk. "Now, me...I choose to embrace my handsomeness." A dimple winked near the right corner of his mouth. "People tend to talk to those who make an effort."

Cassidy rolled her eyes and tore her gaze away from lips that looked as if they would kiss with little provocation. She didn't scare easily, but ice ran through her veins. Would the unsub come after her or was the poem nothing more than a note from an admirer? Could it be that the killer admired Cassidy's way of downplaying her looks or was he toying with her?

Yes, she tried to hide how pretty she was, despite her saying otherwise. Beauty had gotten her mother killed. Now, possibly the same man was bent on erasing more beautiful women from the earth. Downplaying her looks helped her get the job done. She definitely didn't need the distraction of admiring glances from men while women were dying.

"We need to send this to the lab in Little Rock." She handed the bag containing the poem to Colin. "I doubt they'll find anything, but we can always hope."

Something that seemed in short supply lately. Hope. It had done nothing for her mother, a devout churchgoer, nor Cassidy's father who had died when she was too young to remember him. The song phrase that only the good die young ran through her head.

The phone rang. She answered it as Colin left the room. "Officer Monroe."

"Detective?" Laura's voice wavered. "You have a call on line one. Some hikers found another body."

"Thank you, Laura. I'll take it."

She pressed the button on the phone for line one. "Officer Monroe." She listened as a very excited woman explained how she and her girlfriend were hiking and stumbled across a woman tied to a tree. Hanging up, Cassidy grabbed her shoulder holster and dashed off to find her partner.

"Colin, we've got another one." She raced past where he leaned over the receptionist desk, flirting as usual. What would it be like to be so sure of oneself? By the time he joined her, she was behind the wheel of her jeep with the engine running.

He slid into the passenger seat and clicked his seatbelt into place. "You know, my truck is newer." He raised his eyebrows. "Another one in two days?"

"We don't know it's the same guy." She turned onto Main Street and headed for the popular hiking trail on the mountain. "And I prefer my jeep."

He shrugged. "Not yet, but we'll see that it is."

"Are you always this sure of yourself?"

"Always." He cut her a sideways glance.

She wished she were. Cassidy was a good detective, she'd been told so many times, but still that niggling in the back of her mind told her she wasn't good enough. Not good enough for her mother to stay alive, not good enough to have found a permanent family after her death, and now…what if she weren't good enough to catch a potential serial killer?

She parked the jeep alongside the hiking trail and cast a glance at two hysterical women who approached at a run. She took a step back.

"I'll take care of this." Colin grinned and motioned for the women to step beside the jeep.

"Thank you." Calming distraught people was not anywhere close to the top of things Cassidy was good at. She opened the back of the jeep and grabbed her crime scene case.

With one last look at Colin, who had managed to find bottles of water somewhere and offered them to the women, she headed down the trail. Sunlight filtered through tree tops, giving the illusion of a perfect autumn day. The body tied to a tree belied that fact.

"Lizzie Borden took an ax." Cassidy pulled on a pair of gloves, then placed a number beside the bloody murder weapon and snapped a photo before turning back to the victim. "And gave her mother forty whacks."

While the first victim had her throat slit, this one had taken many whacks of an ax to her head and torso almost rendering her features unrecognizable. She shook her head and squatted next to a beaded red purse that matched the woman's gown. If not for the red clothing, she might have thought they were dealing with another perpetrator.

She rifled through the evening purse and pulled out the woman's driver's license. "Pretty. Samantha Meyers" Of course, she would be. Someone wanted all the pretty people dead. The poor girl was nineteen years old and from Oklahoma. What was she doing on a mountain top in Arkansas?

"And when she saw what she had done, she gave her father forty-one."

"Nursery rhymes?" Colin squatted next to her.

"Came to mind when I entered the crime scene." Cassidy handed him the license. "See if you can find out if anyone in Lawton reported this poor girl missing." She straightened and scanned the scene. Something didn't make sense. Why slit one girl's throat and go to such extremes with this one?

"This girl was reported missing yesterday." Colin snapped his cell phone closed. "She disappeared from a party." He glanced around the area. "What are you thinking?"

"That we're dealing with more than one killer."

"Hmm." He stared into the trees. "It's possible. But what would be the motivation?"

"That's what we need to figure out." She sighed. "It's time to bring in the FBI."

He groaned. "They'll take over."

"True, but we need all the help we can get." She dug out her cell phone as the ambulance arrived, sirens wailing. "What about the two who found her?"

"They're waiting for us at the station. I hope you don't mind that I put a case of bottled water in the backseat this morning. If we're going to be taking your car most of the time—"

She waved off his explanation. "It came in handy." She placed a call to the FBI, explaining the two murders, then hung up. "They'll get back to us later."

~

Draco watched from a thick stand of trees as the one he loved and admired found his latest gift to her. Not that Draco personally killed the woman, no, not this one, but he had guided his prodigy. Too bad the silly woman had gone so far overboard in her killing. Still, practice made perfect. Her motive had been warranted.

One day, the pretty people of the world would learn that treating those less attractive with scorn and rudeness had terrible consequences. Someday, they would bow before Draco and his kind. He traced the scar on his face with his forefinger. Just as his love had done minutes before her death. Tears and pleas didn't work to sway one as powerful as he.

The object of his desire turned and stared in his direction. Not that she could see him until he willed it, but he melted further into the shadows, freeing the tail of his shirt from the eager clutches of a bush. Their day would come.

~

Back at the office, Colin tapped a pencil on his desk and stared at the case board. Two deaths in two days. Both beautiful women in red evening gowns. No suspects. He studied his partner.

Cassidy had stood for ten minutes, staring at the board, unmoving, as if she could will a clue to be there that wasn't. He'd read her file. He knew how good she was at what she did, but this time...they were in over their heads.

He straightened and stopped tapping as three agents, all in dark suits, entered the tiny office. The tallest, a large African American, approached Colin. "I'm Agent Ingram, these are Agents Smith and Weston. No wisecracks, please."

Colin stood and shook his hand. "Wouldn't think of it. I'm

Detective Colin MacKenzie and this is Detective Cassidy Monroe, head detective on the case."

Cassidy turned, gave them a nod, and resumed studying the board. "I'm guessing you will want to move to the conference room? It isn't much larger, but we can squeeze in."

Agent Ingram returned her nod. "Are you the Colin MacKenzie that turned down working for the FBI?"

"One and the same." Colin took a deep breath.

Cassidy turned and stared.

He shrugged. "I prefer to dabble in computers in my spare time. Pounding the pavements is more my style." When the FBI asked him to sit at a desk all day and search for cyber crime he had turned them down. Sure, he still searched the internet on his off hours, sometimes sending something suspicious their way, but that type of life wasn't for him.

"Our loss." Ingram motioned his head to the door. "Shall we?"

The other two agents wheeled the case board into the conference room, placing it against a far wall. Once everyone was inside, Cassidy told them of what had transpired over the last two days and her's and Colin's suspicions that they were looking at more than one killer.

Ingram nodded several times during Cassidy's speech. "Agent Weston will provide a press release and make a statement to the press. We'll notify the Lawton police and visit the latest victim's family."

Cassidy crossed her arms. "I do hope you will continue to let us investigate."

"Of course. You've had direct contact from the unsub. We'll keep all channels of communication open and will ask that you do the same. In fact, we insist the two of you follow any leads you may have." With a thin-lipped smile, the three agents left the room.

Follow the leads. He knew darn well they didn't have any. He was amusing himself with the fact Colin chose to hit the streets rather than work for the FBI. He met Cassidy's stern gaze. "Where to?"

"I want to revisit the crime scene. I feel like we're missing something." She grabbed a black hoodie from the back of a chair. "When we were out there before, I felt like we were being watched."

Colin froze mid-stride. "You think the unsub was there?"

"Not sure. It could be nothing more than the heebie jeebies from a dead body, but I'd still like to take a look."

Colin wasn't going to disregard her intuition. Life had taught him to listen to a woman's gut feeling. He dashed into their office long enough to grab a light jacket from the back of his chair and rushed to meet Cassidy at the jeep.

Rain fell in a steady stream, the autumn day dark and drab. Fitting for a murder scene. He clicked his seat belt into place and listened to the steady thump of the wiper blades. He almost requested they wait until the next day to search the woods, but if the rain continued for too long, any signs could be washed away. They couldn't take that chance.

"Why didn't you tell me you turned down the FBI?" Cassidy cut him a sideways glance.

"It was in my file."

"I didn't read your file."

"Maybe you should have." He quirked his mouth. "I read every page of yours."

She frowned. "Good for you." She turned down the road that led to the hiking trail. When they stopped, she grabbed her camera and case from the trunk, and headed into the trees.

Yellow crime scene tape sagged under the increasing rain. After slipping a protective cover over her phone, Cassidy pulled up her hood. She stepped to the edge of the crime scene and looked to her left.

"There," she said. "Earlier, I thought I heard something."

Colin unlatched his gun. "Let's take a closer look."

Shaking the rain from his hair, he led the way in the direction she pointed. He stopped a few feet into a thick stand of trees. "Someone stood here." He squatted. "See the prints? Looks like a size eleven gym shoe." Why hadn't she said something earlier?

"Here is a scrap of fabric. Could be from our unsub."

Colin stood. "If you thought someone was watching, why didn't you say anything?"

"I wasn't sure. It wasn't until I thought more about it that I remembered." She snapped a picture of the fabric on the branch, then used tweezers to pull it free. She dropped it into a small bag. "At first, I thought it nothing more than nerves."

"You've got good instincts, Cassidy. Trust them." He placed his foot beside the print while Cassidy took a picture. "Even if nothing pans out, go with every gut feeling."

"I usually do." She placed her camera and the scrap of fabric into her case. "A second murder in two days rattled me a bit. I'm focused now."

"It was the poem, not the dead body that threw you off kilter."

"Think what you want."

She sure was a prickly woman. As beautiful as the landscape of Scotland and as sharp as a thorn bush. He'd break through her defenses, eventually. He had to. They had to be able to trust each other. But, he had a feeling his partner trusted very few people.

He gave the area another quick scan, hoping they hadn't missed anything else. When the killer struck again, and Colin knew he, or she, would, he'd keep a sharp eye on their surroundings. If he showed up at one crime scene, he'd show up at another.

What was he looking for? Why hadn't he taken a shot at the officers? Did he get off on watching reactions to his deed? Possibly, but Colin thought it might be deeper than that. After the poem Cassidy received, he had a sinking feeling that the women might be some kind of sick, twisted gift for his partner.

4

Cassidy tossed her keys in the bowl on the foyer table and headed to the kitchen. Nothing ended a day on the job more than a glass of wine and a bowl of popcorn. She sipped her Moscato while she waited for the microwave to signal her meal was ready.

She'd messed up. When they'd examined the body that morning, and she'd felt eyes watching her, she should have investigated then, and not chalked it up to nerves and an over-active imagination. They'd lost valuable time. If she had taken her feeling to heart, the killer might be behind bars right that moment.

The microwave dinged, and she withdrew her supper. Maybe not the most nutritious meal, but it was her favorite. Popcorn and a drink was what she needed after the last two days.

She moved to the living room and turned on the television. Agent Weston stood behind a podium, alerting the town and surrounding areas to the possibility of a serial killer in their midst. She was good, telling them what they needed to know, but not giving so much information that she jeopardized the investigation.

Cassidy sat on the sofa and balanced the bowl of popcorn on her lap. Colin could have been one of the agents in charge. Why be content to work for a small town police force? Cassidy would give her eye teeth for an FBI offer. Her partner was definitely an enigma. Just when she thought she had him figured out, he surprised her. It seemed Colin MacKenzie might be more than a handsome face and a killer smile. Too bad she only wanted to know enough about him to work with him.

Popcorn and glass of wine finished, she turned off the television and climbed the stairs to her room. She placed her holster and gun on the bed, then whipped off her shirt. She froze.

The closet door was open about two inches. Meticulous to a fault, Cassidy had a place for everything in her house and never left doors open that were meant to be closed.

She slowly slid her weapon from its holster. Mouth as dry as desert sand, she soft-footed her way to the closet and whipped the door open. Empty, except for jeans, tee shirts, and her few dressier items of clothing. She turned a slow circle in her room. Nothing seemed out of place. Her few pieces of jewelry rested in a crystal candy dish on the dresser. The latest crime novel she was reading sat on the nightstand.

She moved to the bathroom. Towels hung straight, hygiene products in place. Had she been so preoccupied with yesterday's murder that she hadn't noticed her open closet? There was a first time for everything, her old partner used to say. Still, the fact that something seemed off wouldn't leave her. She wouldn't brush it off as she had that morning. Instead, she did a thorough sweep of her home…and found nothing amiss.

There was no other explanation. She was getting sloppy.

Back in her room, she flopped across the bed and stared at the ceiling. She had to have left the closet door open. Her windows were locked, so were her doors. Had her mind been so consumed with the case that she'd forgotten parts of her morning routine?

Ugh. She got up and headed for the bathroom. After turning on the water, she got undressed, dropping her clothes on the floor. She reached over and closed and locked the bathroom door. If someone had gotten into her house, she definitely didn't want to be caught naked.

Her cell phone rang from the nightstand in the bedroom. They could leave a message. She stepped under the hot spray of the faucet and closed her eyes. A big mistake. The faces of the two victims swam across her eyelids.

What if the man who killed them really was the same one who had taken her mother's life? Was it possible that after all these years, her mother's case would finally be solved?

She lathered her hair and turned her back to the faucet. Was Colin right and the perp was fixated on Cassidy? Why? She didn't fit the profile of the victims. Well, not in her day-to-day life. If she dressed nice and put on makeup, she would be just as pretty. She rinsed and turned off the water. Others in law enforcement wouldn't take her seriously if she looked like a Barbie doll.

Still…a momentary thought of luring the perp from hiding by upping her looks flitted across her mind and was quickly dismissed. Jeans and sweatpants were better suited for a law officer in the small town of Clear Springs.

Her cell phone rang again. She sighed, wrapped a towel around her, and hurried to answer it. The caller hung up before she could press the button.

"Why aren't you answering your phone?"

She grabbed her gun and whirled, keeping a tight hold of her towel. "Colin! I could have shot you." She narrowed her eyes. "How did you get in here?"

"I picked your lock." He leaned against the doorjamb, looking as delicious as a slice of chocolate cake. "You don't have a very good security system."

"Why are you here?" She set her gun back on the stand and headed for the bathroom.

"You didn't answer your phone."

She rolled her eyes and slammed the door. Of all the nerve. A smile teased at her lips. The wide-eyed look on his face at seeing her in nothing but a towel almost made her forget her anger. Almost. Darn. She'd forgotten to grab clothes.

She opened the door an inch. "Could you hand me those clothes over the back of the chair, please?"

"You sleep in gym shorts?" He squeezed them through the crack in the door. "Not very sexy."

"No one to impress." She quickly got dressed and ran a brush through her hair. She stepped out of the bathroom and glared. "Explain again why you're here?"

"Oh." He pulled a folded sheet of paper from his pocket. "I was doing some computer searching and ran across this website you might be interested in. Mind if I use your computer?"

"In here." She led him to the second bedroom which she used as a guest room, not that she ever had any guests, and an office. She flipped the top of the laptop and stepped aside.

Colin's fingers flew across the keyboard. What he pulled up make her stomach roll.

"How did you find this?" She watched in horror as the first victim, Amber Wilson, dashed through the forest, glancing with terror over her shoulder. The video went on to film her killer slash her throat.

"Here's the other one." Colin clicked to another link.

"My God." Cassidy's knees sagged. "Snuff films."

He nodded. "I'm not convinced the films are the reason for the murders, but merely a convenient means to let others enjoy the unsub's handiwork."

She leaned against the desk and put a hand over her face. Not once in her years as a detective had she seen something so sick.

Colin grabbed her by the shoulders and yanked her to him. Before she could take a breath, his head descended, his lips claiming hers.

For a second, she responded, before stepping back and stomping on his foot. "What are you doing?"

"Ow." He grabbed his foot and grinned. "I thought you were going to faint. Kissing you was the first thing I could think of."

~

Her lips were as soft and sweet as he thought they'd be. And, for a moment, she'd melted and returned his kiss. His partner wasn't as made of ice as she pretended to be.

"Don't do that again." She poked his chest with her finger.

"No promises." He motioned back to the laptop. "Now that that's out of the way, any ideas how you want to handle this?"

She shook her head. "What made you think to look for these videos?"

"I couldn't sleep. I kept feeling as if there was something we were missing, so I started playing around. If I were a killer, proud enough of my handiwork to send the detective in charge a love poem, what would I do?" He rubbed his hands down his face. "It's disgusting how my mind works sometimes."

"Can we get a trace?"

"I've already notified the FBI agents. Hopefully, they can do more on their end."

"Can we close down the site?"

"Sure, but the killer will just open a new one." He grabbed her elbow. "Let's get something to eat."

"I had popcorn." She yanked free.

"That's not dinner."

"How can you eat after watching that?"

"I'm a healthy male with a clear conscience." Mostly, anyway. "Let's grab a burger."

"Fine. Give me a minute."

He watched as she made sure her closet was closed, checked under her bed, and then made the rounds of the house checking doors and windows. She was thorough. He shook his head at her OCD tendency and held the front door open for her to go ahead of him. "You really need to update your security. I know a guy."

"I'm sure you do." She slid behind the wheel of her jeep and smiled through the window.

Colin laughed and dashed through a lightly falling rain to the passenger side. Working with Cassidy promised to be fun. "You'll have to let me drive sometime," he said, sliding into the jeep.

"You can try if I'm ever incapable." She turned the ignition and backed from the drive. "I know just the place for good barbeque where they won't mind that I'm dressed like a teenage boy."

A sexy teenager, but he wisely kept his mouth shut. They remained silent until she turned into a burger joint with outdoor seating. The smell of roasting beef teased his growling stomach. He loved dive places. They often served the best food.

"I'll order," Cassidy said, sliding from the jeep. "Double bacon cheeseburgers with seasoned fries and lots of sauce. You'll love it. Want a beer?"

"Yeah." He followed her, pulling out his wallet. A man never let a woman pay for dinner. At least not this man. He slid his money through the order window before Cassidy was finished giving their selection.

"Feeling emasculated?" She quirked an eyebrow.

"Not anymore." He grinned and sat at a table for two under the red and white striped awning. The night was cool, but the view in front of him was hot.

Long shapely legs under sagging shorts. A too-big-for-her tee shirt, and a cascade of red hair. Even dressed as she was, Cassidy was definitely the most beautiful woman he'd ever seen. He was one lucky Scot.

Her amazing emerald eyes narrowed as she approached the table. "Are you laughing at me?"

"Admiring the view."

"Right." She shook her head as she took her seat.

"You seemed jumpy when I got to your house." He folded his arms on the table. "Mind telling me why? Don't say it's because I surprised you. You weren't that surprised to see someone in your house. Why?"

She sighed. "My closet door was open when I got home."

He pressed his lips together to keep from smiling. "That's it?"

"I never leave it open. You saw me prepare to leave tonight."

True. She had checked her closet and made sure it was closed tight. "Did you sweep the place?"

"Yes." She shrugged. "I'm sure I was preoccupied this morning."

"Don't brush it off." He'd make sure he checked her home before leaving for the night. It could be nothing, but with the type of person they were dealing with, he wasn't taking any chances. From the stern look on Cassidy's face, she wasn't either, no matter how inconsequential she tried to make things look.

"May I take a look at the case board on your mother's murder?" He asked as a young man brought their food. "I know you have one."

Her gaze could cut steel. "Why?"

"Maybe I'll catch something you've missed."

"I haven't missed anything." She pointed a french fry in his direction. "Now that we suspect she was killed by the same man who killed these women, I'll take a deeper look."

"It can't hurt to have two sets of eyes going over it." He bit into beefy heaven. Bacon grease mixed with cheese on top of a well-cooked burger and a homemade bun. "This is wonderful."

"I come here a couple of times a week."

"I can see why. What's our plan for tomorrow?"

"The morgue. Maybe the medical examiner can tell us something new." She dipped her fry into an orangish sauce. "We've got to get a break soon, or this case will join the cold case files."

He put his hand over hers. "We'll catch this guy. Have faith. My guess is…he'll come to us."

~

Draco watched from his parked car as the detectives enjoyed their food. He'd followed them from Cassidy's home, pleased to see that the man hadn't stayed long and Cassidy left wearing the least sexy and revealing item in her closet. Still, those were her nightclothes. She needed to be careful. Any infraction with the Scot would result in serious consequences. She belonged to Draco. No one else. One day, she would realize this.

He lowered his binoculars, still able to see them clearly, even though Cassidy's gorgeous features were a bit blurred by the rain. The bible said that a woman's beauty should come from within. Her's radiated so brightly, it dimmed the sun. She was truly a jewel among women. Just as her mother had been, before succumbing to the lure of vanity.

His cell phone vibrated in his pocket. Mary Jones. Her killing of the first woman on her list had been sloppy. No finesse. "Yes?"

"When can I do the other one?"

"You need some training, Mary."

"I know I got carried away. It won't happen again." Her smoker's voice rattled, grating on his nerves.

"Perhaps, you can practice on Harold."

"The man who left the first meeting? I don't have anything against him."

"He'll talk. Do you want to go to jail?"

"I don't care. I have nothing. But, I'd at least like to take care of my ungrateful step-sisters first. Fine. What do you want me to do?"

"Make yourself as presentable as possible and lure dear Harold to me. I'll take you through it step-by-step." He hung up before she could argue further. Poor Mary was going to be a trial. Draco expected unquestioning obedience. Something she lacked. After one more look through the binoculars at his heart's desire, he turned the key in the ignition of his jeep and drove home, twirling the pair of black satin panties he'd stolen from Cassidy's drawer on his finger.

5

Cassidy slathered Vicks under her nose, gave Colin a wry smile, and then pushed open the door to the morgue housed in the hospital of a neighboring town. The smell under her nose didn't quite mask the odor coming from the examining table in front of her, but it helped.

Olivia Sparrow, the medical examiner, looked up with a grim expression. "Nasty."

No argument there. "What can you tell us?"

"I don't think these women were killed by the same perp." She pulled the sheet from the first victim. "Here, the throat was slit with one deep slash. A strong person." She moved to the other girl. "This one...some of the axe marks aren't deep...more like the attacker was tiring."

Cassidy stepped aside as Colin leaned in for a closer look. "Any evidence on the perp?"

"No fibers, if that's what you're asking." Olivia shook her head. "Other than threads from the gown she wore. But..." she grinned. "We do have a partial print from the button on Amber Wilson's gown." She handed a sheet of paper to Cassidy. "I've already sent it to forensics."

"I doubt he's in the system, but good job." She folded the paper and put it in her pocket.

"Look." Colin pointed to drops on Amber's ankle. "This her blood?"

"I haven't checked." Olivia withdrew a cotton swab from a nearby jar and took a sample of the blood. "It could be."

Colin straightened. "Or, we could have gotten a break."

Like the fingerprint, Cassidy doubted the killer's DNA was on file. But, if he was the one who killed her mother, the print would prove it. They'd found a partial on the scene then, too. Almost as if the killer left them bread crumbs, then swept everything away when the cops got too close. She'd make a phone call once she returned to the precinct. If it was the same man, then she'd let Colin look at the case board on her mother's murder.

For the first time in years, hope sprang anew. Maybe Cassidy could finally get the justice she'd been seeking.

She grabbed a tissue from a nearby box and wiped the Vicks from her upper lip on the way out the door. "I want to see whether this print is in the database or not. We can do that from the office."

"What do you think about the ME's opinion on multiple unsubs?" Colin held her jeep door open for her.

"I think Olivia is correct." She slid into the driver's seat and waited until Colin got in before speaking again. "My gut tells me the crimes are related, but I haven't put together how. I also want to check the newspaper again and see whether another ad coincided with the second victim."

"I can look for that while you search for the print." Colin clicked his seatbelt into place. "We'll catch this guy."

"There are no guarantees." She drove down the freeway toward town.

Hopefully, Colin was right. Cassidy hated being a pessimist, but life had taught her to never get her hopes too high. When she did, something dashed them into a million pieces. Every time.

She parked in front of the police station and headed inside, leaving Colin to follow. She needed to know without a doubt whether the print found on Amber's dress matched the one at the scene of her mother's murder.

At her desk, she booted up her computer and scanned in the print. While she waited, she chewed the cuticle on her left thumb.

Finally. The print came back as a match. Still no name in the system, but it was definitely the same killer.

She slumped in her chair. "It's the same."

Colin raised an eyebrow. "As your mother's killer?"

"Yes." She ducked her head before he saw the tears in her eyes. She'd waited so long for a break in her mother's case. "I'll show you the case board now."

~

Colin followed Cassidy into her basement. Against one wall

hung a giant chalkboard. He maneuvered through stacks of boxes to get closer.

She swiveled the board to show photos, post it notes, and index cards placed in chronological order. "I've done everything I can to keep up with what was happening before the case was closed. Until today, I had nothing new to add in a very long time." She wrote "prints from Amber Wilson match prints found next to Maureen Monroe" on an index card and tacked it to the corkboard.

"You've managed to collect quite a bit." He peered at the photo of her mother in a royal blue gown. Her throat was slit the same as Amber Wilson. And, like the younger woman, she was quite beautiful. Cassidy was almost a dead ringer for her mother. "You said you grew up in foster care. Where's your father?"

"Mom never told me about him, no matter how many times I asked."

"She was young when she had you."

"Nineteen, almost twenty." Cassidy leaned against a folding table. "I didn't pry. It was clear the subject of my father hurt her to talk about."

"Hmm." He turned and scanned the crowded basement. Most of the boxes were marked as her mother's things. "I think we should start another case board for Amber and Samantha. Keep it close by and compare with your mother's. I think there will be a lot of overlapping."

"Did you find anything in the newspaper?"

"Yep. Another advertisement for modeling. I've asked for a paper to be on my desk first thing every morning." He motioned with his head for her to follow him upstairs. They'd headed straight for the basement upon arriving. "Go through your house and see if anything is out of place." He still thought Cassidy was the killer's target this time around. If he didn't plan on killing her, he had something else planned. It wouldn't hurt to search the house for bugs, then install a better security system no matter how against such measures she was.

He followed her around the downstairs and then up to her bedroom. The closet door was ajar.

"I know I closed it this morning. I was extra careful after yesterday." She moved to close it.

"Wait." He pulled his weapon from his shoulder holster. "Let me check out the closet. You look around the rest of the room."

He opened the door enough to step inside the small walk-in. Clothes filled half the space, confirming that Cassidy wasn't like other women. All the women he knew had jammed closets.

A few shoeboxes and a small safe occupied the top shelf. There. Tucked into the corner was a small hole. As his gaze locked on the camera, he heard a soft hiss. He held his breath too late and toppled to the floor.

When he woke, Cassidy bent over him. Her eyes clouded with worry. "What happened?" she asked.

"There's a camera in the corner and some sort of gas released." He forced himself to cough and crawled out of the closet. "I'm calling my security friend."

"Why didn't the gas release this morning when I got dressed?" She grabbed his arm and helped him to his feet.

"He doesn't want to harm you...yet." He sat on the edge of her bed and cradled his pounding head in his hands. "I held my breath as soon as I heard the release. I'll be fine." If he hadn't been paying attention, he could be dead.

"You need to go to the hospital."

"If I'm not dead now, the gas isn't going to kill me." He dug his cell phone from his pocket and dialed his friend. After getting assurance he'd be there within the hour, Colin held a finger to his lips, then whispered. "No talking until the house is checked out."

"Then, at least lay down." She tried to push him back on the bed.

"Not alone." He winked.

"For crying out loud, Colin! Now is not the time to be a flirt." She rolled her eyes. "You could have died."

"But, I didn't. A drink of water would be nice, though." Anything to wash the bitter taste out of his throat.

"I'll be right back." She ducked into the bathroom.

Colin stared at the closet. The fact the gas released when Colin entered the closet told him a lot. It told him that the suspect would go to great lengths to remove Colin from the picture, and that they were being watched.

~

Draco laughed and turned off his computer. He was going to have a lot of fun with the Scotsman. Happy to have a worthy adversary for once, two if he counted the lovely Cassidy. He headed downstairs to help Mary take care of Harold.

"My dear man." Draco patted the bound man on the shoulder. "I hope you understand that we can't allow you to roam the streets after finding out what our little group is about. Perhaps…God will help you." He laughed, remembering the man's parting words.

Harold squealed under his gag and cast a wide-eyed glance at poor Mary. The woman had made an attempt to appear more attractive, but the mustard-yellow blouse she wore did nothing for her complexion. Some people were doomed to be ugly. People like Draco. He ran a finger over the thick scar on his face. He'd been handsome once. Women had thrown themselves at him. No more. Now, people like him would rule the world; driven and powerful with the need for revenge.

He picked up a filet knife from the coffee table and stepped onto the plastic around Harold's chair. "I'm going to teach you patience, Mary. Now, you don't need to take your time with your victims. A quick, clean death is good enough, but after your overkill…well, you need to learn to take your time, just a little." He ran the thin blade down Harold's arm. Tiny drops of blood beaded in the cut.

"Have you ever fileted a fish, Mary? No? Well, you insert the knife like so…"

Harold screamed under his gag as Draco shaved off a layer of skin.

Draco handed the knife to Mary. "Practice, dear. I'll watch from the sofa. Don't make a mess. The less mess, the less we have to clean up."

Like an indulgent father, he watched his prodigy work.

6

Cassidy filled her mug with coffee and took a seat in the conference room. The FBI wanted everyone involved in the recent murders to watch the latest snuff film together.

It wasn't exactly the way she preferred to start her morning.

Agent Ingram directed everyone's attention to the big screen at one end of the room, then pushed play on his computer. The other two FBI agents stood on each side of the screen like bookends.

Cassidy set her mug down and picked up her pen to jot notes. A person in black approached the woman tied to a tree and paused as if to say something, a hand holding an axe raised in preparation. The victim's mouth opened in a silent scream as the axe fell.

"That killer is a woman," Cassidy said. "She's still dressed in black as the first killer, but definitely a woman. Look at the hands and the way she carries herself."

"Good observation, Detective." Agent Ingram gave a grim smile. "We believe we are dealing with more than one perpetrator. The motive is still unclear."

"The words at both crime scenes gives us the motive," Colin said, taking a seat next to Cassidy. "The pretty must die. The answer we need to find is why? What do these people have against goodlooking people?"

"Revenge of some sort?" Cassidy took a sip of her coffee and grimaced. Their receptionist must make the worst coffee ever. "Perhaps they were wronged in some way?"

"Why are they targeting you, Detective Monroe?" Agent

Ingram crossed his muscled arms. "Yes, we know your house was bugged and that Detective MacKenzie has updated your security system."

Cassidy cut a sideways glance at Colin. Traitor. "I believe these murders are somehow connected to my mother's murder ten years ago. The same words were found next to her body."

Ingram nodded. "I want MacKenzie with you at all times. He'll be moving into your home after this meeting."

"Sir!" No way. Cassidy valued her privacy and independence. She liked things done a certain way. Another person would disrupt all that.

"No arguments. Meeting adjourned."

"Shut up." Cassidy glared at Colin, who grinned like an idiot, and gathered her things. "We have work to do."

"What's on the agenda?"

"Have you checked the newspaper today?"

"Yes, and nothing."

"Why do you think that is?" She moved from the conference room and down the hall to the office she shared with Colin.

"The first killer places the ads for his own reasons. The second killer chose her victim." He perched on the corner of her desk, moving when Cassidy stared at the desk, then him.

"Got another body," Ingram called on his way past the office. "Out near Highway 64."

Colin grabbed the jeep keys from Cassidy's desk and dashed out before she could take them back. She was supposed to live with him? Impossible.

They followed the FBI agents to a culvert that ran under the highway. The air filled with the slamming of car doors as everyone emerged and converged on the crime scene.

Cassidy slid down the embankment and stared at the body of a man skinned like a fish. "This is different." She squatted next to the body. "Every murder is different. The amount of time it took to do this. It can't be the same killer as the one who used the ax." Unless the second killer was evolving, and very quickly.

No one could call the man goodlooking, either. A bulbous nose and overweight, he reminded her a bit of the cartoon character Mr. Toad.

"Not connected?" Agent Ingram stood next to her.

"It doesn't make sense. Until this week, Clear Springs had a low crime rate. Murders were unheard of." She stood. "Now, we have three in as many days." She scanned the treeline, the hairs on the back of her neck standing at attention. She withdrew her weapon and darted into the trees.

"After her, MacKenzie," Ingram called out. "You are her shadow until these killers are caught."

The crashing of the brush told Cassidy that Colin followed without her having to look back. She'd thought she'd spotted a flash of blue. The snap of a twig ahead of her spurred her on.

Another flash of blue.

She ran faster, catching sight of the back of a man's head. "Stop! Police!"

The man didn't pause, instead, firing a wild shot over his shoulder.

Cassidy dropped to the forest floor and aimed. Her shot missed. By the time Colin pulled her to her feet, the man was gone. "After him." She raced away.

The man seemed to have disappeared into thin air. The only evidence he had been there were a few broken branches and her sighting. She groaned.

"He's always at the scene," she said. "I know that now."

"Unfortunately, all we need is another body in order to prove that fact." Colin turned to head back to the crime scene. "We'll catch him. We can set a trap."

"He's been free for ten years." She glared up at him. "What makes you think we'll succeed this time?"

He grinned. "Because ten years ago, you weren't out to get him."

She snorted and ducked her head to hide her smile. The man had a way with words.

"That was the dumbest thing I've ever seen." Ingram confronted her the moment she stepped from the trees. "What part of don't go anywhere alone do you not understand?"

"I saw an opportunity and took it." She put the safety on her gun and re-holstered it. "That's what we do."

"Not anymore. You're valuable to this case. We need you to draw this guy out of the woodwork."

"I'm not going to be bait, Agent." She shook her head and

climbed back to the road to retrieve her case so she could photograph the scene. She'd had the same thought herself, and had decided against it. She'd rather the perp came to her.

Bait. Ha! She'd find this freak and take him down. That was a promise she would do everything in her power to fulfill.

~

Colin had acted immediately when Cassidy ran into the trees. He hadn't needed Ingram's order. He'd been given the tasks of keeping her safe and catching a killer. Both things which he took very seriously. He might joke and flirt, but bringing this perp to justice before more lives were lost, was top priority.

Since the accidental shooting of an innocent bystander two years ago, Colin took every aspect of his job seriously. Too much, sometimes. In fact, he lost sleep over it more times than not.

He strolled slowly around the crime scene. "Cassidy. Here's a footprint. Looks like a woman's size nine."

"You know that by looking?"

"Experience." He squatted next to the print. "The same woman as beside Samantha Meyers, maybe?"

"We didn't find any prints there." She snapped a photograph. "This man is not pretty by any means."

He shrugged. "I still say it's the same perp. Why else would someone watch here, same as the second murder? This man got in the way somehow."

Cassidy stood. "Perhaps. I don't want to jump to any conclusions."

"Are you acting this way because I'll be living with you?" He couldn't think of another reason for the cold shoulder or short answers.

She whirled. "I'm not helpless. I don't need a bodyguard or a live in nanny. But, no, I'm not acting in any particular way because of that."

"Hogswallow."

"Excuse me?" Her eyes narrowed.

"That's a load of bull. You're mad and acting like a child because you can't have things your way for a while." He smirked and headed for the car.

"Trouble in paradise?" Ingram grinned.

"It's your fault. You should be the one living with Miss

Prickles." Colin slid into the driver's seat.

While he waited, he ran through his mind what they knew as facts. Three different murders, three different methods. Two were lured with modeling advertisements. The third did not fit the same MO as the girls. The authorities were dealing with a man and a woman perp. What they didn't know was…were the man and woman working together? Colin felt they were. The first two were killed because of their looks, the third…He rubbed his chin. Had the man known something he shouldn't or simply been in the wrong place at the wrong time? If the later, then why the meticulous skinning? That took time. They could have been caught. They would have needed a place no one would discover them or hear the man's screams.

Cassidy sat in the passenger seat and slammed her door. "I can see the steam coming from your ears. What are you thinking?"

He told her his thoughts. "I know you don't like to hear this, but I think Agent Ingram is right. We need you to draw this perp out."

"He'll never fall for it. He knows who I am. If I show up looking like Barbie, he won't make a move. What I look like won't change his plans."

"I'm sure Ingram is going to want to try."

"Where to now? We have no leads, no suspects, no one to question." Cassidy pounded the dashboard. "The man's a ghost, a vapor that dissipates in the trees."

"He's flesh and blood." Colin started the engine and pulled onto the highway. "Let's take a look at your mother's caseboard again. There has to be something we're missing."

"I've gone over that board a thousand times."

"Maybe so, but I'm new eyes, and this is a new case."

They drove in silence to her house. Colin exited the car first, then scanned the area while Cassidy unlocked the front door and disabled the alarm.

Once inside, he set the alarm and followed her to the basement.

"Someone's been in here," she said. "How did they get past the alarm?"

That was something Colin intended to find out. He pressed the buttons on his phone to the security agency.

~

How Draco loved her spirit! He stared at the photo in his hand. So like her mother in that regard.

He replaced the photo in his shirt pocket, then rolled the man into the shallow ditch. No amount of security could keep him from going where he wanted. A little painful pressure and the man had squealed like the pig he was and revealed the alarm code.

Why must dear Cassie think that something as simple as an alarm would keep him out? Perhaps, it was time to send her another letter. Something to relieve the fear she must feel. Surely, she knew he thought of her every single day of her life?

If only he hadn't rested for ten years, planning to fulfill his calling. Still, now was not the time to reveal himself. He'd been so careful, so meticulous.

He kicked rocks over the body. The cops would start to put the pieces together soon. He needed to make sure Mary took the rap before that happened. Oh, dear, Mary, already chomping at the bit to make her next kill.

The woman's overzealous nature was a hindrance. One Draco would have to curb in time.

He turned on the device in his ear and listened to the Scotsman as he combed Cassidy's house for recording devices. A waste of time. Draco was a dragon. Powerful and invincible. No mere mortal could foil his plans. But, let the little man try. It provided entertainment.

Draco returned to his Mercedes and headed to his luxury apartment in a nearby town. It wouldn't do to live too close to his darling. After his disfigurement so many years ago, he'd worked hard to amass a fortune in computer software. Now, while he sought his revenge against those who looked down on the less attractive, he had no worries about money. He had all the time in the world.

He laughed and cranked up his radio. Beethoven's Fifth shot from the disc player. Draco drummed his fingers along with the beat and sped home. Things were about to get exciting!

Pressing a button on his steering wheel, he sent a text to his followers.

Delete after reading. Consequences are tough. Meeting in usual place at nine a.m.

Things were gonna get shaken up for sure! He turned the volume on his radio higher and increased his speed. It was a good day to be a dragon.

7

Cassidy stared at the spot on the case board where her mother's picture had been. Scrawled in red sharpie was the word Dragon. Stories said dragons could be killed. She wanted to be the dragon slayer. She *would* bring this beast down. "I'm checking the rest of the house."

"There's no answer at the security agency." Colin slipped his phone in his pocket. "I'm coming with you, then we're paying a visit to my friend."

She nodded and headed upstairs, weapon in hand. Not that she expected to find anyone. This particular dragon came and went like a whisper.

Her bedroom closet was closed, same as her drawers. She opened them anyway and went through the items one-by-one. "I'm missing a pair of underwear."

"Laundry?" Colin peered into the drawer.

She slammed it shut. "I just did the laundry." She definitely didn't want him ogling her panties. "I don't know when they went missing, only that they are. Sick pervert." Some criminals took souvenirs, she just hadn't expected something of hers to be valuable enough to anyone. Why was this unsub fixated on her?

If she were to suffer the same fate as her mother, why hadn't he come forward and made a move? Why flit in and out of her house or spy on her at crime scenes? What had the man had against Cassidy's mother?

She moved into the bathroom. Everything looked to be in place.

"I'm taking the room right next to yours," Colin said. "Anyone after you, has to pass my room first."

"Fine." She still didn't like it, but saw the need for protection with every passing minute. "Let's go see why your friend's security measures didn't work." Although locking the door seemed a waste of time, she did it on their way out anyway. The Dragon had proven he would go where he wanted. "The next stop is the pound. I'm adopting the biggest, meanest dog they have. That's the best security."

Colin shrugged. "I'm the best security, but I like dogs. Instead of the pound, I know a guy who sells German Shepherds. They're well trained to listen to commands and not to take food from anyone other than their owner. That way, they can't be poisoned."

"How far?"

"About an hour."

They made the drive to Colin's security acquaintance in silence and pulled up in front of a modest bungalow. Cassidy cut the engine. "He works out of his home?"

"Yep. Wait until you see what's in his garage." Colin bounded from the jeep and hurried to the front door. He knocked, then peered through the front window before trying the doorknob. The door swung open. He exchanged a grim look with Cassidy, then pulled his gun.

"Stay behind me," he said.

Cassidy pulled her own weapon and walked so close to him she could smell his aftershave. Tension radiated off Colin's back, rippling his muscles.

They made their way through the three bedroom house, eventually ending up in a garage filled floor to ceiling with computer monitors and surveillance equipment. This was no small time security company.

Colin moved to the monitors and typed something on one of the computers. Video of Cassidy's house popped up. A few more buttons and the video showed a man in black punching in the security code on the keypad inside her front door. Seconds later, he headed down the basement steps, took a few minutes to study the case board, then snatched the photo and strolled out of the house as if he had all the time in the world.

"This killer has nerves of steel." Colin pounded the desktop. "Let's go get that dog."

"What about your friend?"

"I have no idea where to look for him. Either he's out on an innocent errand or he's dead. We won't know until he answers my phone call or we find his body." He stormed out of the house.

Cassidy took one more look at the video feed of her house, then followed. The killer was always one step ahead of them. They needed a huge break in the case.

"I'm sorry about your friend," she said, sliding into the passenger seat and letting Colin drive.

"We don't know that anything bad has happened." A muscle ticked in his jaw.

Cassidy knew, deep in her gut, that the man was dead. The Dragon didn't leave witnesses. He'd found out about the security, killed Colin's friend, then strolled into her house as if he were an honored guest.

Their next stop took them to a ranch in the mountains. Colin drove the jeep down a dirt road and stopped in front of an A-frame log cabin. While dogs milled around the yard, not one barked as Cassidy and Colin exited the jeep.

A man stepped onto the porch. "Hey, Scot! This the lady that needs a protector?"

Cassidy pasted on a smile. "A female dog, if possible." The last thing she needed was a dog lifting its leg on everything in sight.

"I've got the perfect girl for you." He motioned for them to follow. "Her name is Rosie. She won't bark unless you tell her to guard, then she'll alert you the moment someone steps foot on your property. If you want her to attack, say Angriff, that's German for attack, and motion toward the person you want a hurting put on. Say watch 'em for her to watch. If you want any other command words, teach her. She's a smart girl, two years old, and will catch on quick."

He unlocked a gate leading into a large dog run. "Take care of her and she'll take care of you. Rosie!" A beautiful dog with straight ears, a regal head, and a prominent black saddle against a dark tan body trotted toward them.

Cassidy held out her hand, already in love with her new best friend. "Hello, Rosie. How will she know I'm hers?"

"The moment I clip her leash on her collar and hand it to you, she'll know. She'll be loyal to death, ma'am." He clipped a bright red leash to a matching collar and handed it to Cassidy.

The moment the dog stared up at her with trusting, wise eyes, Cassidy knew she'd do everything in her power to keep Rosie safe. "Thank you, girl. We'll make a good team."

~

Colin couldn't help feeling a twinge of jealousy at Cassidy's words. He wanted her to think of him as a good partner. What held her back? While she remained professional at all times, he often wondered why her hesitancy in opening up to him. They'd be together twenty-four seven until the silly dragon was caught.

His cell phone rang the same time Cassidy's did. He pulled it from his pocket and read the text. "Another body." He'd bet his teeth it was Seth Jargon, his security friend.

"That dog will track, too," the trainer said. "Not much my furry children can't do. They're as docile as lambs until you want them to work."

"Great. Come on, girl. We have a job to do." Cassidy opened the back door of the jeep for the dog, then slid back into the passenger seat.

Colin informed Agent Ingram they were an hour out, then took his place in the driver's seat. "Let's see what our new partner can do."

Driving above the speed limit, they reached the location where the FBI agents waited in forty minutes. Colin headed into a ditch, leaving Cassidy to bring the dog.

"A new friend?" Ingram motioned his head toward Rosie.

"I thought it a good idea." Colin peeled back the blanket covering the body and stared into the lifeless face of his friend. "This is Seth Jargon. He owns Secret Eyes Security. I hired him to install an alarm system in Detective Monroe's house. A security system that the perpetrator got around, strolled in, and stole a photograph of Monroe's mother." He straightened. "That's been our day."

"The victim died from what looks like a single gunshot to the heart. The ME can tell us more, but if it's the same perp, he's all over the place in his MO."

"The Dragon." Cassidy led the dog around the perimeter of the body. "He calls himself The Dragon."

Rosie's ears perked up, and she froze, staring into the trees.

"Let's go, Colin." Cassidy unhooked the leash and motioned

for the dog to go. Like a rocket, Rosie shot into the trees, Cassidy following at a run.

Colin dashed after them. Just like the last time, they crashed through the brush to no avail. If anyone had been there, they disappeared, which became evident the moment Rosie stopped and looked up at Cassidy with a whine.

She glanced over her shoulder at Cassidy who patted her on the head. "Good girl." She reattached the leash to the collar, then turned to Colin. "I'm getting very frustrated with all this." She stomped past him.

"We'll get a team out here to scour the woods. Maybe they'll find something to help us. The man is bound to have left something behind." Not that it would do much good to find DNA on someone not in the system. But, it would tell them they were chasing the same person responsible for the other deaths.

"I'm going to have the locks changed on my house and change the security code. If he doesn't have anyone to kill in order to get the needed information, it might make it harder for him to get inside."

"Have Rosie at your side at all times. Between me and the dog, you'll be safe."

She sighed. "I'm not worried about me, Colin. I want this man caught so the murders stop."

She might not be worried about herself, but Colin was losing sleep at night. He couldn't lose a partner. Between worrying about Cassidy and the nightmares that plagued him, it was a wonder he could think straight.

They rejoined the FBI agents as the body was being loaded into an ambulance. He hadn't known Seth well, not being in the states more than a year, but his heart lurched to see someone he'd shared beers and laughs with zipped into a black bag and stowed away. He didn't want that to happen to Cassidy. He steeled his heart against caring too much and marched to the jeep.

~

Draco looked over his group of nine. He preferred an odd number. Every form of art looked better in odd numbers. But, Harold had betrayed them. Soon, Mary would have to go, once she'd served her purpose. Then, he'd need to recruit another.

"When will I have my turn?" Ben, a man whose face was

pitted with acne scars, scowled.

"Patience. Mary has almost completed her tasks, right Mary?"

She nodded. "One more. I'm ready. I've proven myself with Harold."

Draco sighed. "We do not say the names out loud of those who have left us."

Silence descended over the room as the implications of Mary's slip of the tongue registered on the attendees. No matter. They needed to know the price of disobedience.

"It is often difficult to mete out punishment," Draco said, "even when the person needs it. In order to help you all take the next step, I've designed some tasks for you to fulfill. Jobs that will help you face your adversary and inact your revenge without showing that you are a novice. In the jar on the table are slips of paper. Each of you are to draw one. On it, you will find your assigned task. Don't disappoint me, people." He fixed a stern gaze on them. "Show me you can do these things. Show me you can stay one step ahead of the police. Only this will prove that you are worthy to be my follower."

Chairs scraped along the floor of Draco's rented house. Not the place he called home, but rather his place of business. His followers formed a line and each took a slip of paper that would cause chaos in the town of Clear Springs.

A grin spread across his face. If his beloved Cassidy could continue with her bravery despite the coming disasters, she would prove her worth.

8

Cassidy sat on the basement floor, boxes piled around her. Rosie lay staring at her with big dark eyes.

She hadn't slept a wink. Colin might have been in the next room but Cassidy couldn't have been more aware of him if he'd snored in the same bed. What was wrong with her? She'd sworn off men for the sake of her career. Why would one handsome Scotsman with a sexy brogue and deep blue eyes rock her plans?

"Coffee?" As if her thoughts had called him, the object of her lack of sleep handed her a steaming mug. "What are you doing?"

"Thanks." She took the drink. "Going back through my mother's files. I must have missed something. With the new evidence, I thought it worth the time."

Colin sat cross-legged across from her and pulled a box to him. "It's as good a plan as any."

Concentration was in short supply. Cassidy sneaked a peek at the man across from her. His dark hair was ruffled from sleep, his tee shirt faded, and baggy plaid lounge pants covered his long legs. She'd never seen anyone sexier. She sighed and dug further into the box.

"I haven't looked through everything," she admitted. "Some of these boxes are my mother's personal effects. It was too painful...until now." It was still painful, but needed to be done in the light of the current situation.

"I can do this if it's too hard." Colin gave her a lopsided grin. "I had to go through my parents' things a few years back. Most difficult thing I ever did."

"I'm sorry about your parents. How did they die?"

"House fire." He sighed. "It was arson. They arrested a

disgruntled neighbor a few days later. The man was angry over boundary lines."

"That's rough." They shared the fact both of their families were murdered. In an uncharacteristic gesture, Cassidy reached over and placed her hand on his. "The pain never goes away, does it?"

"Never." He handed her a leather book. "This looks like a journal. You should be the one to read it."

Her hand shook as she took the journal and flipped it open. "It's my mother's." She scooted against the wall and started to read while Colin continued looking through the boxes. An hour later, she froze. This couldn't be right.

She read the words again. "I'm a product of rape." She flipped through the pages again. "No name of her attacker, though." The book fell into her lap. "Why didn't she ever tell me?"

"What?" Colin stopped what he was doing.

"My mother wrote about the experience. She chose to keep me despite the violent act. Fought and injured the man and got away. That's why she became a cop, so she could help victims." Her eyes burned as her heart sank to her knees. "When I asked about my father, she always put me off, saying she'd tell me about him someday."

Who was Cassidy's father? Had they ever caught him? That was one mystery she might never know. Still, her gut told her she knew the man, had seen him before. Would she recognize physical traits they shared?

She shook off her thoughts and set the journal aside. They had multiple murders to solve. She could explore her genealogy at another time.

"Here's something." Colin handed her a yellowed newspaper page. "Your mother answered an advertisement. The same as our first two victims."

Cassidy snatched the paper. "But our victims weren't sexually assaulted."

"Maybe he's too old." Colin gave a wry grin. "Can't...you know."

"Don't be crude." She set the paper next to the journal. "My mother was almost twenty when she had me. Right around the same age as our victims. He's evolved. More in control of his actions."

"I agree. It was a poor joke." He closed the box and reached for another one. "We need to check the police records at the time your mother was attacked, then later when she was murdered. See what the officers thought about the situation."

"I've read everything I could find on her murder, but didn't know about the rape. We'll go when we've finished these boxes." They might find something else to help them in their search.

They didn't. By the time they finished going through the boxes they'd uncovered nothing more of interest other than the journal and the newspaper. "I'm hitting the shower," Cassidy said, "then I'll be ready to dig through the police files."

"I'm making more coffee and omelets. You have to be starving." He unfolded his lean frame and took her hand, pulling her to her feet.

Handsome and could cook? "I am hungry." She bounded up the steps, taking the book and paper with her and hurried to the bathroom.

She couldn't help but glance in every crevice and corner for hidden cameras. No way did she want The Dragon, she smirked at his name, to see her in the shower. She turned the water to hot and disrobed, draping the shorts and tee shirt she'd slept in over the toilet.

Adjusting the faucet to a comfortable temperature, she stepped into the shower, wrapped her arms around her middle, and cried. No wonder her mother hadn't wanted to talk about Cassidy's father. How horrifying the experience must have been. A young woman right out of high school, her future promising, attacked and left pregnant by a monster.

She raised her face to the spray and let the water wash away her tears. She'd managed to hold it together with Colin, but now, alone, she let the grief swamp her. When her tears were spent, she washed her hair and body and toweled dry.

She stepped out of the room to the aroma of frying bacon. So far, having Colin around hadn't been a hardship other than her heightened awareness of him. She took a deep breath and squared her shoulders. She couldn't let her emotions run rampant around him. Caring for another only opened one's heart to ache.

~

The vulnerability on his partner's face when she'd read the journal had ripped at his heart. He'd wanted to comfort her, but knowing that wouldn't go over well, had told a bad joke instead. What was wrong with him? He wasn't usually an insensitive person.

He flipped the omelet onto a plate and set it in the oven to keep warm while he cooked the second one. When Cassidy perched on a stool at the breakfast bar, he removed the first omelet and slid it to her. "Feel better?"

"A little."

"Must have been a shock." He wanted to comfort her the same way he did the relatives of murdered victims. But, Cassidy was different. No simple pat on the hand would suffice. Not when he wanted to pull her into his arms and cradle her against his chest. With her standoffish attitude, that wasn't a good idea.

She fed a bite of egg to the dog. Having the biggest German Shepherd he'd ever laid eyes on, one that was trained to protect, eased his mind somewhat. He wouldn't need to keep his eyes on his partner every second if Rosie was around.

His omelet finished, he sat on a stool next to Cassidy and dug into his breakfast. "Scanning old newspapers will be time consuming, but all we need is a little something to help us along."

"I think we need to question the friends." Cassidy left a few bites on her plate and set it on the floor for Rosie to lick clean. "I know we did preliminary questions, and that they all said they hadn't seen the victims the night they died, but I want to dig deeper."

"I don't think they know the killer. The victims were both visiting family here."

"I know, but I'm at a dead end here, Colin." Her face was lined with stress.

"I'm starting to agree with Ingram." He eyed the loose pants and shirt she had on. "I think you need to start dressing like one of the pretty people and lure this freak out of hiding."

She sighed. "Such a bother. I worked hard to get where I'm at in my career. Looking like a fashion plate won't help me be taken seriously."

"It's all about the attitude." He grinned. "If you act kick ass, people will think you are. You can do that in stilettos as well as work boots."

"Stilettos are out of the question. I'll break my neck." She slid from the stool. "I'll go see what I have in my closet. There may be a shopping trip in my future."

He laughed. "You make that sound like a death sentence."

"It is." She motioned for Rosie to follow, and left the kitchen.

The doorbell rang. Colin waited for Cassidy to give the order for Rosie to guard. When it didn't come, he peered out the peephole in the door. Most killers didn't ring the doorbell.

Agent Ingram stood on the porch, the other two agents waiting by the car. This did not look good.

Colin opened the door. "Sir?"

"Mail for Monroe." He handed Colin a large Manilla envelope. "We've scanned it for anything hazardous. Seems clean, but we thought she should open it right away."

"She's upstairs getting dressed. Come on in." Colin turned and almost stumbled over Rosie. Good girl. Silent as a wraith and as vigilant as the best cop. Her eyes never left Ingram.

"There's coffee in the kitchen," Colin said. "Will Smith and Weston be coming in?" He couldn't say their names without grinning.

"No. They're on guard duty, but I'd love a cup."

Soon, they sat at the breakfast bar, sipping coffee, waiting for Cassidy to come downstairs. Colin told Ingram their plans on looking through old newspaper articles, but left out the full reason why. He also explained about wanting to question friends and family deeper.

"This case is a tough one," Ingram said. "Bodies are piling up, no evidence is left behind, we're dealing with more than one perp, and we're getting nowhere."

"We can't give up." Cassidy stepped into the room. Her makeup had been artfully applied, her hair straightened down her back in an curtain of fire. A navy blue suit fit her as if tailored for her. A sea green blouse complimented her eyes.

Colin's gaze flicked to her feet. The same black work boots. Still, the woman was stunning.

Ingram smiled. "You clean up nice, Monroe."

"This had better work." She poured coffee into a travel thermos. "It takes three times as long to get ready when I have to go to this kind of trouble."

"At least the view is better." Ingram clapped her on the shoulder. "Let's go to work."

~

Draco stood in the shadows between two buildings across the street from the bank and watched as two of his followers tossed a pipe bomb through the open door of a vacant building. No one would be injured...this time, but it would bring his darling Cassidy running to the scene.

The two doing his bidding jumped into a waiting car and sped away as people flocked onto the sidewalk to see what the commotion was about. Fifteen minutes later, the FBI crows in the black suits and black SUV pulled up, followed by Cassidy and her partner in the jeep.

Draco smiled as his darling exited the vehicle, looking like one of the FBI agents. Only, her beauty shown as radiate as the fire spewing from the bombed building's shattered windows. Yes, he had a personal grievance against beautiful people, but despite her professional demeanor, Cassidy Monroe was more beautiful on the inside than out. He'd seen her care for the citizens of Clear Springs. Watched as she put in more than one hundred percent effort in catching criminals. Beautiful, yes, but smart, and...his.

With one last adoring glance at her, he turned and headed down the alley toward his car. The pipe bomb was only the beginning. He needed to supervise the next follower's orders. He rubbed his hands together. It was going to be wonderful!

"Hey, mister! You can't park there." A man in a white apron exited the back door of the bakery. "Employees only. Can't you read?"

Keeping his face averted, Draco tossed the man a flippant wave and sped from the alley. Now, he'd have to drive his second favorite car. The baker was bound to have gotten the make and model of the car. Not the license plate, though. He grinned. That he kept too dirty to read.

9

"Stay." Cassidy commanded Rosie to remain in the car and shut the door, leaving the window open against the warm morning, then turned to survey the hectic scene.

Flames billowed from the storefront and ate at the roof. Glass littered the sidewalk like confetti. "Was anyone injured or killed?"

One of the first responders, an EMT she had yet to meet, answered, "No. Just an explosion."

"Any witnesses?"

"That baker over there came running over a minute ago. He's waiting to talk to someone."

She nodded and headed for the man in a white apron. "Sir, I'm Detective Monroe. Do you have information for us?"

He glanced toward the alley. "I'm not sure it's related, but right after the explosion, I saw a man in a dark Mercedes speeding out of the alley. I called to him to stop, but he kept going. Customers are not allowed in the alley."

"License plate?"

"Too dirty to see." The man frowned. "That was the strange part. The rest of the car, and the man, were immaculate."

"Rosie!" Cassidy motioned for the dog and Colin to join her. "Thank you, sir. You've been very helpful."

Rosie bounded from the car window and sprinted to Cassidy's side a second before Colin joined her. The three of them headed into the alley as Cassidy explained what the witness saw.

The alley was empty of all but a few cars, none of them a Mercedes. Not that Cassidy expected to see the perpetrator still hanging around. While Colin studied the tire tracks, she began the arduous task of knocking on business doors.

She hit pay dirt on door number three. An elderly lady who smelled of chocolate answered.

"I saw a rusty pickup truck pull away from across the street seconds before the explosion," she explained. "It had two men inside. I think they were men."

"Why didn't you report this when the authorities showed up?" Cassidy's pencil poised over her notepad.

"I didn't know if there would be more explosions. I'm a simple candy store owner, not a vigilante. Finding these people is your job."

"Yes, ma'am, and we're doing our best but we can always use the help of the community."

"That's not what my tax dollars pay for." She slammed the door.

Cassidy shook her head. Two vehicles, one luxury, one not, were seen fleeing the scene. Which one, or both, were involved?

She scanned up and down the alley. "Do you think it's The Dragon?" How she hated that name.

"No clue. He didn't leave us much to go on, if it is." Colin straightened and snapped a picture of the tire tracks. "Let's head back to the station. I still need to look through the morning's paper, and you can get started on the old issues."

She nodded and glanced in the direction the Mercedes had gone. A sheet of paper danced on a slight breeze. Following her instinct, she darted for it, chasing the paper until it stopped against a cement wall. She lifted it by the corner. Printed on it were the words:

Detective Monroe:

Are you enjoying our little game? Can you prove yourself worthy to be my assailant? We have more in common than you know.

Draco

"It *was* him." She said, hurrying back to Colin and handing him the note. "He's playing a silly game."

Colin's mouth twisted in thought. "No one died, which leaves me to believe he didn't want them to. When he kills, it's personal."

"Personal to his accomplices, too." Cassidy sighed. How could she keep up with the man without clues? A single sheet of paper and a set of tire tracks wouldn't reveal his identity. "I can look for someone in the system named Draco, but I'm sure it's an alias." They didn't even have enough for Rosie to track. She bit back a curse. Her mother had once told her that if you had to curse to be interesting, then you weren't interesting to begin with. Still, times that like this made it difficult to keep a civil tongue.

Most people in law enforcement cursed with regularity. Cassidy was determined to be different. Not only in the way she handled herself, but in how she did her job. She glanced heavenward. *I could use some help right about now.* From her mother, from God, she wasn't picky.

After letting Agent Ingram know about the note and statements from the witnesses, Cassidy opened the door to the jeep to let Rosie in, then climbed in herself. The note proved The Dragon was responsible. Thus, the FBI could supervise casing the scene, freeing her and Colin to head back to the station.

Once there, she made a pot of coffee, filled two mugs, and joined her partner in front of the case board they worked on with the FBI. After handing Colin his coffee, she tacked up the note and two cards with the descriptions of the vehicles. Perching on her desk, she sipped her coffee and studied the board. Nothing but murders and games.

She sighed and sat at her desk, opening her laptop and logging into the site that gave her access to old newspapers. She typed in her mother's name and started searching.

She stopped on the article about her mother's rape. Not a rape by a stranger, but one at a college fraternity party. Her mother said she hadn't known the man, but had fought back until several other college young men heard the ruckus. By that time, Mom was covered in blood...not hers.

Cassidy needed to find the young men who found her. No names, but someone at the college had to know something. She picked up the phone and called Arkansas State. Fifteen minutes later, she had the name of a teacher who had been there at the time of the rape who agreed to speak with her.

"Let's go to college." She grabbed her purse and weapon, clipped the leash on Rosie's collar, and headed out the door.

"I really hate when you do that," Colin said, jogging to catch up.

"Do what?" She cut him a sideways glance.

"Take off like I'm going to follow like an obedient puppy."

"Aren't you going to follow?"

"That isn't the point." He scowled, his brows lowering over his amazing eyes. "It's rude."

"Sorry. I'll try to do better, but we have an appointment." She explained what she found. "Maybe this teacher saw or heard something that will take us a step further in this investigation."

~

They parked in front of the administration building, then asked the receptionist inside where to find the cafeteria. She glanced at Cassidy's badge before pointing them in the right direction. She frowned at Rosie, but didn't say anything, then turned back to her work.

The cafeteria was virtually empty that time of day. Cassidy headed for a man who looked to be nearing his retirement years. "Mr. Laraby?"

"Yes. I presume you're Detective Monroe." He waved them to the two empty chairs at his table. "Beautiful dog. A service animal?"

"In a sense." Cassidy took her seat. "You knew Maureen Monroe?"

"She was one of my students. A very bright girl. I was saddened to hear of her murder." He straightened in his chair and crossed his arms. "You believe her rapist killed her?"

Cassidy nodded. "What can you tell us about the night she was attacked?"

He sighed. "It was a frat party. Your mother came with a friend. The other gal ditched her and ran off with her boyfriend. Not sure how Maureen occupied herself. All I know is that three young men came running, one of them carrying her. She was covered in blood. We discovered it wasn't hers. When the cops arrived, she told them what happened and that she cut her attacker." He gave a wry smile. "She was one tough girl."

"We know all this. I was hoping you could tell us something new. Who were the boys?"

"Only one is alive right now. One died in a car crash, the other in Desert Storm. Bruce Main lives a few blocks from here." He scribbled an address on Cassidy's notepad. "I doubt he can tell you much more. I don't think anyone got a good look at the attacker."

"Was he as student here?"

"Very possible. It wasn't a secret party, but you did have to be enrolled here to attend. Still, it wouldn't have been impossible for someone to sneak in." He slid a thick book across the table. "A yearbook I 'borrowed' from the library. Good luck."

Cassidy shook his hand, thanked him, and glanced at Colin. "Ready to make one more stop?"

"No stone unturned." He grinned.

~

Colin stared at the small white house. A tricycle sat on a well-manicured lawn. If the man was married with children, he might not be happy to dredge up something horrible from his past. Still, Cassidy deserved to know as much as possible. He shoved open the car door.

"Stay." Cassidy left Rosie on the front porch and rang the doorbell. The yearbook was tucked under her arm.

A man in a business suit opened the door. "I'm heading to work. Not buying whatever you're selling."

Colin flashed his badge. "We have a few questions. Are you Bruce Main?"

Surprise registered in the man's eyes. "Yes, but..." He closed the door and joined them on the porch. "I really have no idea why you're here."

"Mr. Main." Cassidy stepped forward. "You helped a woman who was attacked almost twenty-five years ago at a frat party. That woman was my mother. She was later murdered. I'd like to know what you can tell us about that night."

He rubbed the back of his neck. "Not much. Me and the boys heard her scream. When we got there, a dark-haired man was running into the bushes. I gave chase, but he got away. I'm afraid I'd been...intoxicated, and not too quick on my feet. I'm sorry."

"It wasn't your fault. Is there anything else you can tell me about her attacker? Did you recognize him? Would he be in this book?" She held out the yearbook.

Main glanced at Colin. "Man, this is bringing up some stuff I never wanted to think about again."

"I'm sorry, but it's important." Colin took the book from Cassidy and handed it to Main. "Please. Is there a place we can sit?"

"There's a table on the back porch. My wife has already left and the babysitter is inside. Will that suffice?"

"Perfect." Colin took Cassidy by the elbow and escorted her after the man. They sat quietly while he flipped through the thick book.

"I think it might be one of these two men." He tapped two pictures. "Loners, both of them, but they were at the party. I hate to accuse anyone when I didn't get a good look at his face, but the profiles...yeah, it could be one of them."

Colin glanced at the names. Daniel Haler and Vince Smith. Could one of them be the man they were looking for?

"Neither one of them returned to school after that night. With as much blood as Maureen had on her..." Main shuddered. "She hurt her attacker. If he would have come back to school, we would have known."

"Thank you." Cassidy stood and offered her hand. "You've been a big help."

He returned her shake and offered his hand to Colin. "I hope so. That's a night I'd rather forget. One more thing. There was a knife next to Maureen. We left it there. I'm not sure whether we ever told the cops. Like I said, we were drunk."

"Can you tell us how to get to where the attack took place?" Colin asked.

"Sure. It isn't far, but nature would have taken over. Or the police could have found the knife."

Cassidy shook her head. "Nothing in the files about a knife."

He gave them directions. "I really need to go. Good luck." He bounded down the stairs and to his car.

Cassidy grinned. "We're getting closer to slaying a dragon."

10

Cassidy knew the chances of finding the knife her mother used after that many years was slim. Still, she wanted to see the place she was conceived in violence. The place that changed everything she thought her life growing up had been. She glanced around the small patch of trees behind the college.

How dark it must have been. How frightened her mother must have been. Still, she'd fought for her life, not preventing her rape, but wounding her attacker. Fatally? Perhaps, but not likely. He was seen fleeing the scene. "I want to check emergency room and hospitals for knife wounds on that night," she said, turning to Colin. "If he'd been injured badly, he would have had to seek medical attention."

Colin glanced toward the college. "Not the first aid office here, most likely. We can make some calls back at the office."

She glanced around the area, trying to envision what had happened that night. Years of nature reclaiming her territory would have covered the knife in dirt and leaves. Without the proper equipment, if the knife was still there, they'd never find it.

"I'm ready to go." With a gentle tug on Rosie's leash, she headed back to the car.

They stopped for lunch at a fast food burger place and took their food to the conference room where the FBI agents waited for them. "About time," Ingram said.

"We were following a lead to nowhere." Cassidy opened her food sack and explained about their visit to the college.

Ingram frowned. "You think your biological father is this Dragon?"

She froze. She hadn't put the thought into words, but now that he said it, it made sense. "I don't know. Who else had a reason to kill my mother? The man she injured. If he's killing pretty people, maybe his knife wound was disfiguring. I'm going to check hospital records for that night."

"MacKenzie, what do you think?"

Colin exhaled sharply. "It's all connected somehow. Why else would The Dragon be focused on Cassidy?"

Ingram shrugged. "We'll go with it for now. Monroe, get a DNA sample on you. We'll have something to compare this Draco with if we ever get lucky. Maybe your DNA will match with that on the first victim's shoe."

She nodded and bit into her burger. "I really hope I'm wrong."

Colin opened the morning's paper while he ate. The agents left the room to process anything found at that morning's bombing and, hopefully, pursue Cassidy's hunch about Draco. Figures that she'd found out her biological father wasn't a military hero, but rather a sick, twisted killer.

Retrieving her laptop from her desk, she set it up on the conference table and began her search for knife victims almost twenty-five years ago. Eye strain set in almost immediately, and her focus wavered.

"Found another advertisement." Colin handed her the paper. "He's specifically asking for a red head. You, perhaps?"

She scanned the personal ad. "Red haired model wanted. Competitive pay. Come to 506 Oakwood Drive at eight p.m." It showed today's date. "It looks like I have an appointment tonight."

"Not without me and the agents." Colin took the paper back and tore out the ad.

"He won't be there." She shoved a French fry into her mouth. "It's a test to see if I'll show."

"Doesn't matter. You still aren't going alone."

"I wasn't planning on it." The Dragon was just crazy enough to kill her.

~

Oh, this was going to be good. Draco rubbed his hands together. He had no doubt sweet Cassidy would show. He'd hide behind a two way mirror and let one of his minions take the fall, if it came to that. A new man arrived to that morning's meeting, eager to prove his worth. If he could get in and out of a warehouse full of cops trying to hide, he'd be worthy to be a follower. If not, he'd die in a hail of bullets. Draco didn't care either way.

He placed a folding chair behind the wall size mirror and settled down to wait. That night's photographer sat quiet next to him, awaiting orders.

"Be vigilant, Mark. A precious woman will soon enter that cavernous room. She'll be beautiful…and armed. Do not harm her. Convince her that you are a photographer. If you can't, then find a way to flee. While you won't see the cops, they'll be there."

"I have a way out. A hidden door in the wall behind the backdrop. I won't fail you." The acne scarred, balding man met Draco's gaze. "I'll do this, then you help me rid the world of a witch."

"I promise." Draco smiled with pleasure at the thick scar running from the man's jaw to his collar bone. Cassidy would think this poor example of himself to be Draco. Imagine her surprise when she finally meets the real Dragon. "Get into place."

Mark nodded and stood, exiting through a side door as Cassidy stepped into the brightly lit room. "Welcome," he said, grinning. "My name is Mark, and I've a variety of gowns for you to wear."

~

Cassidy's gaze landed on the scar running along the man's neck. Was it possible Draco was actually showing himself? "I'd like a red one. Do you think it will clash with my hair?"

"No, I think it will be wonderful." His grin never faltered. "There's a changing screen there. We can start with red and move to other colors. You'll be a fabulous model. Those cheek bones…" he kissed his fingers.

Cassidy rolled her eyes and stepped behind the screen. What in the hell was going on? This man did not act like a cold blooded killer. Was it possible he really was a model scout? She chewed the inside of her cheek.

Outside, Colin and the others waited for her signal. What if she made a mistake and they converged on an innocent man? She needed to discover a way to determine whether this man was Draco or not?

"How did you get that scar?" she asked, stepping from behind the curtain. The red dress she'd chosen hugged her curves.

Mark turned his head and fiddled with a camera on a tripod. "Car accident."

"I'm sorry. It really isn't any of my business." She stood in front of a background depicting a misty forest. "I think my father has a similar scar." She forced a smile. "But, I've never actually met him. He got his in a fight, I heard."

Mark turned on a high powered fan. "Sounds like a bad ass."

She shrugged. "What would you like me to do?"

"Act sexy and stop talking."

Act sexy? One of the few things she had no idea how to do. She pursed her lips and lifted her hair from her neck while he snapped pictures. This was getting them nowhere.

"Have you been a photographer long? Do you have a portfolio?" She did her best to act empty-headed and flirtatious.

"Why are you talking to me?" Mark's friendly demeanor faded to be replaced with anger. "Don't I repulse you?"

She stopped moving. "No, should you?"

"The acne pits and scar doesn't turn you off?"

"No one is perfect, Mark. Some people's scars can't be seen."

"You seem to be perfect." He snapped another picture, then glanced at the mirror on the wall.

Cassidy smiled and approached the mirror, holding her fingertip to the glass. Ah ha. A two-way mirror. She turned. "Tell my father to come out and speak to me."

Mark's eyes widened.

The lights cut off.

"I need back up!" Cassidy called.

A door slammed somewhere in the dark.

She grappled for something to use as a weapon, her hand closing on the camera tripod. It would work in a pinch. She clutched it in one hand as she searched with the other for the changing screen. Her holster and gun hung on a hook just inside...there. She dropped the tripod and clutched the gun as the lights flickered back on.

Colin raced toward her, grabbed her arm, and tried to drag her from the building. "Let's get you safe."

"Wait." She grabbed her clothes. "It's the only suit I have."

They dashed outside as a dark-colored sedan sped away.

Cassidy groaned. "He wasn't Draco, but the man was there.

That mirror is a two-way. What kind of game is he playing?"

Colin's gaze warmed as it raked over her. "You look very beautiful."

"Stop it. We're working."

~

Colin had listened to the recording coming clear through the wire Cassidy wore with interest. Realizing that Mark the photographer was not Draco The Dragon had been a brilliant move. "I don't know what game he's playing, but he's trying to get you to do something."

"He needs to face me and stop wasting our time." She leaned against the jeep as the FBI agents exited the building.

"I thought you looked good in a suit," Ingram said, grinning. "But, this…ooh, la la."

"Let's hurry this up so I can go home and change." Cassidy scowled. "Did you find anything?"

"A door behind the backdrop. That's how he got away. Good move on asking him about Draco. He also took the camera with him. Looks like dear old Dad wanted photos of his darling daughter."

"Let's go." Cassidy opened the door to the jeep. "I left Rosie at home and it feels weird without her."

Colin joined her. The agents would finish with the scene, as always. All Colin and Cassidy were good for was doing the grunt work. "Do you feel as if tonight was a waste of time?"

She shook her head. "We discovered that Draco does, indeed, have others working with or for him. I say that's a huge discovery."

They only needed to figure out what to do with the information. Colin started the ignition. "I think you were supposed to think Mark was Draco."

"He's not old enough or sure enough of himself. I figured out Draco was there by the way Mark's eyes kept darting toward the mirror." She propped her bare feet on the dashboard. "Draco wanted to see whether he could pull my strings. Fine. I'll play along. Maybe by doing so, we can prevent more deaths."

"I agree." But, he didn't like it. Not one bit. It was a dangerous game. One that could get them all killed.

He cut a sideways glance at the beautiful woman next to him.

What were the thoughts and feelings running through her head? They had to be momentous. Finding out your father might be a serial killer had to do things to her head. He reached over and grasped her hand. "Are you okay?"

"I'm fine." She stared out the window.

"It's okay to not be fine." He gave her hand a squeeze.

She pulled it away. "I've got a lot on my mind, Colin. Leave it alone. I'll deal with it all once this maniac is behind bars."

"Don't push me away. I can help you through this." He'd do whatever it took to keep her safe, help her sort out the information that had to have her reeling.

They stopped at a stop sign. He grabbed her hand again and pulled her close, staring into eyes illuminated by the street light.

"Don't," she whispered.

"Oh, but I'm going to. You need something else to think about." He pulled her a little closer.

"No."

"Yes." He moved his hand to the back of her head and placed his lips on hers. Gently, like a trainer would touch a skittish horse. He deepened the kiss, cupping her face.

She moaned and put her arms around his neck.

A horn honked behind them, pulling them out of the increasingly heated moment.

Cassidy jerked as if stung. "I can't do this. You can't distract me this way."

He chuckled. "I think I can." He pulled away from the stop sign, fully intending to continue distracting her from the myriad of problems running through her mind. She needed to focus on one thing—catching Draco. Their biological relationship needed to take a backseat right now.

If she sunk into a depressed state, which Colin suspected she was headed toward, they'd accomplish nothing.

11

"Let me get out of this dress," Cassidy said the moment they stepped into her house. "I'll meet you in the living room."

"I'll make popcorn." Colin grinned.

Still clutching her suit and boots, Cassidy hiked the dress to her knees and climbed the stairs to her room. Wadding the gown into a ball, she stuffed it into a paper bag and placed it in the corner before donning a pair of cotton shorts and a long tee shirt. The dress would go to the station in the morning for evidence. Not that they would find any prints other than hers and those of the man named Mark.

When she joined Colin in the living room, he had the lights low, a bowl of popcorn and two glasses of wine on the coffee table and was dressed in nothing more than a pair of cotton plaid lounge pants. Gracious the man looked good.

"Wine. The perfect thing after a day like today." She sat on the opposite end of the sofa and grabbed one of the glasses.

"I even found a movie in your stack of DVDs. Something called P.S. I Love You."

"One of my favorites." She peered at him over the rim of her glass. The man was up to something. "Tomorrow, I need to research the two names we were given at the college."

"No work talk. You need time off. Morning will come fast enough." He pressed the TV remote. "Come closer. You're too far away."

"I'm fine where I am."

"It'll be hard to share the popcorn." He sat the bowl in his lap.

The man played dirty for sure. Sitting that close to him was asking for trouble. "I can get another bowl."

"Are you afraid of me, Cassidy?" His eyes darkened.

She snorted. "No way. You're the softy in this partnership. The good cop. A real boy scout."

"Let me show you how bad I can be." His brogue deepened. "Let me help you forget your pain. Snuggle close and watch this chick flick with me."

What could it hurt? She could use the distraction. Sitting next to him, smelling his heady cologne, breathing in...him. She scooted closer and let him put his arm around her shoulders. "You said you wouldn't be a demanding roommate."

"You make it hard in some cases." He grinned down at her. "The sight of you in that red dress did things to my mind. I cannot be held responsible."

"Stop it." She slapped his chest, freezing when he held her hand there. Heat radiated through her palm. Her gaze clashed with his. Before she did something stupid, like kiss him, she gulped her wine.

He moved her hand holding the wine glass from her mouth. She jerked. Wine spilled down his naked chest.

Colin jumped to his feet, almost tossing her to the floor. "Oh, that's cold."

"I'm sorry." She dashed to the kitchen and grabbed a handful of paper towels. Hurrying back, she dabbed at his chest.

"It's fine. I'll take a shower." He chuckled and strolled away, muttering something about taking her mind off unpleasant things.

Oh, he did that all right. She laughed softly, refilled her wine glass, and settled back on the sofa. The man was definitely a distraction. Funny how that didn't seem to upset her as much as it had at first. It was nice having him around.

She glanced to where Rosie watched them. "A little bark when things start to get heated would be nice, my girl. You're supposed to be here to protect me." And she definitely needed protecting from Colin.

Her ears twitched.

"Seriously, us girls have to stick together." She got to her feet, motioned for Rosie to follow her, and headed upstairs to bed where she would be safe from the distraction of handsome men.

~

Cassidy's eyes popped open. A horrible moaning came from

Colin's room. "Stay," she whispered to Rosie as she got out of bed.

Barefoot, she plodded to the room next door, pushed the door open, and peered inside. "Colin?"

He thrashed, tangled in the sheets. She rushed to his side and placed a hand on his shoulder. "Colin, you're having a nightmare."

Moonlight streamed through the open curtains, highlighting his features. Perspiration coated his chest and face. He gripped her arm, his eyes wide. "I didn't mean to."

"Shh. I know." She had no idea what he meant, but sat on the side of his bed and smoothed a dark curl away from his face. "It's going to be okay."

"Never. I can never forget." His eyes closed. The sheet he covered with slipped, revealing a taut stomach and the fact Colin preferred to sleep in the nude.

Oh, boy. It also became evident he was talking in his sleep. What should she do? She tried to remember whether she'd read that you are to wake up the person having the nightmare or try to comfort them in their sleep? Since he didn't seem as if he would do harm to himself, Cassidy chose comfort.

She pulled the sheet higher on his chest and caressed his cheek. Stubble rasped against her hand. A tear slid down his cheek. She leaned forward and brushed it away with her lips.

And found herself flat on her back with Colin on top of her. His lips claimed hers, his hands running up and down her body, lifting her shirt.

For a moment, she contemplated giving in. No. Going through with what he was offering would complicate their relationship beyond repair.

"Colin, wake up." She pushed against him. "Colin!" Her palm stung from the force of her slap.

~

Colin jerked awake and rolled off Cassidy. "I'm sorry. I'm so sorry." He lowered his legs off the bed and buried his face in his hands.

"You were asleep." Her voice held a definite chill as she sat up.

Whether from his forcing himself on her or because he'd withdrawn, he was afraid to find out which had made her angry. He'd woken in time. "Why are you in my room?"

"You had a nightmare." The rustling of the bedsheet told him she got up.

"I have them a lot."

"This is the first time I've heard you."

He turned his head as she stood in front of him.

"Colin, look at me."

He sighed and glanced up. Her hair was mussed, her lips swollen. He shook his head. "How's that for a distraction?"

"Don't get crude." She put a hand on his arm. "It was a mistake. Are you all right?"

After what he'd almost done, she was worried about him. Asleep or not, he'd betrayed her trust and a vow he'd made to himself a long time ago. Never get physically entangled with a partner. He'd come too close to stepping over that line.

He shrugged off her touch. "Please go." He turned away so he wouldn't have to see the pain flickering across her face.

"All right." Her soft words tore at him. "Please don't sleep in the nude anymore."

He didn't get up until her heard her bedroom door close. Then, he flopped back on the bed and flung his arm across his eyes. What a fool!

How would he face her? He groaned and rolled onto his side, hugging a pillow to his chest. *I'm sorry, Cassidy.*

~

Well, that was a first, Cassidy thought as she slammed her door. No one had ever regretted making out with her before or sent her packing from their room. Not that there had been many men. Just one in college and she had sent *him* away when she'd discovered she was one of many notches on his bedpost. She'd vowed to stay celibate after that, but Colin's vulnerability had shot down every defensive brick in the wall she'd built around herself.

"Now what?" she asked Rosie. "Do I pretend it never happened?" She couldn't. What an idiot she was.

If they were members of a larger police force, she'd request a new partner. As it was, they were stuck with each other.

She lay on her bed and stared through the dark at the ceiling. What a predicament. Shame washed over her like a cold winter rain. She shouldn't have kissed him. Stroking his hair had seemed to be working. Why had she gotten so close?

Rosie growled deep in her throat.

Cassidy shot to a sitting position and reached for the gun on her nightstand.

Something crashed through her bedroom window.

She dove to the floor, scooting under the heavy bed as something exploded. "Rosie!"

The dog yelped and scurried to her side.

Cassidy slapped out burning fur and fought to see through the smoke.

"Cassidy!"

"Under here."

A hand grabbed her and yanked her out and to her feet. "Let's go." Colin dragged her along, Rosie following.

"What happened?"

"Looks like a pipe bomb."

"My house!" Cassidy grabbed a fire extinguisher from the wall and headed back to her room.

"I'll do it. Get back." Dressed again in his plaid pants, but barefoot, Colin aimed the extinguisher at the wall opposite Cassidy's bed.

With one hand on Rosie's collar and her tee shirt pulled over her nose, she watched through streaming eyes as Colin put out the fire. When that was done, she retrieved her cell phone and called 911.

"Stay close by me. We're going downstairs." Colin gripped her arm. Gone was the tender lover, replaced by a grim Scottish warrior.

In the kitchen, he ordered her to sit at the bar, then proceeded to pick slivers of glass from the bottom of his feet. "He hasn't wanted you dead before. What changed?"

"It was risky to think a pipe bomb would kill me. How did he know I was in my room?" She shrugged.

"What. Changed?" He enunciated each word.

"Us. That's what changed." She glared at him. "Is that what you wanted to hear?"

"How does he know? Think. You have to be aware of everything happening around you. All the time."

She quieted, running through each room in her mind. Her eyes widened. "Your curtains were open. He watched us."

~

How dare she! Draco gunned his engine and sped into the night. His precious girl was soiled now.

She was no longer any good to him. Not for the purpose he wanted anyway. How could she lead his followers when he was gone? They needed someone pure in mind, if not in body. Someone like him. After Maureen, he'd had no other women. He thought his daughter kept the same values. What if she didn't share his blood? What if Maureen had not been the nice girl she'd seemed?

Cassidy was no better than the others he targeted. Using her pretty face and lovely body to lure others into her web. He needed to find out for sure whether he had fathered her. If not, his plans would have to change.

The Scot had been sleeping! Deep in the throes of a nightmare. She'd taken advantage of him and needed to be punished. The pipe bomb was a warning.

Maybe her partner had led her on earlier in the day like Maureen had toyed with his affections a long time ago. Let her know he was open to her charms. Perhaps he wasn't innocent in their night time romp. He'd have to be eliminated. No more games.

Draco would still lure Cassidy to his clutches. Somehow, he'd get her DNA and have a test run. Any fool could purchase the kit off the internet. He couldn't make further plans until he knew for certain.

He sped home, closing the grey Lexus in the garage. He needed a consoling drink. He needed to kill someone!

In the house, he poured a double shot of whiskey and headed for his office and his list of names. He'd said he'd leave the killing to others, but in this case…

He chose a woman who had laughed in his face at a bar, calling him a freak. All he'd wanted to do was buy her a drink, have a little conversation. He'd planned on saving her for later, but tomorrow was not her lucky day.

12

Wrapped in a blanket too thick for the summer evening, Cassidy watched as Colin, still shirtless, spoke with the FBI agents and firemen raced into her house to make sure the fire danger was over. Colin had known when he'd asked how The Dragon knew about what had almost transpired. He'd wanted her to come to the same conclusion.

Whatever sweetness might have been from Colin's kisses and tender endearments had been sullied, tossed into the dirt and stomped on. It was for the best. It shouldn't have happened and the consequences were now more dire than she would have imagined. The target on her back was as big as the Ozark mountains.

She glanced at the trees bordering her property. Was he watching? Wanting to view his handiwork? The temptation to go and see was strong. But, she stayed perched on the hood of her car. Heading off alone would be stupid. There were times she might be impulsive, but stupidity was not a trait she wanted others to think of her as having.

Sarah Robertson, reporter and all around nuisance, approached Colin with a wolf whistle. He said something to hear, leaving her with a scowl on her face, and donned a shirt handed to him by Agent Ingram, then marched Cassidy's way. "Are you all right?"

"I'm fine. The house is fine. Everything's great."

He sat next to her, his weight popping the hood. "Don't sulk. There isn't time for a pity party."

She glared. "I never feel sorry for myself. It's a wasted emotion."

"We could see you sulking from the front porch." He straightened the blanket around her.

"It's too hot."

"You might be in shock."

"I'm not that weak. Nothing is damaged but my room." And her pride. "I can deal with that."

"Are you up to finding and interviewing the other two college students who didn't return to the party the night your mother was attacked? The fire department will clear the house soon and we can grab some sleep. I'll take the sofa."

"No, you stay in the guest room." She wouldn't get a lick of sleep in that bed. "I've slept there plenty of times watching TV. You'll hang off the edge. I'll call someone to repair my bedroom."

"They'll have to be checked out by the FBI before we'll allow them in," Agent Ingram said, approaching the jeep. "I'll have Agent West find someone. Glad to see you're doing fine."

"Except for the fact this perp stays one step ahead of us." She shrugged off the blanket and slid from the jeep's hood. "What do we do? Wait for him to come for me again?"

"He'll slip up eventually." Ingram clapped her on the shoulder. "In the meantime, keep hunting." He flashed a thin-lipped smile and left to join the other agents.

Without glancing at Colin, Cassidy headed for the house to prepare a bed on the sofa, knowing without asking that Colin would sleep on the floor next to her.

~

Surprised that she had actually slept, Cassidy woke to the now familiar smell of breakfast and brewing coffee. She stretched, popping the kinks from her back and made a vain attempt to smooth her hair into place.

Colin, frying pan in hand, gave her a smile from the doorway that didn't quite meet his eyes. Those were still shadowed with shame.

She sighed and returned his pasted on smile. Two could pretend nothing had happened, but there would come a day when they had to talk about what had almost happened in detail. Especially if they were to continue being partners. Nothing would be the same between them. They'd almost crossed a line she'd promised herself to never step over. She had no intention of leaving her home. If they couldn't work together as professionals, he would have to be the one to leave.

"Omelets," Colin said. "You have time to take a quick shower if you want. I took mine earlier."

"I want." She bounded up the stairs and through her room smelling strongly of smoke. Someone had taped plastic over the shattered window. The opposite wall was burned black, along with most of the bedding. Refusing to let the sight break her, Cassidy moved to the bathroom where, hopefully, a hot shower would clear her head and help her forget the night before.

When she'd finished and dressed in her customary baggy clothes, no suit today, she joined Colin in the kitchen.

His eyebrows rose at her outfit, but he wisely held his tongue and slid a plate full of omelet and bacon toward her. "I found the addresses for Daniel Haler and Vince Smith, so we're ready to go once you've eaten."

"Did you sleep at all last night?" She cut her fork into the fluffy omelet.

"Not much," he muttered, turning away.

They ate in silence, the tension thicker than an autumn fog rolling across a lake. Cassidy tried not to take peeks at the man sitting next to her, and failed. She wanted to tell him it was okay. What had almost happened wasn't the end of the world. Just an unfortunate mistake that, if they'd gone through with it, could have been dealt with.

She finished her breakfast, set her plate in the sink, and grabbed her badge and gun. "I'm ready."

Colin nodded and followed suit, then set the alarm on the front door and followed Cassidy to the jeep. "Who's driving?"

"I will." She climbed into the driver's seat.

"Haler lives in Little Rock, Smith in Conway."

"Smith first then." She backed the jeep from the drive and headed down Interstate 40. "Are we going to his home or work?"

"I don't know where they work. I'm hoping neighbors can tell us." He rubbed his unshaven chin. "You don't need to make aimless conversation, Cassidy. I'm over my temper tantrum."

"Good."

~

He chuckled wryly. Cassidy seemed determined to pretend nothing had changed between them, so he'd follow her lead. If he didn't, guilt would consume him. He couldn't work efficiently under those circumstances. "Take the second exit," he said, glancing at his GPS.

"What's with the nightmares?"

"I don't like talking about them." He adopted the cocky attitude that always made her stop talking. "Of course, you coming to my room and all helped erase some of that."

"It won't work."

"What won't?"

"Making a joke of it. Tell me about your nightmare." Her hands tightened on the steering wheel.

She was like a bulldog. He glanced out the window. "I shot an innocent woman."

"Okay, I wasn't expecting that. What happened?"

"Do we really have to do this?"

"I think so."

He grinned. "Not going to come comfort me anymore?"

"If you don't stop with the jokes, I'm going to punch you in the throat." She whipped the wheel to the side and swerved into the parking lot of a grocery store before facing him. "I am not a pain killer for you. I am not a nurse maid. I am not your comforter, although I lost myself for a minute. I am your partner, and I want to know what your nightmares are about so I can find a more healthy way of helping you."

Ouch. "On a professional basis."

"Yes." Her look could cut steel. "Sometimes, talking about these things actually help them stop. Have you seen a counselor?"

"Many times." He didn't believe in them, which is why they probably didn't work. "We had a hostage situation in New York shortly after I arrived in the states and entered the police force. A man was holding two women and a small child inside a dress boutique. One of them was his girlfriend and her daughter, the other the store clerk. My sergeant ordered me to take the shot. I squeezed the trigger right as the man pulled the woman tighter against him. The shot went through him and into her, killing them both."

"That wasn't your fault." She made a move to put a hand on his arm, then drew back.

Now, she was afraid to touch him. Way to go, MacKenzie. "I should have waited."

"You didn't know. You were following a direct order."

"Are you always going to make excuses for me?" He narrowed his eyes. "I was asleep, I didn't know what I was doing, I almost forced myself on you, I didn't know he was going to pull the woman close? Stop making excuses for me."

"Fine. It's all your fault." She drove back onto the road. "Maybe you need to learn to forgive yourself."

The load was too heavy. Forgiving himself didn't seem harsh enough in light of the things he'd done. "Can we forget personal conversation and keep things strictly professional? It'll be a heck of a lot safer."

She rolled her eyes. "That was my intention all along."

~

Draco strolled into the bar, Mary trailing a few feet behind him. If he wanted the woman off his back, he needed to let her finish deleting her enemies.

She pointed out the target, a pretty blond around the age of twenty-five sitting alone at the polished mahogany bar. She was turned to face the men playing pool, her emerald slip of a dress sitting high on her thighs.

He knew her type. He'd approach her, ask to buy her a drink, and get laughed at. Then, he'd pester her until she made the excuse to use the restroom, where he'd grab her, drag her through a back door and turn her over to Mary. So simple these pretty people. So predictable.

"Hey, pretty lady. Can I buy you a drink?" He was careful to keep the scarred side of his face away from her. Let her think him handsome for a few seconds more.

She tilted her head, a sliver of a smile on her glossy lips. "Sure. Chardonnay, please."

Motioning to the bartender, he placed the order, then faced her full on, knowing how the scar twisted his lips on the one side. "Do you come here often?"

Her eyes widened. "Um, no. Excuse me. I'll be right back."

Just as planned, she headed for the glowing red sign marked restrooms.

Just once, he'd like to know what it felt like for a woman not to look at him with revulsion in her eyes. He paid the tab, took the glass of wine, and followed Mary's prey, motioning for the other woman to follow.

He dropped a tablet into the wine and waited. "You forgot your drink," he said, when the woman emerged.

"Oh, thank you, but I must decline. My boyfriend..."

"One of those playing pool?" Right. Liar.

"Yes." She smiled. "I really must get back."

"Please take your drink. No hard feelings." He held out the glass. "You can at least spare me a few minutes since I bought it for you."

"I...suppose." She took a sip, then another, as if by hurrying, she could rid herself of his company. She swayed on her feet. "Oh, I must have drank it too fast."

"Here, let me help you. No strings attached." He clubbed her on the side of the head, then propped one shoulder under one arm while Mary moved forward to take the other.

They helped their victim outside and into the trunk of Mary's twelve-year-old Dodge Charger. "You make it look so easy," Mary said.

"It is easy. You need only learn to read people. Who is this woman to you?"

"My father's youngest daughter by his new trophy wife. She's done nothing but point out how much better she is than me. Thinner, more attractive, more successful. I can't wait to rid the world of her." Mary slammed the trunk.

"Be patient and take care."

"Aren't you coming?"

Draco shook his head as he slid behind into the driver's seat of his car. "I'll be sure to watch the video. You should know what to do by now." With a toss of his hand, he drove away. He couldn't babysit the woman forever. She knew the consequences if she messed up. Either he would dispose of her or turn her over to the authorities. Either way, she'd no longer be his concern. He had bigger things to take care of.

13

Cassidy followed Colin's directions to a large apartment complex on the edge of Conway. From the looks of the place, Vince Smith had fallen on hard times.

Wood trim in need of paint, white siding grayed from the weather, a pool thick with slime, and more rusty automobiles than should be in one place. Weeds claimed every patch of ground that sported a bit of dirt. The sign out front stated luxury apartments for lease. Must be a lot less.

Side-by-side, she and Colin climbed stairs to the third floor. Cassidy stood off to one side while Colin rapped sharply on the splintered door. The man who answered had more tattooed skin than not. A scar, covered by a snake tattoo, disappeared down his shirt.

"Vince Smith?" Colin flashed his badge. "Mind if we ask you a few questions?"

"What about?" The man reeked of cigarette smoke.

"Something that happened at college a long time ago. The attack of Maureen Monroe ring a bell?"

"That night haunts me." He stepped aside and waved them into an apartment so clean Cassidy had to take another look outside to make sure she hadn't entered an alternate dimension. "Have a seat," he said. "Y'all want a soda or water?"

"No, thank you." Cassidy perched on the edge of a dark brown leather sofa.

Colin took a chair across from her.

Vince sat in a chair angled to face the one Colin had chosen. "That was such a long time ago, man." He rubbed both hands down his face.

"Did you know Maureen?" Cassidy kept her gaze glued to his

face.

"Yeah, we went out a time or two. Sweet girl." He shook his head. "She wasn't much of a partier, but wasn't a prude either. She could have fun…when it was called for."

"Did you see who she left the party with?"

"Nah, I was drunk as a skunk. Spent most of my college life that way. Ended up getting dropped from my classes. Me and my buddies heard her scream, then some guys carried her out of the trees. She was covered in blood." He shuddered.

"Was there anyone there you didn't know? Anyone who stood out?" Cassidy glanced at Colin, glad to see him taking notes, then transferred her attention back to Vince.

"A lot of people." He frowned. "It was one of those mixer things where students could get to know each other. We had Freshmen to Senior there. There's no way I could have seen everyone." He drummed his fingers on the arm of his chair. "There was this one guy. Pretty good-looking, I guess. He kept going from girl to girl, flirting and offering them drinks."

"Can you describe him?" Cassidy leaned closer.

"Dark hair, blue eyes, maybe. When he came up to the girl I was hanging with, I run him off."

"Did he talk to Maureen?"

"Yeah." His eyes widened. "I could tell she was only being polite. Wasn't really into the guy. I looked over there a couple of times, just in case she needed me to get rid of him, but they were laughing and seemed to be getting along. When they disappeared, I didn't think much of it. Man, do you think it was him? Could I have saved her?"

"You were one of the male students who didn't return to the party when Maureen was found. Where were you?"

"Passed out with the girl I was hanging with. After seeing Maureen, finding out what happened, well, I drank a lot more." He hung his head. "I had to erase the image of her, you know? I'll never forgive myself if I could have done something."

In his condition, Cassidy doubted he could have done much. She handed him a business card. "Please call if you think of anything else. Anything at all that might help us find this guy."

He took the card. "Why are you looking after all these years?"

"We believe he may be responsible in the death of another

young woman." She stood and offered her hand. "Thank you for your time."

He shook her hand. "I'm sorry I couldn't do more."

They at least had a description of sorts. Not that they could take the word of a drunken college student twenty-five years after the fact, but it was more than they had when they arrived. That, and the fact her mother might have left willingly with her attacker.

"Do you know whether they did a tox screen on my mother?" she asked Colin once they stepped outside. "What if this man she was laughing with slipped her something?"

"The same thought occurred to me. I didn't see anything in her file, though."

Since she hadn't been killed, most likely the screen hadn't been scheduled. Either that or her mother hadn't gone to be tested. She sighed and climbed back into the jeep.

Their next stop was an expensive community in North Little Rock. They pulled into the long drive and parked next to a red Ford convertible.

Cassidy squelched a bit of car envy and led the way to the front door. She pressed the bell and waited. When several minutes passed, she knocked. "Where to now?"

Colin dug through the mail in the mailbox. "He's probably at work. We need to find out where that is. Nothing here." He replaced the mail.

"Can I help you?" An elderly man came around the corner of the house, a shovel in his hand. "The Halers are working."

Colin flashed his badge. "We need to speak with Mr. Haler. Do you have the address of his job?"

He shook his head. "It's something, something, Haler. A law firm."

Colin grinned. "We'll find it from that. Thank you." He started to take Cassidy's elbow, then dropped his hand.

Good grief. It wasn't like touching her would burn him or anything. Oh, that's right. He didn't need his painkiller right now. Well, next time he had a nightmare, she'd yell loudly from the doorway! No more getting too close. She was the one who would get burned.

~

Colin rolled his head on stiff shoulders and wished for a good night's sleep. He had a prescription from the last counselor he'd seen, but after Cassidy's nighttime visit, then the pipe bomb, he needed to be alert. Hopefully, he'd sleep that night from sheer exhaustion.

"Haler looks like he does well for himself," he said, studying the brick two-story office building in front of him. "Funny how people in the same class at college can take such different routes."

Cassidy made a noise in her throat and pushed open the double glass doors. "Let's hope he has a minute to speak with us."

Colin shot out an arm to hold the door open, then followed Cassidy into the plush waiting room. Their shoes clipped across the marble floor.

A receptionist smiled at them from behind a oak desk. "Welcome to Larson, Moore, and Haler. How may I help you?"

Colin showed his badge again, thinking he might as well wear it around his neck. "We need to speak with Daniel Haler, please."

"Let me see if he is available." Her smile never wavered as she punched buttons on her phone. "Mr. Haler, the police are here to see you. May I send them in? Thank you, sir." She beamed up at them. "He's busy."

"Tough." Cassidy glanced at a sign. "We'll show ourselves in." She marched down a long hall.

Colin shrugged at the lovely receptionist, smiled, and followed the Bull Dog. "You get more with sugar than vinegar."

"I've heard that." She continued to the elevators and pressed the button for the fourth floor. "You can remain the good cop. I'm comfortable with my role."

The elevator doors opened and they stepped inside. Immediately, tension filled the space as the doors closed.

Colin kept his gaze locked on the numbers flashing above the buttons. He would have to find a way to be alone with Cassidy without feeling like a boy with a crush. One who had snuck a kiss while playing Truth or Dare. He remained still while the doors opened and she stepped out, then followed her to the right.

A brass plate on a glass door announced they'd found Daniel Haler. Cassidy shoved open the door, bypassed a wide-eyed girl behind a counter and marched into the man's office. "We're Detectives Monroe and MacKenzie. Thank you for seeing us."

The man's face darkened. "I said I was busy."

Colin stepped forward to diffuse a situation that could spiral out of control. "Sir, this is important. We only want a few minutes of your time." He closed the door and took a seat across from Haler, motioning for Cassidy to do the same.

"We're here about an assault on a Maureen Monroe that happened while you were at college." Cassidy tossed a business card on his desk.

"I had nothing to do with that." The man scooted his chair back a foot. "I barely knew her."

"Where did you go that night?" Gone was the nice officer who had questioned Smith. Cassidy was sharp as nails and about as friendly as a pit bull.

Colin bit back a grin. This was the woman he'd met over the first victim's body. This hard-nosed partner he could deal with.

"I was at the party." Haler's brows drew together.

"After Maureen was brought to the on-campus clinic, you were one of the few men not spotted again for several days."

His gaze flicked around the room. "I...don't know where I was."

"Do you have any scars, Mr. Haler?" Cassidy gave him a shark-like grin. "From a knife, perhaps?"

"No, nothing, I swear." Terror filled his eyes.

"Do you mind visiting the restroom with Detective MacKenzie? Or would you prefer a search warrant?"

"I have nothing to hide." He lunged to his feet. "Fine." He unbuttoned his shirt. "I was stabbed a few years ago by a disgruntled client. You can check my medical records. I pressed charges. What's this all about anyway." He fixed his shirt. "That girl's attack happened a long time ago."

"Sir." Colin held up his hand to halt Cassidy from further questioning. "We believe her attacker may have recently killed another woman. Anything you can tell us will be greatly appreciated."

He settled back in his chair. "I was there as a spy." He shook his head. "The dean wanted to know who brought drugs to the parties on campus. I'd drink, then go in the bushes and throw up, then start the process all over again. I was purging when I heard a girl scream. I didn't know at the time that it was Maureen. When I parted the bushes, a guy was running away holding his face. Blood was everywhere. I got sick for real and fell in my vomit. By the time I was conscious, it was all over and she was being cared for."

Colin glanced at Cassidy. Hope shone in her eyes.

"He was holding his face?" she asked.

"Yeah, like this." Haler cupped his cheek. "That's all I could tell. Oh, and he had dark hair."

Cassidy jumped to her feet and reached across the desk to shake his hand. "Thank you." She took a deep breath and left the room.

Colin shrugged at Haler and joined her in the hall. "Talk about doing a one eighty."

"We now know any injury my mother caused him was to the face. I say that's a huge step forward. Now, we can check hospital records of that night without questioning every single person stabbed that night."

"Do you get many stabbings around here?"

"We didn't get much of anything around here…until recently. Not in Clear Springs, anyway." She pressed the button on the elevator again.

The tension was somewhat relieved as Cassidy continued to talk of what they'd learned. Excitement laced her words. "We can get the FBI to help us track down knife victims and interview the names we find. I mean, I'd like to have a go at all the names we find, but the interviews will go a lot faster with five people instead of two." She glanced up at him and fell silent.

He hadn't meant for her to catch him looking at her as if she were the most beautiful thing he'd ever seen. He hadn't wanted her to see in his eyes how he was growing to feel about her. Especially after the other night. He cleared his throat and looked away.

"I think having help is a good thing." He closed his eyes and prayed for strength.

14

The conference room echoed as five people made phone calls to hospitals and clinics within a fifty mile radius of the college. Cassidy set her pencil down and stretched. It would have definitely taken just her and Colin forever to go down the list. Once they had their suspects, she prayed she would be the one who got her mother's attacker. She rubbed her hands together. She'd love to get her hands on him.

Colin looked up from his phone and laughed. "You look pleased with yourself."

"Plotting revenge." She smiled. "Two more locations on my list." She reached down and scratched behind Rosie's ears.

"I'm finished. I have five names to visit."

She frowned. It wasn't a competition, yet she looked at it as one. She quickly made the remaining calls, came up with zip, and then stood, glancing at Ingram. "Do we take the names we each have?"

"You two take yours. We'll take the rest. No one interviews anyone alone," he said. "Understood?" He cast a stern dark-eyed gaze around the table. "In fact, I think it wise that the two of you take Weston with you. The danger to Monroe is too great."

They all nodded and gathered their things.

While Cassidy didn't need a babysitter, having a third person around would help keep things less tense between her and Colin. Maybe her and Weston could be friends. She could use a girlfriend. Especially the other night. Hashing over her feelings for Colin, sharing a bottle of wine, talking about…what did close friends talk about?

She studied the cool, but beautiful features of the FBI agent. She didn't look like she was in the market for a friend. Smith and

Weston rarely spoke, unlike Ingram.

"We'll take the rented SUV," Weston said. "The killer knows Monroe's vehicle. Knocking on the door and flashing our badges is all the announcement we need." She marched out of the building ahead of them.

Cassidy tossed Colin a surprised look. "Do you think she's upset to play bodyguard?"

He shrugged. "Let's just get through the day." He leaned close, giving her a teasing whiff of his musky cologne. "I think she has a thing for Ingram."

"Really?" Cassidy glanced at the other two men. "Interesting."

"Maybe we can get her to open up to us." He winked and held the front door open.

Her heart did a somersault. Relieved to not feel the usual tension between them, she hurried to the SUV and got in the backseat with Rosie. The dog had found an empty spot in Cassidy's heart. She couldn't imagine going anywhere without her now.

The moment Colin's seatbelt clicked into place, Weston began barking orders. "I do the talking. I knock, announce myself, and enter any residence first. There are vests in the back. Each of you are to wear one. Do not pull your weapon for any reason unless I pull mine first."

"What if the suspect fires first and you're down?" Cassidy couldn't help the jab. "Can we think for ourselves then?"

Weston glared at her through the rearview mirror. "Keep your wits and sarcasm. Today could very well be the day we catch a killer."

Cassidy squelched any thought of them being friends. Oh, well. She had Rosie. She didn't need anyone else. Instead, she stared at the back of Colin's head and thought of things that might be possible...if she let her guard down. Which she had no intention of doing.

"Remember. I take the lead," Weston reminded them as they pulled in front of a well-maintained home built in the 1950s. She cast a warning look over her shoulder at Cassidy, then exited the vehicle.

Cassidy told Rosie to stay and followed the agent and Colin to the front door. She stood a few feet away from Weston and peered through a crack in the curtains. "Television is on, but I don't see anyone."

"Get away from the window." Weston shook her head. "Bullets shatter glass."

Cassidy sighed. She wasn't an imbecile, but unless they were very lucky and the killer was actually at home with open curtains, she didn't think they were in much danger.

They were just turning to leave when an African American man answered the door. A knife scar ran from his temple past his eye.

"FBI." Weston showed her badge. "We'd like to ask you a few questions."

"I've not had any trouble in years," the man said. "Ask what you want from out here."

"How did you get that scar?"

"Gang fight." He crossed his arms. "But I don't live that life no more."

"He doesn't fit the profile." Weston thanked him for his time and headed back to the SUV.

It went that way for most of the day. One after the other they ticked off the names on their list as non-suspects.

Frustration gnawed at Cassidy the way Rosie chewed on a rawhide. The killer had to be close. He had to have a scar down his face. While all the men they'd interviewed were the right age, it was obvious most of them weren't the killer. Half of them had never gone to college and had received their wounds in fights and accidents.

They stopped for lunch at a fast food Mexican place and ate in the car. Colin had been unusually quiet the first half of the day.

"I have two names left on my list. One is a man in his mid-fifties," he said. "The age is right. He received thirty stitches on the left side of his face twenty-five years ago. The other man is also in his fifties and the scar is along the neck. He almost bled out, according to the ER records. My guess…we visit the first guy. Maureen may have wounded her attacker, but I just don't feel like she could have gotten in a good enough whack to almost kill him."

Weston turned in her seat. "I've read your file. You have good instincts. Both of you do. So, if that's what your gut is telling you, that's where we'll go next. I need to check in with Agent Ingram."

She exited the car and punched numbers into her cell phone. Immediately a grin spread across her face.

"So she can smile," Cassidy said. "I was starting to wonder."

"You don't reign as Ice Queen anymore. Not with her around."

"Who calls me that?" She stabbed a piece of carne asada with her plastic fork."

"Everyone. I did, too, until..." he sighed. "Now, you're the Bull Dog."

"Ugh. I prefer Ice Queen."

"Sorry, but you've been knocked off your frigid throne." He leaned forward and peered closer at Weston. "Something's wrong."

The agent slid back into the driver's seat. "We have another body. Interviews will have to wait." She cursed, thrust the vehicle into drive and sped down the highway.

~

"This isn't The Dragon's work." Colin stared at the knife wounds to the victim's face. "He would never mar her beauty."

"One of his followers?" Cassidy squatted next to the body. "There has to be either followers or copycats either doing his bidding or with agendas of their own."

Which would make it extremely hard to find and arrest them all. He knelt next to his partner and studied the body close up. "She reeks of alcohol. We need to visit the bars in the area. See if anyone recognizes her." He glanced around the area. "No purse."

Cassidy tapped the woman's hip. "I think her ID is in her underwear." She shrugged at Colin's glance. "Where else is she supposed to carry it? Turn around."

He averted his gaze while she fished out the woman's ID. "Same last name as one of our other victims."

"Sisters?" He took the driver's license. "We might have finally gotten a break."

"Find a common enemy." Cassidy pushed to her feet. "Do that first or interview scar face."

"That's cruel."

"It's nothing compared to what I'm going to do with the man when we catch him." She stepped aside while the emergency personnel zipped the body into a bag. "I think he distracts us with dead bodies to keep us from getting too close."

"How so?" Colin leaned against the side of the SUV.

"Well…" She took her bottom lip between her teeth.

Colin took a deep breath to halt the effect of what even that small gesture did to him.

"We find out that he's scarred in the face and start interviewing. We find a body—" She held up a hand to stop him from saying anything. "I know this woman was killed before we started knocking on doors. The point is…he's one step ahead all the time. He's smart enough to know we're low on law enforcement personnel and that dropping crumbs like some perverted Hansel and Gretel, he can keep us from zeroing in on one thing."

"She's right." Ingram joined them. "I've called for reinforcements. We're stretched too thin. They should arrive in the morning. I know all this is out of your jurisdiction, Monroe, but I appreciate the hard work."

"Why not Colin's jurisdiction?"

"He's been a detective a lot longer and was almost recruited by the FBI." He gave Cassidy an indulgent smile. "You're learning on one case what it took us to learn over several."

"Lucky me." She exhaled sharply. "Let's use those computer skills of yours, Colin, and watch this latest video before we knock on more doors. We can visit the bar later."

"Yes, boss." He grinned at Ingram. "At least she's pretty."

The agent laughed. "Lucky man. You've got both the women."

There was only one he wanted, though, and she shied away like a skittish horse if his hand so much as brushed hers. He chuckled along with the other man, hiding his feelings, then left to join the women.

Several minutes later he'd located the video. "See how the killer stands? It's definitely the same woman who killed this victim's relative."

"Why haven't we seen videos other than The Dragon and this woman?" Weston asked. "Do you think she's his only accomplice?"

"No. There were the ones who set off the bomb on Main Street, then the man pretending to be a photographer. There's no telling how many followers he has." Colin kept his gaze glued at the screen. "Last time, it was almost as if she was performing for someone. I don't think our dragon is there this time."

"She's flying solo?" Cassidy leaned closer, her hair brushing Colin's cheek.

He took a deep whiff of floral-scented shampoo. "That's why she's taking her time with the face."

"That looks like a scalpel." Cassidy tapped the screen. "She could work in the medical field."

"We can't call every doctor's office in the state of Arkansas. We need something else to narrow our search." He scanned the edges of the video feed. Trees, trees, and…wait a minute. He squinted. "Does that look like a car in the bushes?"

Soon he was flanked on the other side by Weston. If he wasn't so enamored by his partner, he'd be in any man's dream. He shook off his thoughts. "A dark blue sedan?"

"I can't make out the license plate." Weston straightened. "Forward to this email. I'll have our technicians take a look. Maybe they can zoom in enough to read the numbers."

A mere second later the video was soaring through cyber space. They may have gotten another break.

He crooked both arms to the women. "Let's go catch a killer."

15

"This is it." Cassidy glanced at the name on the paper, Russell Ball, and the expensive looking apartments in front of them.

"Same orders as before," Weston said as she marched through the double glass doors of the building.

Cassidy was getting tired of her bossy attitude. Counting to ten, she followed the agent into the elevator and pressed the button for the third floor. A penthouse apartment, at least in these parts.

When the elevator stopped, Colin ushered the women out first. "Let's make this quick. It's been a long day and we still need to talk to the bartender."

"Quick *and* thorough," Weston pointed out.

"That's right, Colin." Cassidy smirked, teasing. "Remember your priorities."

"Yes, ma'am." He grinned, sending her insides quivering.

"You two stop playing around." Weston pressed the doorbell and held her badge to the peep hole. "FBI."

The door cracked open and blue eyes peered out. "One second, please." They heard the sounds of a chain being removed and the door swung open.

Russell Ball's scar started right below his left eye and into the curve of his lips, twisting them into a joker-style grin. "Come in." He waved his arm in a grand gesture.

Cassidy glanced around a modern, immaculate apartment. If not for dishes containing the remnants of the man's meal, she'd doubt anyone lived there. She returned the man's stare, keeping her features impassive at his disfigurement.

"I'm Agent Weston. This is Detective Monroe and Detective MacKenzie. I see we've disturbed your dinner and will be as brief as possible." She flinched and averted her eyes from his face.

"Have a seat." Ball's eyes narrowed as he motioned to the pale gray sofa. "I was finished eating. How may I help you?"

Weston sat on the edge of the sofa and leaned her elbows on her knees. "Let's start with how you got that scar?" She swallowed hard.

"That's a bit rude, but all right." His smile faded. "A terrible car accident many years ago."

Weston flipped through pages on her clipboard. "I have no record of you being in a car accident. Only that you went to an Urgent Care facility twenty-five years ago for what they described as a knife wound."

He shrugged. "The facility was overworked that night. An honest mistake."

"Did you know a Maureen Monroe?"

He thought, placing a finger on his lips. "I don't believe so."

"From college? A frat party, maybe?"

"Definitely not. I stayed to myself in college. My education was more important than chasing skirts. My college transcripts will attest to that." His gaze flicked to Cassidy.

"Mr. Ball." Cassidy took a deep breath. "On the night you received that wound, a woman was viciously attacked. A woman that happens to be my mother. She cut her attacker. You are one of three men who were at the party, but not seen again after her attack. Where did you go?"

He scratched his chin. "You're investigating an attack that happened twenty-five years ago? How should I know where I went?"

"You strike me as an intelligent man," she said. "I think you know very well where you were. An attack on a woman would leave an impression on anyone."

"Fine." He bent and hung his hands between his knees. "I was at the party. I left to snort a line of coke and passed out next to the pool. I can't let this mar my record. I'm a successful businessman."

"Do you have an alibi?"

"Detective Monroe." He stood. "When a student of my caliber does something like that, they are careful not to be seen. Now, if you'll excuse me, I need to clean up the remnants of my dinner."

Effectively dismissed.

Ignoring the sharp looks from Weston, Cassidy approached Ball and held out her business card. "If you can think of anything that would help our investigation, please call. My personal cell number is on the card, along with the station. Thank you for your time."

He took the card, his fingers brushing hers. A chill slithered up her spine at the cold look in his eyes. This man did not like the police. "I will." He dropped her card on the coffeetable, then opened the front door.

"One more thing." Colin stopped in the doorway. "Maureen Monroe's attacker would not have wanted to be seen either, yet he was. Are you sure no one can back up your story? There's also one thing that is bothering me...the college had no Russell Ball on their roster. Your name only appears on the clinic records. Why is that?"

A muscle jerked in Ball's undamaged cheek. "Another unfortunate mistake made twenty-five years ago by a second-rate college. Good day, officers. I'm sure if you dig a little harder, you'll find your missing answers. But not here."

~

Well played, Detective MacKenzie. Draco closed the door behind them with a definitive click. He'd almost panicked to see Cassidy at his door, but held his wits rather well, he thought.

Her gaze had landed on his scar without any trace of revulsion. Not so with the FBI agent. He'd seen her disgust and attempts to divert her gaze anywhere but at him. Perhaps the lovely agent would like to meet The Dragon in all his splendor.

They acted as if Maureen was the victim. Not so! He caressed his scar. He was the one left disfigured, his life ruined.

He opened his coat closet and ran his hands over the leather jacket with the embroidered dragon. All his followers would receive the same jacket once they'd proven themselves. Unfortunately, it wasn't happening as quickly as he'd like. Mary was very close, though.

At first, her work had been sloppy. Her last kill had shown a patience and finesse that gave Draco pleasure. He'd taught her well. Perhaps it was time to reward her. He picked up the phone from the end table and punched in her number.

He would wear his jacket when he killed the agent. Mary

would wear hers on her next assignment. It was time for the world to become better acquainted with The Dragon and his minions.

~

Colin grabbed Cassidy's hand for a quick squeeze before she could pull away. "Don't worry. We'll catch the killer."

She slipped her hand free. "You keep saying that, and we keep coming up against dead ends."

"Faith, my dear." He held the back door open for her.

Rosie bounded out and lunged against the glass doors of the apartment complex.

"Rosie!" Cassidy dashed after her. She grabbed the dog's collar and glanced up.

On the other side of the glass, fear etched across his face, was Russell Ball. Draped over his arm was a leather jacket. She got a glimpse of a multi-colored design, but couldn't make out what it was.

"I'm sorry!" Cassidy tossed him a wave and dragged the barking dog back to the SUV. "What has gotten into you?" She glanced back to see Ball scurry into a parking garage. She'd be lucky if he didn't press charges over her brute of a dog.

"What's wrong?" Colin helped her get the struggling animal into the vehicle.

"I don't know. She's never acted like this before."

He stared in the direction of the parking garage. "They say dogs are good judges of character."

"Not so much." Cassidy climbed in and smiled. "She likes you, doesn't she?"

"Very funny." He closed the door and got into the front passenger seat.

"To the bar?" Weston asked.

"Onward, chauffeur." Colin clicked his seatbelt.

Cassidy laughed at the woman's uptight expression. She really needed to learn how to relax. If not, this case would kill them all.

~

Colin stared out the window and watched the trees pass. The dog's reaction to Ball stirred something in his gut. Could she be reacting to the man's fear or something else entirely? Maybe he wasn't her target. He tried to remember seeing someone else close by and drew a blank.

"What's going on in that pretty head of yours?" Weston asked.

"Did you see anyone else around when the dog went berserk?"

"A doorman, I think."

"What did he look like?"

"I couldn't see his face. Not past Ball, anyway. I noted the fancy red jacket and got in the car." She cut him a sideways glance. "Do I need to turn around?"

"Did you see the doorman when we went into the building?"

She shook her head and squealed tires turning the SUV back in the direction they'd come. "He's probably gone, but maybe someone can give us a description."

She drove right up to the doors and parked. "Monroe, stay with your dog. We don't need a repeat."

Colin sent Cassidy an apologetic look and jogged after Weston. They barged into the lobby of the complex. No doorman in sight.

"Excuse me." He approached a young man at a vending machine. "Does this place have a doorman or a security guard?"

"We have a guard, why? No fancy doorman, though."

"Does the guard wear red?"

The kid laughed. "Seriously? Have you ever seen one wear anything but blue or black?" The only one we have wearing red around here is crazy old lady Ethel. She wears a red cape with yellow fur every day, no matter what temperature it is. A real kook that one."

"Do you know where we can find her?"

"Nah. She leaves every day and comes back at odd times."

Colin clinched his fists. Another waste of time. Still, they needed to follow every lead.

"I'm sorry," Weston said as they returned to the SUV. "I'm originally from New York. We have doormen."

He exhaled sharply. "Did you see anyone out here, Cassidy?"

"Nope. Just me, Rosie, and the birds." She kicked the back of his seat. "Don't leave me again. I'm just as capable at investigating as either one of you and a whole lot safer with you than alone."

"Again, my apologies." Weston headed them back to the highway and to the bar as dusk descended over the trees.

A pink and green neon sign flashed Bar and Grill in twelve foot letters above the building. Colin hadn't stepped foot in a bar in several years. Not after having frequented one far more than was healthy after the shooting. He took a deep breath and shoved open the door to the SUV.

Flanked by Cassidy and Weston, he entered the bar and paused to allow his eyes to adjust to the dim light inside. The place was packed and several conversations halted as heads turned to study the newcomers. While some of the men might take it upon themselves to approach the beautiful women at Colin's side, anyone looking hard enough would be able to tell by their no-nonsense demeanor that they weren't there for a good time.

"I hate these meat markets." Cassidy marched to the bar and pulled a picture of their latest victim from her pocket. "Have you seen this woman?"

"Who's asking?" The bartender kept wiping the bar, not even glancing at the picture. The flamingo-style pink neon light behind him highlighted his bald head.

"FBI." Weston flashed her badge.

"In that case." He glanced at the photo. "Yeah. A real looker. She was in here the other night."

"Alone?" Cassidy asked.

"It started out that way, then some man approached her. I could tell she didn't want anything to do with him, but she was polite. He bought her a glass of wine." He tapped his temple with his forefinger. "I remember all the beautiful ladies."

"What did the man look like?" Colin leaned against the bar, directing half his attention to the bartender and the other half at those watching them.

"A real ugly dude. Massive scar on his face. He came in with a plain Jane. She took a seat at the opposite end of the bar, and he approached our beauty. What did Miss Lovely do?"

"She was murdered."

The bartender blanched. "Seriously? Wow. Let me think a minute." He wiped his sweating scalp with the same rag he'd wiped the bar. "Yeah. She went to the restroom. I was helping another customer, but when I looked up, all three of them were gone.

"Is there a backdoor to this place?"

He pointed them to a sign that stated restrooms.

Cassidy went into the women's room, Weston studied the

short hallway, and Colin shoved open the backdoor. No alarm sounded despite the warning sign on the wall. He glanced around, spotting a security camera. He'd bet the thing was disabled, too. Still, he called back to Weston to check on video footage before stepping onto the gravel paved alley behind the bar.

Several different tire tracks marred the gravel. Still, if they could get one to match the tread from the one they'd picked up at the crime scenes, they'd have proof the killer had stalked Megan Goodall, and murdered Lacey Goodall before that.

He pulled out his cellphone and placed a call to the office asking someone to tell him whether the two women were related. Turned out they're sisters. Interesting.

Now, all he needed to do was find out who would want to kill the sisters. He made a mental note to dig into their family history.

16

Back at Cassidy's house, Colin headed straight for the living room and his laptop. While he worked, the aroma of brewing coffee filled the place. Good. He'd be up late trying to make sense of all the pieces.

Cassidy set his mug on the coffee table next to his laptop. "Let's talk about it."

His head snapped up. "Now?" She couldn't be serious. Now was not the time to discuss what had almost happened between them.

"Why not?" She sat in an easy chair across from him and propped her feet on the coffee table. "We need to connect the dots."

"Wait. You're talking about the case?"

She frowned. "What else would I be talking about?"

"Nothing." Relief washed over him like a warm summer rain. "Let me check one more...yes. The Goodall sisters have a half-sister. A Mary Jones." He pulled up her picture and turned the computer so Cassidy could see the woman's photo. "Does she look like a Plain Jane to you?"

"The Dragon's accomplice?" She peered at the screen.

"Maybe." He jotted down her address. "You're a woman. How would you feel if your father married a woman then had two beautiful daughters."

"Sort of like Cinderella."

"What?"

"It's like the fairy tale, only The Dragon might be Mary's Prince Charming." She sipped her coffee. "Still, I'm not the type to get jealous over looks. I'm not a good person to ask."

"Pretend."

She stared over his head. "If I thought myself ugly, and scarred, I suppose I'd be jealous. Especially if a father that once lavished attention on me no longer had me at the center of his universe. But to kill someone? That's a stretch."

"If she's a follower of The Dragon, she might have the same outlook on pretty people that he does." Colin reached for his mug. "Maybe her half sisters were mean to her. Taunted her. Made fun of her."

Cassidy shrugged. "Let's assume she's deranged enough to go there. Other people have murdered after being bullied. We add her to our suspect list. Along with Russell Ball and our other scarred friends. Who else?"

"That's about it. We have tire tracks, fingerprints with no match in the system, and words drawn in the dirt." He ran his free hand through his hair. "I've never seen anything like it. I have a feeling the perp is right under our nose but we can't see him."

"What else do we know about Jones?" She reached down and rubbed Rosie's ears.

"She works as customer service at a department store. Turns out she doesn't have a medical background at all." He glanced at his monitor. "Lives on the outskirts of town in a trailer park. She lives a pretty unassuming life. Easily overlooked." Unlike the gorgeous woman wearing sweatpants and a loose tee shirt sitting across from him. Even in the most unsexy attire, he couldn't help but notice the heads turn when she'd entered the bar.

"You're staring." She raised her eyebrows.

"Sorry." He ducked his head. Careful man. *You're wearing your heart on your sleeve and she's made it more than clear what she thinks of a relationship with you.* His head agreed. Partners should never cross the line, but his heart had something else in mind. "First thing in the morning, we go visit Mary Jones."

She nodded, still absently scratching the dog's head. "Why do you suppose Rosie went berserk today?"

"Instinct? She saw someone we didn't or sensed something we missed?" Her behavior had nagged at him all day. So had the fear on Ball's face. "We need to take a closer look at Russell Ball. It bothers me that he isn't listed on the college roster. We need to find out what his name was before he changed it." He sent an email to Ingram. "I also want to talk to his neighbors. Someone might know something they don't know they know."

"He's your number one?"

"Yep." He settled back on the sofa. His cell phone vibrated the same time Cassidy's beeped. He glanced at the text. "Help."

Cassidy jumped to her feet. "Mine says the same thing. It's Weston's number."

Their phones rang. Colin answered. "MacKenzie."

"Agent Ingram. I got a text from Weston. Isn't she with you?"

"She dropped us off an hour ago."

Ingram cursed. "Get to the motel. Now."

~

"Agent Weston?" Draco grinned when she opened the door to her motel room. "I have some information on the killer that is ravaging Clear Springs."

"How did you know where I was staying?" She peered past him into the parking lot.

He pushed his way inside, holding a Tazor to her ribcage. She jerked and fell like a board. "Why, I followed you, pretty one. You really should be more careful."

Her blue eyes blinked up at him. Words gurgled in her throat.

"You FBI agents think you're so smart, so above the rest of us." He grabbed her under the arms and dragged her to the bathroom.

He rolled her into the tub and tazed her again. No sense in letting Miss Beauty have the upper hand. He turned and tied her hands to the shower head, stretching her arms to an uncomfortable position. He then dug in her pockets, pulled out her cell phone, and sent a group text to all important contacts on her list.

"I really wish I had more time to play." He sat on the closed toilet. "You really are quite lovely."

"Why?"

"Why you?" He turned the damaged side of his face to her. "I saw the revulsion in your eyes earlier. You're no better than the other women I killed. Stay there. I'll be right back."

He dashed to his car, donned his leather jacket, then hurried back inside. He set up his video camera on the bathroom sink and pressed record. "We don't have much time." He pulled a knife from his pocket, careful to keep his face averted from the camera. "But, I can't disappoint the others, can I? They'll be expecting a video. I guess we have three or four minutes before I need to disappear." He shoved a washcloth in her mouth.

Using the knife, he popped the buttons from the white blouse she wore, revealing creamy skin. He softly drew the blade over her, counting her ribs as she screamed against her gag. Each scream sent his heart soaring! He closed his eyes and inhaled her fear.

After he'd had his fun, he put a bullet between her beautiful eyes and left, crushing her cell phone under his boot.

~

They made the fifteen minute drive in seven. Cassidy cut the jeep's engine and sprinted for the lobby, mere steps behind Colin. With one hand wrapped in Rosie's leash, she barged inside.

Ingram and Smith, their faces grave, turned from the counter to face them. "I want her found before I watch her death on camera," Ingram said. "I've tried her cell phone several times. Straight to voice mail. She doesn't answer a knock on the door of her room. Follow me." He grabbed a key from the shocked manager's hand and led the way.

"Find something," he barked, unlocking Weston's room door.

"What's her name, sir?" Cassidy withdrew her weapon. "We only know her as Weston."

"Maggie." He choked on her name.

They stepped into a ransacked room. The quilt from the bed lay half on the floor. A chair lay on its side. "Maggie Weston?" Cassidy moved toward the bathroom.

She froze. Maggie lay in the tub, a bullet hole in the center of her forehead and thin cuts across her ribcage. Written on the mirror in what looked like blood were the words, 'The pretty must die'.

"In here." Cassidy stepped over a shattered cell phone.

Ingram joined her and groaned. "Maggie." He knelt next to her body. "Why you?"

"No offense, sir," Cassidy said, sliding her gun into her holster, "but she fits the profile. She's quite beautiful." She turned to Colin. "For her to be targeted, she had to have met her killer and been repulsed by him, or at least he thought she had been."

"Russell Ball."

She nodded. "He's the only one we know of that she questioned for any length of time."

Ingram glanced up with red-rimmed eyes. "I want that bastard hung by his testicles."

"We're trying, sir. We don't have any solid evidence against him." Cassidy backed from the bathroom as emergency responders arrived.

"Find some! Get him behind bars. And, Monroe...get out of those sweats. We want this guy coming to us."

He had come to them and look what happened. She glanced at Colin as fear slithered up her back and wrapped its tentacles around her throat. "He's better than me, than us. We can't catch him. He's like a ghost." She'd known all along she didn't have what it took to be a good detective. This proved it.

Colin placed a hand on each of her shoulders and shook her. "Stop it. You will catch this guy. You're a great detective. One of the best I've ever worked with."

"How do you do that? How do you always seem to know what I'm thinking?" She locked gazes with him as if turning away would cause her to lose her grip on reality. "I don't think I can draw him out. He knows where I am. He can come get me any time he wants. He doesn't want to. He's toying with me." How could he? Especially if he was her biological father as they suspected? Who treated their child this way? If The Dragon wanted her, he could have her.

"Let's head to his apartment. If he's gone, I want to call a press conference." She pulled away from Colin. "We'll give out his description and name. Somebody out there has seen him and knows where he is."

"That's my girl."

They headed to Ball's apartment. Cassidy wasn't surprised in the slightest to find him gone. The manager let them into his apartment, a place Cassidy doubted he would return to.

With Colin starting at one end, and her at the other, they made a slow sweep of the place and came up with nothing. No photos, no books, nothing personal in any way. It was if the man had never been there.

"Who are you?"

Cassidy turned to see an elderly woman in a bright red coat with a fur collar died a sunshine yellow. Weston's doorman? "I'm Detective Monroe, this is Detective MacKenzie. Do you know the man who lived here?"

"No one lived here, dear. Well, there was a poor soul who came in and out, but he never slept here."

"Did he have a scar?"

"Oh, yes, the poor thing. I've often wondered how that came to be. That man has a story to tell, mark my words." Without actually entering the apartment, she poked her head in and looked around. "Very clean."

"When was the last time you saw Mr. Ball?" Cassidy took her by the arm and drew her into the hall.

"Why…" she plucked at a stray hair on her chin. "Less than an hour ago, I'd say. He told me goodbye as we passed in the hall. It sounded pretty final. What am I supposed to do with all his newspapers?"

"Newspapers?" Cassidy peered into her face.

"Why yes. He was always placing ads and said he kept them for prosperity's sake. Since he came and went so often and hired a cleaning crew for the apartment, he asked me to hold on to them. Shall I give them to you?" She clapped a white-gloved hand over her mouth. "Is he dead? Did he have an accident? Oh, dear."

"No, ma'am. He's fine. The newspapers?"

"Oh, yes. Right this way." She unlocked a door across the hall.

Cassidy was immediately assaulted by the odor of several cats. Breathing as shallowly as possible, she followed the strange woman into the apartment. Next to a rickety kitchen table were several newspapers.

"See? The man was always placing ads. I couldn't find out which ones, though," the woman said. "He didn't sign his name."

Cassidy knew which ones would be his. "What was he wearing when you last saw him?"

"A leather jacket with a dragon stitched on the back. Quite fetching. He carried more of the same jackets in his arms."

17

Cassidy woke early the next morning, made a pot of coffee, poured herself a cup, and then headed to the basement. Something had been teasing at the corner of her mind. She'd missed something that would, without a doubt, point to Russell Ball as her mother's attacker. Time would tell whether he was also the one who had murdered her, although her suspicions ran strong that he was. There couldn't be two evil masterminds out there who left the message 'the pretty must die' next to his victims.

She dug back through her mother's things and pulled out a shoebox full of photos. She'd seen some from her mother's college days and hadn't thought much of them…until that morning.

One after another the photos were set aside until she came across the one haunting her. She peered at the young man with his arm around her mother's shoulders. Russell Ball, handsome, grinning, and scarless. Mom had known her attacker. No wonder she'd gone away from the party with him.

"What are you doing?" Colin came down the steps. "I got worried when I didn't see you on the sofa."

"Look." She handed him the picture. "I think they might have dated. They at least knew each other."

His eyes lit up as a grin spread across his face. "This is a great find."

She glanced away before doing something she'd regret, like throwing her arms around his neck in celebration. Instead, she petted Rosie, craving physical contact with a breathing being. "All we have to do now is find him."

"And Mary Jones." He sat on the bottom step. "This case is coming to a close. Can you feel it?"

She felt a lot of things, one of which was the tender feeling she got when he slept and she could watch him without getting caught. She'd heard him cry out again last night, but had done no more than peek into his room. What she'd wanted to do was lie beside him and comfort him.

"I hope so," she said. "I've never been challenged this way before. It's…unsettling the way the body count is adding up."

He held out his hand. "Come. Let's have breakfast and then visit Mary Jones."

Her gaze clashed with his as she put her hand in his larger one. Heat infused her. The moment she was on her feet, she pulled free. Close contact with Colin only muddled her mind.

That morning, he'd cooked pancakes and sausage. At this rate, Cassidy would have no other choice than to wear her sweats.

After eating, she donned her suit, clipped her hair back from her face and applied a smattering of makeup. A lot of bother to hunt down criminals. Still, Ingram had ordered her, and with him grieving the loss of Weston, she'd do as he wanted.

"I do like you in a suit," Colin said, handing her Rosie with her leash attached. "Gorgeous."

Her face heated. "Thanks." This type of attention was why she dressed in clothes suited for cleaning out the garage. She didn't welcome the attention. Beauty got her mother killed. Why advertise the fact she'd inherited her mother's looks?

"I know what you're thinking."

"Oh, yeah?" She slid into the front passenger seat, surprised at how easy she gave over control of the driving to Colin.

"You think beauty is something to shove aside, hide under the rug." He started the ignition. "It won't work. Your beauty shines through even in sweats. Embrace what God gave you. It's a gift."

She supposed he accepted his good looks with open arms. She'd seen him use his manly assets to distract witnesses upon finding a dead body. Even Weston had faltered in her chilly attitude a time or two when he poured on the charm.

"What do you think about Ball fleeing his apartment with an armload of matching jackets?" She cut Colin a sideways glance.

"I think we need to be vigilant and worried. It sounds like he's outfitting a small army."

That's what she thought, too, and the idea sent dread flooding through her. How many followers did he have? Even a few could leave a path of destruction worse than Clear Springs, or even the state of Arkansas, had ever seen. She clicked her seatbelt. They'd already seen more death than she'd ever thought to experience on the job in a small southern town.

While Colin drove, she called Ingram to check in and give him their plan for the morning. "We're headed to the last known address of Mary Jones."

"You shouldn't go without backup."

"You're welcome to meet us there, sir, but every angle needs to be explored immediately. We also found a photo of my mother at the college frat party with Russell Ball. I don't think that was his name back then."

"I'll have someone check on that. If he changed his name legally, there'll be records. Be careful." Click.

He'd no sooner hung up than her phone rang again. "Detective Monroe here."

"Detective this is Mr. Laraby, from the college. Do you remember me?"

"Yes, sir, I remember you."

"You said to call if I discovered anything. Well, I remember something."

She heard the rustling of papers.

"Your mother's roommate here was Allison Bergeron. Since I didn't have her as a student, her name skipped my mind until I started going through school rosters."

"Why would you be doing that, sir?" She glanced at Colin.

"Something about that night was bothering me. Not just the violence of your mother's attack, but that no one did anything about it afterward. Those boys dropped her off at the clinic and left the party."

"We have a photo of my mother with the man we believe attacked her. Do you think you could identify him?"

"Maybe. If he was one of my students. I'm here until noon if you want to stop by."

"Thank you." She hung up. "Detour," she told Colin. "Head back to the college." She called Ingram back and gave him Bergeron's name. "Call me when you have an address."

"Will do." Click.

The man was short on words that morning. She sighed. The

death of someone who meant a lot to you did that.

~

Colin parked in front of the cafeteria and walked next to Cassidy and Rosie. Mr. Laraby sat at the same table as the last time they'd spoken to him.

The man looked up with a grim smile. "I'm sorry for having you drive all the way back out here."

"If it helps us solve the case, it was time worth spent." Colin pulled out a chair for Cassidy then took one to the man's right.

"This is the picture." Cassidy handed the photo to Laraby.

"Yes, I know this man." Laraby leaned back in his chair. "Smart. A real ladies man, back in the day. His name is Blake Russell."

Colin exchanged a glance with Cassidy. "You're sure? He registered here under that name?"

"Yes, but he wasn't enrolled here at the time of the attack. He received his bachelor's in business early. I always figured he would be a very wealthy man someday."

"Would that have kept him from being invited to the party?" Colin rested his folded arms on the table.

"Not at all. Not with his popularity."

Hmm. Being a handsome, sought after young man, the disfigurement to his face could easily have sent him into a psychotic rage. He could have harbored a grudge for years until deciding to kill Maureen. All they had to do now was find out where he was hiding.

Cassidy checked her phone. "We have an address for Allison."

"You've been a big help, Mr. Laraby." Colin stood and shook the man's hand. "Please call if you think of anything else."

"I will. Good luck."

Colin and Cassidy hurried back to the jeep. "I still think we need to check Mary's address before questioning Allison," he said.

"I agree. A killer in one hand is worth a potential witness from twenty-five years ago in the other."

They sped back toward Clear Springs and the rundown trailer park at the edge of town. Colin drove slowly through the mobile homes until he spotted Mary's address. He passed the rusty trailer and parked a few homes down.

"If you're looking for weird Mary, she ain't home." A

toothless old woman in the mobile home next to Mary's blew a plume of smoke into the air. "Packed up her Ford and skedaddled this morning before sunup."

"Are you sure she left?" Colin stopped and faced her.

"Had a couple of suitcases. That's good enough for me."

If they hadn't had breakfast…no, missing Mary was just one more broken link in the chain. One more thing that kept The Dragon and his minions one step ahead of the authorities.

He thanked the woman and continued to Mary's trailer. They might find something. No stone could be left unturned.

The door to Mary's trailer hung open by a couple of inches. Withdrawing his weapon, Colin motioned for Cassidy to stay behind him.

"Send Rosie in first." She unhooked the leash from the dog's collar. "She'll alert us if anyone is inside. Search, Rosie."

When minutes passed and no warning bark came from inside, Colin entered the trailer, wrinkling his nose at the sour odor of spoiled food and the mustiness of mounds of newspapers and magazines. "What a mess."

"It figures she'd be a hoarder. A lot of hurting people are. We'll be in here forever searching through all…this." Cassidy waved an arm at mounds of clutter that barely left enough room for a person to walk.

"We'll start by looking for something that seems out of place or of significance." He reholstered his gun and headed down the short hallway to a bedroom.

Rosie nosed in a closet and gave a short wuff when Colin approached.

"Back, girl."

Colin squatted and shoved aside a mound of clothes to reveal a calico cat and five kittens. He glanced around for a basket or box of some kind, finally emptying a clothes basket and moving mama and babies inside. He carried the basket back to the front room and set it on the crowded kitchen table where Cassidy flipped through a small pile of newspapers.

"We've been looking through larger editions. What if there's something important in these smaller presses? What's that? Oh." She picked up one of the kittens, nuzzling it against her cheek. "You poor little thing."

"I guess we'll be making a stop at the pound." Colin sat and pulled several of the papers to his side of the table.

She placed the kitten back with its mother and opened another newspaper to the classifieds. A few minutes later, she gasped. "I know how he's getting his followers." She shoved the paper at Colin.

Circled in red was an advertisement that read:

Mistreated?
Pretty people treating you unfairly?
Has your life been forever changed because of THEIR treatment?
Call 555-212-3456
I can help if you're willing to do the work

18

After calling in and securing the crime scene at Mary Jones's trailer, Cassidy and Colin drove toward the address they had for Allison Bergeron. Strange how so few people moved out of the area after college. Perhaps, they'd gone, realized life wasn't greener outside of Arkansas, and moved back.

"I spent my childhood convincing myself that my father was some kind of hero killed while saving people. Maybe a fireman or the military. Mom never talked about him, so I built up this fantasy. Wow, was I wrong." Cassidy took a shuddering sigh. "I couldn't have been further from the truth." An ache took up residence deep in her heart. Not only was she the product of rape, but she was the child of a serial killer.

Colin took her hand. "We can't help where we come from. We only have control over where we're going."

"You're wise for such a pretty face." She tried to smile, and failed. How would she react when facing her father for the last time? Could she pull the trigger? If she'd known Russell Ball was the man who'd fathered her and killed her mother, she would have shot him where he stood. Yes, she'd be able to pull the trigger.

"Let's grab some coffee." Colin swerved the jeep into a drive thru coffee shop. "You need something to bolster your spirits."

She glanced at him, studying the strong jaw line, the etched lips, the concern in his eyes. "Kiss me."

A crooked smile spread across his face. "Needing a distraction?"

"I know it's not professional, and I told you to keep your—"

He cupped the back of her head and kissed her long and hard until she could think of nothing but breathing. When they were both gasping, he drew back. "Did it work?"

"Thank you." She chuckled. "You're good medicine, Colin MacKenzie. I'm sorry about what I said the other night, you know, about being your pain killer."

He squeezed her hand. "Let's help each other through this, then we'll have time to explore us." He released her and pulled up to the window. "You can use me for whatever you need to in the meantime."

"Excuse me?" The barrista at the window widened her eyes.

"Sorry." Colin laughed and placed their orders.

Soon, they were back on the road, still chuckling over the expression on the poor barrista's face. "I think you disappointed her," Cassidy said. "She would have loved to be your plaything, I think."

"She was cute, but I prefer a more mature woman." He winked.

Was there a future for them? Cassidy stared out the window at the thick trees zooming past on the sides of the highway. She'd never really considered a man in her life. Her career, proving herself, those had always taken precedence. Dare she hope for something more?

What kind of man wanted a woman with her blood line? If she'd thought proving herself in a predominantly male career in the south was hard before, once people found out who her father was, it could become near to impossible. She could move. Start fresh somewhere else. It was a thought.

They parked in front of a modest ranch-style home in a neighborhood of cookie cutter houses. On the front porch sat assorted shoes in varying sizes. A tricycle lay on its side on the freshly mowed lawn. A porch swing moved by a gentle breeze. A scene of tranquility. One which Colin and Cassidy were about to disrupt.

"Let's go meet your mother's bestfriend." Colin shoved open his door.

Cassidy's heart went into overdrive. They were about to speak with the woman who had known her mother better than anyone. She squared her shoulders, commanded Rosie to stay, and marched to the front door. On second thought, she snapped her fingers for Rosie to follow. They might be in the house for a while and the day was heating up. If Allison didn't want a dog in the house, Rosie could stay on the porch.

The door opened before Cassidy's finger pressed the bell. A pretty woman with a stylish blond bob haircut answered the door. "Baby is sleeping." She smiled. "I hope you aren't selling anything."

Cassidy showed her badge. "We have a few questions for you. Are you Allison Bergeron?"

The woman's brows drew together in a frown. "Not anymore. I haven't been her in twenty years. I'm Allison Carson now. What's this about?"

"May we come in or would you prefer the porch?" Cassidy glanced at a set of whicker rocking chairs.

"Come in." She eyed the dog, then her gaze rested appreciatively on Colin. "The dog won't make noise will it? I have a three year old inside that would love to play with it."

"She's well trained," Cassidy said, drawing the woman's attention back to her.

Allison opened the door wide and allowed them to enter. "Can I get you something to drink?"

"We've coffee, thank you." Colin smiled, putting the woman at ease.

How did he do that with a look and a grin? Cassidy shook her head and sat on one end of the sofa. "We were told by a Mr. Wilson that you were Maureen Monroe's bestfriend in college."

"Yes." Allison sat in a stuffed chair covered with a floral fabric. "Benji, play nice with the dog."

"Gentle, Rosie." Cassidy watched as a tow-headed little boy squatted next to the dog.

"I haven't seen or heard from Maureen in…at least ten years. We used to keep in touch, then nothing."

Cassidy took a deep breath. "She was murdered ten years ago. We believe by the same man who attacked her during the frat party."

"Oh." Tears sprang to Allison's eyes and she glanced at her son. "Benji, go get a juice box out of the fridge, okay?" Once he'd gone, Rosie trotting at his side, she turned back to Cassidy. "He'll probably give your dog cookies, I hope that's okay." She sighed. "I had no idea Maureen was dead. And…that awful night." She covered her face with her hands. "I've done everything possible to forget that night."

She hadn't wanted to go to the party. I coerced her. It was all my fault. If she hadn't been there…"

"If I know my mother, she had a mind of her own."

"You're her daughter? Of course you are. I can see the resemblance." She reached over and placed a hand on Cassidy's arm. "You're just as pretty as she…was."

"Can you tell me about her?"

"A great gal. Oh, the fun we had. I was the troublemaker, Maureen the logical one. Still, she had her wild side. She went to the party because a boy she thought was handsome was going."

"Blake Russell?"

"Yes, that's the one. Your mother wasn't a prude, but she was one of the good girls. That's why her attack affected so many of us the way it did. I was promiscuous. It should have been me in the woods that night." Tears trickled down her face. "I've never forgiven myself. If I hadn't been with my own boy that night…well, things can't be changed, can they?"

"No, ma'am." A knife stabbed at Cassidy's gut. "If only they could. We have reason to believe that Blake was her attacker that night and the one who later killed her. We also believe he is responsible for the deaths of a couple of other women."

"Oh, no." Her sobs increased.

Colin knelt next to the woman's chair. "None of it is your fault, Allison. You can't force someone to do something they don't want to. Things got carried away at that party, things that resulted in future destruction. You weren't at fault. We're not here to make you feel bad. We're hoping you can give us some answers. Maybe tell us more about Blake Russell."

"He was a handsome enigma. Smart, finished college early. All the girls wanted to be noticed by him, but he only had eyes for Maureen. Called her his Fire Princess. I would never have figured him for a killer."

"My mother wounded him that night." Cassidy stared at the freshly vacuumed carpet. "Gravely wounded him. We think that is what set him on his path of destruction."

Rosie barked from the kitchen.

Cassidy lunged to her feet at the same moment Colin did.

They dashed into the kitchen.

Rosie lunged at the kitchen door, keeping her body between the door and the child. The twisted features of Blake Russell stared through the window, then vanished.

Colin unlocked then yanked open the door. "Give the command, Cassidy."

"Angriff!"

Rosie darted outside, Colin and Cassidy on her heels. They chased her around the corner of the house.

Blake grabbed for the door of a dark sedan left running. With his other hand, he tazed the dog, then slid into the driver's seat. He squealed tires backing from the driveway.

Colin knelt and fired off two shots while Cassidy called Ingram and knelt beside the helpless Rosie.

The shots shattered the back window of the sedan and Cassidy watched helplessly as Russell sped away. "Good girl." Once Rosie was back on her feet, albeit a bit wobbly, Cassidy turned and headed for the kitchen.

Allison clutched her son to her chest while a baby screamed from a room on the other side of the house. "Thank God I keep that door locked. Was that Blake?"

"Yes." Cassidy glanced out the front window. He'd followed them. "We'll need to put your family in protective custody."

~

Oh, the game was getting fun now! Draco grinned as he sped away from the blond woman's house. He remembered her from college. Pretty, but in no way close to Maureen's beauty. He wanted to go back after the cops left and show her who he was now, but the innocence in the little boy's eyes wouldn't allow him to.

He didn't harm children. They weren't responsible for any revulsion they might show. If they cried when seeing him, he blamed the parents for not raising them better. He caressed his scar. He'd always wanted a son. Instead, he had a daughter, beautiful like her mother, who hunted him like an animal.

Someday, when the time was right, they'd face each other in a final, epic battle. The strongest would survive. He had no qualms that they would ever be a loving family. He was meant to be alone. The last of a dying breed. The lone dragon on a quest to rid the world of the unworthy.

He popped Beethoven's Fifth into the CD player and drummed his hands on the steering wheel in beat with the music. The next few weeks would be glorious as he continued his diabolical game. He laughed, the sound ringing loud over the music.

Sweet Cassidy, can you hear the music? He'd make sure it was the last thing she ever heard, his face the last thing she saw. Just like Maureen.

19

Mary Jones checked into a motel in the next town and cursed The Dragon. She immediately repented. She couldn't stay mad at the man who gave her back her purpose in life.

She tossed her suitcases in the corner and threw herself across the bed. How had the cops found out about her? Draco had promised there was no way to be discovered. It had to be because of her hateful sisters. They were at the root of all her problems.

Well, no more. She laughed, the sound manic in the small room. They couldn't create problems for anyone anymore.

She glanced at the water-stained ceiling. What did she do now? She had no others on her list. Most people were kind, if not sympathetic to Mary's plainness. It wasn't her fault she had mousy hair and mud-colored eyes. Nor was it her fault she'd struggled with being overweight her entire life. Her mother had been attractive, her father handsome. It was nothing more than the luck of the draw.

Sighing, she pounded the mattress and dug her cell phone out of her purse. "What do I do now?" she asked the moment he answered. "I have no other purpose."

"Find one." Draco's deep voice resonated over the air waves. "But we don't kill those who don't deserve it. You must remember that. Find a new identity for yourself. All the information you need is in the packet I gave you at the first meeting. Our time of working together is complete."

"No." Her heart beat in her throat. "I want to continue helping you. Tell me what to do. Please."

"Find your purpose again, Mary." Click.

She grinned, knowing exactly what she would do. Something

that would make her Draco's favorite.

~

Rosie seemed to suffer no ill effects from being tazed, much to Cassidy's relief. She sat on the porch of Allison's house, her arm around the dog, and waited while Ingram and the crime scene investigators prepared her and her family to be moved.

A navy Toyota Camry pulled into the driveway. A harried man shoved open his door and, leaving it hanging open, bounded up the porch steps, not sparing Cassidy a glance. Mr. Carson, she presumed.

Colin met the man at the door, saying something to him in a low, soothing voice. Her partner would be a wonder in hostage negotiations. He had a way about him that put the most anxious person at ease. Except for her. The deep rumble of his voice sent her senses into overdrive instead of soothing them.

Since The Dragon seemed to be mirroring Cassidy's steps, Ingram had asked her and Colin to take the Carsons to the safe house and leave the rest of the investigation to the FBI. The order raised the hackles on the back of her neck. This was her case! It was personal. The last thing she wanted was to be hidden away in some mountain cabin with a guard watching her every move.

"But, my job. Our life," Mr. Carson argued. "We can't leave it. This killer isn't after us or he would have harmed my wife and son."

"Sir, it's only until he's caught. It's a precaution. Think of your family."

Cassidy turned her head as Colin placed a consoling hand on the man's shoulder. She pushed to her feet. "The killer wants me, Mr. Carson. Rest assured we'll do everything in our power to keep us all safe."

He narrowed his eyes. "Yet, you're the officer going with us, right?"

"Yes, sir, I've been ordered to hide the same as you." She motioned for Rosie to follow and pushed into the house. She approached Ingram. "I'd like permission to go to my home and pack a few things."

"Smith and MacKenzie, take Monroe to her place. Be back in an hour. We're wasting daylight." He gave Cassidy a nod and marched to the kitchen where Allison packed a box with food.

"Ma'am we only have so much room in the jeep."

"My babies have to eat."

Cassidy smiled and joined her bodyguards outside. An hour later, a few changes of clothing, toiletries, her mother's journal and her case notes, and Cassidy sat in the idling jeep while FBI agents she had yet to meet loaded her vehicle with everything a family thought they couldn't live without. When the jeep was full, they loaded the family's silver mini-van. She shook her head. A lot of baggage to cart up the mountain.

"This is ridiculous," Colin said, getting into the driver's seat. "That woman doesn't want to leave anything behind."

"She wants her family comfortable." Which would be a lot more than she and Colin would be. The two bedroom safehouse left the two of them sleeping on the floor in the front room in much too close proximity to each other. Still, the family would provide a safe buffer between the tension radiating between her and her partner no matter how much they tried to pretend as if nothing was happening between them.

"It bothers me that Ingram is removing us from the case, so to speak." Colin backed out of the drive. "We were beginning to make headway."

"I agree. If one of us had to go into hiding, it should have been me, leaving you to continue the investigation."

"No way." He frowned. "Where you go, I go. It's been that way since day one." He took her hand. "I'd go crazy not knowing how you were or whether Blake was getting close."

His words warmed her to the bone. "I appreciate the thought, but I trust you to help me more than anyone else."

He grinned. "I don't intend to stop investigating completely. I'll just be doing it through cyber space. Everyone leaves a trail. We just have to find Blake's."

"Don't forget Mary."

He chuckled. "How could I forget our crazy Plain Jane? No, I'll be searching for her right along with her leader."

"Why do you think none of his other followers have come forth? He has to have them. Why else have an armload of jackets? Do you think he's working with them one-by-one? Other than Mary, we've only met the one posing as a photographer and nothing on him since." Nothing about this case was easy. It was one for the history books. They could have saved so much time if her mother would have mentioned her attacker's name in her journal.

Why hadn't she? Why keep it a secret? Had her mother had a personal vendetta against Blake that led to a showdown she lost? So many questions, so few answers.

"What do you think about Ingram sending the Carsons to the safehouse?" she asked. "If Blake had wanted to harm them, he had the opportunity. At least with the little boy."

"Allison is a good-looking woman. I don't think Ingram wants to take any chances. Maybe Blake has a few morals and doesn't harm children. But, if he wanted to go after their mother...well, you know what it's like to have your mother murdered."

She did. Her later teen years had been ones full of difficulty, pity, and rebellion. She wouldn't wish that on anyone. "I still don't like being sent away."

"We'll manage." He squeezed her hand and pulled free as he turned the jeep down a side road that didn't look as if anyone had driven there in a long time.

Weeds covered the dirt road, hiding the ruts. The jeep bounced over one hole after another until Cassidy thought her teeth would break from clacking together. She breathed a sigh of relief when they pulled in front of the rustic cabin. "Home sweet home for however long we're destined to stay." She opened her door, then Rosie's. "Check it out, girl."

The dog bounded away, nose to the ground as Cassidy turned to survey their surroundings. Thick trees and underbrush provided plenty of places for a person to hide. Someone should have kept the place up a bit more. It might prove to be more of a danger than a safe place.

She scanned the tree line. The sun barely cut through the thick branches overhead. Several trees hung low over the cedar roofed cabin. There'd be no fires until they were trimmed back. It was a good thing it was summer and not winter. "I'll head inside and open the windows to air the place out," she told Colin as the mini-van pulled behind the jeep.

She marched to the front door and pushed it open with a loud squeak. Two mice darted across the floor, leaving tracks in the thick dust on the floor. At least she'd keep busy cleaning.

Who was she kidding? She didn't want to clean. She wanted to hunt down and confront her murderous father.

20

Cassidy and Allison had the cabin liveable by nightfall. Then, boredom quickly set in. While Colin worked his magic on the internet, Cassidy set her mother's caseboard up in the cabin's dining space. She hoped that by taking everything down and putting everything back up, she'd discover something she might have previously missed.

"What is that?" Bill Carson stood next to her, arms crossed.

"A case board on a cold case related to the one we're working on now." She leaned against a small wooden table and stared at the board.

"These photos look old." He peered closer at the ones saved by Cassidy's mother. "Is the killer here?"

Cassidy pointed him out. "We have no idea where he is now."

"That's Blake Russell. I went to high school with him."

"What?!" She whirled, sloshing hot coffee on her hand. She hissed and wiped it on the leg of her jeans.

"Yeah. He comes from a rather influential family, at least for this area. A bit of a spoiled brat, smart, and athletic. Leader of the popular group. Last I heard, he'd made a bundle of money for himself in real estate."

She couldn't believe their luck. "You wouldn't happen to know the name of his company, would you? He's changed his name since you knew him. He goes by Russell Ball."

"Wyvern Incorporated."

Of course. Cassidy clapped him on the shoulder. "Thank you." Maybe being locked up with the Carsons wouldn't be so bad after all. She headed to the living room where Colin sat hunched over his laptop. "Look up Wyvern Incorporated. Bill said it's Blake's corporate name."

"Wyvern as in dragon? How dense could we be?"

"In our defense, I didn't expect him to be a wealthy owner of anything."

Colin's fingers flew over the keyboard. "The company was sold for five million dollars last year." He leaned back on the sofa. "Another dead end."

"No." She sagged next to him. "He planned this. He built up the business, sold it, and started creating havoc."

"He has the money to lay low for a while, too." He started typing again. A few minutes later, he groaned. "Most of his funds are in an off-shore account."

"Of course, they are." They were never going to catch him. Not usually given to self-pity, Cassidy blinked back tears. She'd been sad and cried at her mother's death, devastated for months, but these were tears of frustration and helplessness. Sometimes, when the day seemed darkest, she almost turned to the God her mother believed in.

Colin put his arms around her and pulled her close. "Please don't cry. Don't give up on me, sweetheart." His thick brogue smoothed the edges of her pain.

She rested her head on his shoulder and closed her eyes, suddenly exhausted. If only she could stay there. If only she were worthy of having a career and love. But, she wasn't. It took everything she had to do her job the way she thought it needed doing and in one fell swoop, Blake Russell took that all away. Now, even if she felt there was room in her life for romance, she couldn't foist her bloodline on anyone. Most of all any possible future children.

Squeezing her eyes tight, tears trickled down her cheeks. Enough pity. She swiped the tears away and sat up. "What's our next move?"

~

"We pass on any information we have to Ingram." Colin felt an immediate loss when she pulled away. At least she was no longer treating him as if he were going to attack her or give her some fatal disease. It seemed as if she's chosen to pass off their...misunderstanding and continue as friends, if not close partners. He'd take what he could get. There was plenty of time for more in the future. "At least we've gone a few days without another death." She pushed to her feet and spread a sleeping bag on the floor. "I'm bushed, Colin. I'm going to sleep."

He nodded. "I'll take first watch and wake you in four hours."

While she settled in the close area between the sofa and the wall, Rosie curled up next to her and the rest of the cabin's occupants headed to their prospective rooms. The Carson's youngest wailed in protest at going to bed but settled down within minutes. Soon, soft snores drifted from Cassidy's makeshift bed.

He shifted in his seat so he could see her in the light of the laptop monitor. Shadows flickered across her face. Long lashes rested on soft cheeks. Lips, begging to be kissed, parted slightly in sleep. Her beauty did things to him that no other woman had ever done. Not only her outward appearance, but the beauty within. Her strength and determination. Still, he saw her vulnerability and knew he'd die protecting her if it came to that.

A board creaked overhead. Bill Carson most likely paced the floor in his own attempts to protect his family. Moments later the man joined him downstairs.

"You should sleep, Mr. Carson." Colin closed his laptop to prevent the man from seeing confidential information.

"I can't. Not when there is a madman out there who might want to harm my wife." He ran his hands through his hair. "Agent Ingram let me bring my pistol. I haven't fired the thing in years."

"Can you shoot another person?" A lot of people couldn't.

"If it means them or my family, I won't hesitate." He pulled up one of the four straight-back kitchen chairs and swung it around, straddling it and resting his folded arms on the back. "I hope it doesn't come to violence."

"We'll do our best to keep it away from you." Colin glanced at Cassidy. "It's her he wants, not your wife. If he were to go after your wife, it would be to get to the detective."

"It upsets me to think the FBI would put my family in more danger by sending the detective with us." The corners of his mouth turned down.

"She's good at what she does. If we're wrong, and the unsub has targeted your wife for a reason known only to him, Detective Monroe is an asset you want on your side."

"I guess I'll have to take your word for it, won't I?"

Colin understood the man's anger. He felt his own. "You should get some sleep."

The man smiled. "I know a dismissal when I hear one. Good

night, Detective." Bill replaced the chair and headed back up the stairs.

Colin watched him leave then opened up his laptop. He needed to find the one needle in the haystack that would give them the upper hand in a case quickly growing out of control.

"Don't blame him for being angry," Cassidy mumbled from the floor. "I'm angry, too. None of us asked for this."

He nudged her gently with his foot. "I don't. Go back to sleep. I'm sorry we woke you."

He eyed the backpack next to the front door. His prescription sleep aids were in there. While he hated to take one, he wondered whether having a nightmare in a houseful of strangers might be worse.

~

Mary backed down the rough dirt road and onto the highway. Cackling, she parked on the shoulder and dialed Draco. "I know where she's hiding," she said in a sing-song voice.

"I thought you were going to disappear and start over."

"I want to help you. Without you, I'm nothing." Why couldn't he see that? Start over? He'd given her a new life, a new purpose. Why would she want to be anywhere else?

Silence screamed from the other end of conversation.

"Draco?"

"When I give you a direct order, Mary, I expect you to follow it. Do not engage Detective Monroe. I will deal with her myself. Do you understand?"

"Yes, sir." She understood perfectly. He wanted something done with the detective and the fact she still walked the earth meant he didn't know what to do about her. Mary could read between the lines better than most people. She understood the need for secrecy. "I'll do as you say." Click.

She drummed her hands on the steering wheel in a beat of celebration. When she did what needed to be done, Draco would love her above all others.

~

Imbecile! She was going to ruin everything.

Draco leaned back in his leather chair. What to do about Mary? She was going to ruin everything.

He needed to give her a job to do. One that would get her

captured, or better yet, killed. If that didn't work, he'd have to dispose of her himself. Poor Mary. He saw the look of longing in her eyes. She was so desperate for love she'd take even a disfigured man such as himself. Perhaps there really was someone for everyone in this world. If only she weren't so…annoying, and a little more attractive. He would never desire a pretty person again. Not after having discovered the ugliness inside them. Still, he wanted someone that he could stomach looking at over the table at mealtime. Perhaps, he was a bit of a hypocrite.

Pushing to his feet, he crossed the small amount of space in the cramped apartment and stared out the window at the mini-mart across the street. He could have rented a much nicer place, but a dump like this one would be the last place the authorities would suspect. Living in the seedy side of town had its benefits and after putting a bullet between the eyes of a young gang member without batting an eye, the locals left him alone.

Draco needed a distraction. He shoved his arms into the sleeves of his leather jacket and headed outside. Even he could buy companionship with the right amount of money. He had ten tons of stress bottled up inside of him and desperately needed a release.

He scoured the streets looking for a woman with a bit of class. So many of them were skanky or shied away when they saw him coming. Unfortunately, the shooting of the gang member had made so many of the women afraid of him.

Keeping the good side of his face to them, he approached a group where a young woman of about eighteen smiled shyly up at him. He didn't recognize her. While sweet, she wasn't beautiful in the typical sense and wore tight jeans and a shirt that didn't show every one of her assets. Just the type of girl to wile away a few hours.

"Are you eighteen, and can you stomach this for a hundred dollars?" He showed her his scar.

Her eyes widened. "As long as you don't do that to me, I can."

"I like your style, young lady." He crooked his arm. "Two hours company is all I desire. Do you prefer red or white wine?"

"Pink champagne." She batted her lashes.

He laughed. "Then pink champagne it shall be." He bowed to the other prostitutes. "She'll be back in a little while, safe and sound."

After stopping at a liquor store on the corner and keeping his face turned from security cameras, he purchased the best pink champagne the store carried and escorted his little friend back to his apartment.

"Have a seat, darling. There's a change of clothes on the table. What is your name?"

"What do you want my name to be?"

"Maureen." He grinned. "You wouldn't happen to have red hair under that black wig, would you?"

She giggled and yanked off the wig. Strawberry blond curls tumbled to her shoulders.

It might not be the same shade as the woman he'd once idolized, nor was Little Maureen anywhere close in the beauty department, but if Draco turned off the lights, he could pretend they were anyone in the world.

He filled a bowl with ice, shoved the bottle of champagne inside and then lit a candle. "Let's get this party started."

"Can you kiss with your lips all twisted like that?" Little Maureen twisted a curl around her finger. "What happened to you?"

"An evil woman took a knife to me." He sat next to her on the sofa. "If you don't want to suffer the same fate she did, you'll stop asking questions." His blood boiled, and he fisted his hands to keep from striking her.

21

"I'm calling to keep you up-to-date on the case," Ingram said on the phone the next morning. "We've had another...incident."

"What happened?" Cassidy waved Colin over.

"The body of a young prostitute was discovered this morning."

"Why do you think her death is related?"

"Written in the dirt next to her body were the words 'pretty is as pretty does'. I know it isn't exactly the same as the others, but the word pretty—"

"We'll be right there." Cassidy grabbed her holstered gun from a peg high on the wall out of the reach of children.

"No, we'll do the investigating. You're in hiding and protective service."

"You can't do this." She flopped onto the sofa. "This is more my case than anyone's. I need to be there when this guy is caught. Bill Carson is armed. If anyone comes snooping around—"

"I gave you a direct order."

"Then call my supervisor." She lunged to her feet and paced. "I'll do this with or without your permission." She waved a hand as Colin opened his mouth to speak. "You know as well as I do that Blake Russell does these things to draw me out. So, let me be there. We won't catch him otherwise. You know it."

Bill Carson grabbed the phone from her hand. "Sir, I would appreciate her leaving this cabin. If this maniac wants her, then having her close to my family puts us in danger." He handed the phone back to Cassidy. "You're welcome." He marched into the kitchen.

"Sir?"

"The man has a point." Ingram sighed. "As much as I hate to say this, go ahead and investigate this lead with MacKenzie. I'll send Smith to watch over the Carsons." He gave her the location of the body and hung up.

Cassidy grinned and fist pumped the air. She might be walking into a trap, but it was better than sitting there wondering what was going on.

She glanced at Rosie who sat looking up at her with intense eyes. The Carson's little boy laughed and threw his arms around the dog's neck. "Stay, Rosie. Guard." It would leave an empty spot in her heart not having her faithful companion with her, but the child could use the protection more.

"Are you sure?" Colin glanced from her to Rosie.

"I'm sure." She heaved a sigh and glanced at the Carson family. "If I don't return for her, take good care of her. She's the best protector you'll ever need." She knelt down and hugged her furry friend. "Be good. I'll be back by dark." God willing.

Rosie whined, confused, as Cassidy strolled out the front door.

Without looking back, she climbed into the jeep, grateful for the chance to search for The Dragon rather than wait for him to come to her as she hid in a cabin in the woods.

"You're either the bravest woman I've ever met," Colin said, "or the dumbest. That dog is the best warning you can have that someone is coming."

"Which is why I left her behind. If something happened to the children because of my presence, I'd never forgive myself." She stared at him. "You should understand about not forgiving yourself. You can't get over something that was an accident. My staying here is not the same thing."

"Low blow." He started the ignition and turned the jeep around in the small yard.

"You didn't have a nightmare last night."

"I took a pill, and I'm still feeling the effects. They leave me grouchy, so don't start in on me."

"All righty then." She fought a smile and glanced out the window. Perhaps the always grinning Colin wasn't so perfect after all. How long would his bad mood last? She glanced at her watch.

~

Colin parked next to the yellow crime scene tape in the city's poorest, and most crime ridden, area. Several gang members and prostitutes stood on the civilian side of the tape and craned their necks to get a look.

"Pardon me." He lifted the tape to let Cassidy through.

Lying on the gravel strewn alley next to a dumpster was the body of a young girl. She didn't look more than fifteen or sixteen. If she was older, she was lying. His heart sank at the loss of such a young life. Red hair fanned out from a face that was more cute than pretty. A short leather skirt barely covered what should be hidden.

He knelt next to her and looked up into the tear-filled eyes of a much older girl. "What's her name?"

"All we know her by is Angel."

"Who was her last trick? Did you know the man?"

She shook her head. "He wasn't a regular." She shuddered. "He was a monster. Handsome on one side, scarred on the other, like Two-Face, the character from the Batman movies. She was wearing jeans when she went with him."

That cinched the fact that Blake Russell was most likely the murderer. Colin pushed to his feet, noticing a young African American man standing off to one side. The man motioned his head, calling Colin closer.

"Do you have information for me?" Colin stepped over the tape.

"That man was here before. A couple of days ago. Me and some of my homies tried to harass him. He pulled out a gun and shot one of us right between the eyes. He's cold. Didn't even flinch when he pulled the trigger, then just walked away."

"Did you see him with the girl?"

"They went into that liquor store for a bottle. I don't know where they went after that. Me and the homies been trying to find him to exact payback, but he's like a ghost."

"He calls himself The Dragon. Stay away from him."

"Dude." The man held up his hands. "We got to pay him back. Just call us the dragon slayers. We'll send you his head."

"Then you'll most likely die." Colin almost threatened to lock the guy up in order to save his life. He glanced at the man's 'homies'. He couldn't lock them all up. He shook his head and headed for the liquor store while Cassidy spoke with the crime scene techs.

A bell jingled over the door when he entered. He glanced up and noted a security camera. "That thing work?"

"Yes, sir. We keep it running on a loop. It doesn't pay to not be vigilant in this neighborhood."

"Do you have the footage from last night?"

"Yep." He motioned Colin to come around the counter. "You can see it all on that monitor."

Colin backed up the video feed until he came to the approximate time Blake had entered the store. The man kept the scarred side of his face away from the camera and grinned, or grimaced, at the young girl at his side. Was it possible he'd slipped up and not noticed the camera?

"How did he seem to you?" He asked the clerk.

"Happy. The girl was giggling. They seemed to be having a good time."

"She didn't seem afraid of him?"

"Nope."

Hmm. Colin glanced at the video again. What had changed? Had she said something to set Blake off? In the video her hair was dark, but outside her hair was red. Was that the trigger? He ejected the tape and slipped it into a paper bag. "Thank you for your cooperation."

"Any time. Angel was well liked around here."

Colin headed back out and joined Cassidy. "Any word on her real identity?"

"We're checking her against missing teens. It will probably take a while. Poor thing." She scanned the area. "Doesn't make sense that Blake would go for one so young."

"Look around. She was the prettiest one here. He probably thought she'd give him the least resistance. The weird thing is, the store clerk said they were laughing while making their purchase. Angel hadn't seemed frightened of him at all."

"She said or did something that got her killed. I guess we start knocking on doors. Not the safest thing in this neighborhood."

"The gang members are out for revenge. I'm sure they'll help." If they didn't kill him before alerting the authorities to his location. In moments like that one, Colin didn't care if they found the man alive or dead.

"I need some coffee."

"There's a gas station on the corner. They'll have some. Then we can plan our next step. Did you find any clues around the body?"

"Not a thing, just like all the others." She glanced at her watch. "Are you still grouchy?"

"No. Why?"

"Your bad mood lasted two hours."

"Seriously? You timed it?"

She shrugged and laughed. "It's out of character for you."

She was something else. He grinned and put his arm around her shoulders.

The gang members parted like the Red Sea as the two of them strolled down the sidewalk. A couple of them gave Cassidy appreciative glances, but no one said anything. Their silence gave Colin the creeps. The authorities needed to find The Dragon before the dragon slayers did.

~

Draco removed every trace of Little Maureen from the shoddy apartment. He cleaned the surfaces with bleach, vacuumed the sofa, and tossed the bedding into a pile to be laundered. Her jeans he tossed out the window after dousing them with bleach. They'd find them and link them to the girl, but he didn't care. He'd be long gone by then.

Not that he didn't expect Cassidy and the Scotsman to not figure out he'd killed her, but because it was what he did when he had a victim at his house. Although he hadn't planned on killing the girl, he wanted no traces of her anywhere around.

Once he was certain he'd taken care of anything relating to her, or him, he gathered his things and closed the door. Time to find a new place to live.

He scooted out the back door of the building and headed for his rented Lincoln. Popping the trunk, he tossed his suitcase in the back.

"Hey, Dragon."

He whirled, coming face-to-face with five gang members. "Walk away."

"The cops are looking for you. We told them we'd bring them your head."

"Good luck with that." Draco re-opened the trunk and pulled out a bag. "I'll give you one more chance to walk away."

"Now, that ain't going to happen, Dragon." The leader said his name as if it were a cuss word. "We got to make amends for you killing our friend. Now, it doesn't seem likely that you can shoot all five of us."

Draco pulled a lighter from his pants pocket. "Perhaps not." He set the paper bag on fire and leaped behind the dumpster.

The bag exploded.

Screams filled the air along with the stench of burning flesh.

He sighed and came out of hiding, stepping over the nearest gang member howling on the ground. "You should have listened to me." He gave the man a kick, then climbed into the driver's seat of his car, now showing the effects of the pipe bomb he'd set off. No matter. He'd ditch the car and get another one.

The gang members wouldn't die. The bomb hadn't been powerful enough. But, they would sport a few scars of their own.

He cranked up the radio. Classical music burst from the speakers as he pulled out of the alley. When would the masses learn not to mess with The Dragon? He glanced at the clock in the dashboard. He had thirty minutes before his meeting with his followers.

He spotted the detectives strolling down the sidewalk as if they were on an afternoon excursion. They stepped into the gas station store. Draco parked across the street and watched through the window as the Scotsman bought two coffees.

It would be so easy to pick them off. He thought of the gun in his glove compartment and almost reached for it. No, he had a different end in mind for them. Cassidy needed the opportunity to join him, to share his vision. If not, she would suffer the fate of her mother.

He would wait.

22

An explosion rattled the store window.

"That came from the alley." Cassidy turned to the store clerk. "Where's the back door?"

The young woman pointed. "Should I call the cops?"

"We are the cops!" Colin barged down a short hall and out the back door, Cassidy on his heels.

The five gang members they'd spoken to earlier lay writhing in agony on the ground. The leader clutched a leg missing several layers of skin.

Cassidy placed a call for an ambulance and squatted next to one young man with a stick poking out of his forehead. "Looks like y'all had a run in with The Dragon, and he was breathing fire." She shook her head. "At least everyone here is still breathing. This one barely." She moved the man's hand away from his face. "Don't pull it out. You'll bleed to death."

"I warned you, didn't I?" Colin helped the leader to a sitting position and used the man's belt as a tourniquet.

The young man cursed. "He's bad news for sure."

"So, it was the same guy?"

"Yep. Came out of that apartment complex behind us."

As soon as the ambulance pulled into the alley, Cassidy followed Colin into the apartment complex. A few moments spent with a drowsy manager and they knew which apartment Blake Russell had rented.

"The man always paid cash," the woman said, tightening a stained yellow terry cloth robe around her faded nightgown. "Kept to himself and never gave me a lick of trouble. Not like some of my other tenants."

She led them up the stairs and into an apartment reeking of

bleach. "See? The place is spotless. Just like him."

Cassidy cast her an incredulous look. If only the woman knew. "Don't you do background checks on your tenants?"

"I done told you he paid cash. That's all I care about. Y'all let yourselves out." She turned and shuffled back down the stairs.

Cassidy stepped into the sparcely furnished room, snapping gloves onto her hands. "He cleaned it in anticipation of us coming."

"Probably to remove that poor girl's DNA." Colin moved to the window. "He's got a clear view of the street and the prostitutes from here. My guess is...he'd chosen her, whether to die or for company, I don't know."

"He did a lot more than that." Cassidy peered under the sleeper sofa and pulled out a slip of paper torn from a receipt. In girlish scrawl was the name Maureen. "Either she shared my mother's name or that's what he chose to call her."

Blake Russell seemed to be spiralling into decline, especially if he had taken to naming his victims by Cassidy's mother's name. She pushed to her feet and headed to the one other room in the place. The bathroom.

She opened the medicine cabinet to find it empty. Same with the small closet on the other side of the wall. It was as if no one had lived there. Another deadend as far as clues went. Still, they'd have the crime scene investigators scope the place. They knew Blake was their man, but every clue that backed that up made putting him behind bars easier.

"Cassidy." Colin's voice called her from the front room.

She joined him at the front window. A dark Lincoln idled in front of the building. She knew without being able to see through the tinted windows that their killer sat in the driver's seat. She opened the window and leaned out. "Come on up and let's talk."

Her cell phone rang. "Blake?"

"Hello, dear. Have you found the item I left you yet?"

"The slip of paper with my mother's name?"

"No, I didn't know about that. Silly little girl." He chuckled. "She and I got along just fine until she had a slip of the tongue. Very unfortunate."

"What's the item, Blake?"

"I go by Draco now, dear." He sighed. "I thought you were

better than this. I hate to make things too easy for you. I need a worthy adversary."

"Come up here and I'll show you how worthy I am." With a bullet in the heart.

"Tsk tsk. When the time is right." Click. The car pulled away from the curb and drove off.

"He said he left us something." Cassidy turned from the window. "There aren't many hiding places here."

"So we look closer. I'll start at this end, you start in the bathroom."

She'd just come from there, but anything was better than standing around guessing. She returned to the small room containing a shower, a toilet, and a pedestal sink. If someone were to hide something, where would they put it? She glanced at the vent overhead. Climbing onto the toilet seat, she removed the screw holding the cover in place. Empty, like everything else.

She jumped down and lifted the lid from the toilet tank. Bingo. Inside was a plastic bag. She pulled it out, shook off the water, then removed the contents and stared at the photos of a smiling, handsome Blake and her mother. They both looked so happy. Were these taken at the same party as the photo Cassidy carried in her pocket?

Had her mother and Blake been an item? Not according to Allison Carson. Rather Blake had wanted her mother and her mother had only tolerated him. As time went on, the more convinced Cassidy was that Blake had had an unhealthy obsession with her mother. An obsession that drove him to kill.

She turned the top photo over. Written in red ink were the words, "Join me or I kill the Scotsman."

~

Colin leaned against the doorjamb and watched as Cassidy's face paled. "What did you find?"

"Pictures and a warning." She handed him the photos. "He's coming after you."

"I've been expecting him to. He won't catch me unawares."

Her eyes glistened. "Being my partner could get you killed."

"Hazard of the job." He held out his hand. "Come on. Let's meet with Ingram, tell him what we have, and head back up the mountain. Don't worry about me."

He could tell his words didn't soothe her. She would worry, because that's who she was. She'd grown to care for him, despite her struggles to the contrary, and this note would only make her worry more.

Slipping her hand into his, she allowed him to pull her to her feet and out of the room. He gathered her in his arms, breathing deep of her scent, only for a moment, then released her. He tilted her face to his. "I'll be fine. No dragon is going to end me." He grinned, fighting back the urge to kiss her. With a woman as opposed to romantic entanglements as Cassidy, it was best to let her make the first move. "I'm glad you aren't considering the contrary."

"Which is?" Her voice shook.

"Joining the family business."

She choked back a laugh. "This is serious."

"We've known from the beginning the risks of this job." He chucked her on the chin. "Chin up, Bull Dog. We've a killer to catch."

"Don't call me that." She stepped back, her gaze locked on his. "If something were to happen—"

"We'll deal with it when and if." He moved out of the apartment, pulling the door closed after Cassidy. The crime scene techs would come here when they finished with the alley.

The message on the photo bothered him, he wouldn't lie. Draco the dragon stayed one step ahead of them all the time. The only thing going for Colin was instincts and a desire to live. It would have to be enough.

They met Ingram in the alley. Cassidy handed him the baggie and photos. "This is why I can't hide. The clues are for me to find."

"You've made your point." Ingram dropped the evidence into a bag. "The toilet, you say? Doubt there's anything on it after being in the water."

"We didn't find a hair in the place. Just a slip of paper with the name Maureen." Colin nodded for Cassidy to hand it over. "We're heading back up the mountain to try and come up with another plan to draw this perp out."

"Good luck," Ingram said. "We're batting zero. If you're a praying man, tell the big guy upstairs we could use a break"

Colin nodded and placed his hand on the small of Cassidy's back. They made their way back to the jeep, ignoring the curious looks of the bystanders. Maybe the gang's pals would help bring The Dragon down.

"I don't want to go back to the mountain," Cassidy said. "Blake may not know where the cabin is, and I want him to come to me."

"Your house? What about backup?"

"Call Ingram and tell him where we're going. We've got the security system. We'll know Blake is there the moment he steps foot on my property."

He didn't like it. Not a bit. "It's too dangerous."

"I'm not going to have a war at the cabin where a baby and innocent people are. You should understand how painful it is to be the cause of an innocent's death."

He knew all too well. "This is different. I pulled the trigger that killed that woman."

"It'll feel the same to me if one of the Carsons is hit." She gave him a sharp look. "You can't stay awake forever. The moment you fall asleep, I'll be in the jeep and headed home."

"Fine." He whipped the steering wheel and turned the jeep around.

~

"Where are they going?" Mary whispered, narrowing her eyes as the jeep swung and drove in the opposite direction of the mountain cabin. Surely they weren't headed back to town. Bringing down Draco's nemesis would be much harder under the watchful eyes of nosy neighbors. She cursed and followed.

Sure enough, less than an hour later, the two cops pulled into the female's driveway. Minus the dog, which would be a huge plus when Mary needed to break in. She needed to find a way through the security system. There were bound to be cameras and alarms.

No worries. She was a smart woman, one of the most intelligent she knew. The only thing she had over her step-sisters. She smiled. Former step-sisters.

She'd find a way in. If not, she'd simply ring the front doorbell and have them invite her in. Draco would be amazed at her prowess, her ingenuity, her bravery, her *worth*. He might even make her his second-in-command.

A thrill shot through her. She had found her new purpose. To become the most important person in Draco's life. He would love her. After all, the man wouldn't care that she was plain. He, himself, was scarred. No, they'd become the most formidable duo in the history of the world.

She laughed and drove past the house. Life couldn't be better for Mary Jones.

Before returning to her motel room, she stopped for fast food burgers. The largest they had. She was celebrating her good fortune, after all.

In her room, she set the food on the round table for two and headed for the bathroom to change into a flannel nightgown and a terry robe. Once she and Draco became an item, she'd need something more…feminine. Her face heated at the thought. She'd bet he was a generous lover. Not rough and hurtful like her father had been.

Some would say the hate inside Mary was caused by life. She knew it was because she was being fashioned into someone worthy of Draco. Unless she could overcome the tragedies of her past, she couldn't welcome the future that promised to be more than she'd ever dreamed.

She plopped across the bed and opened the food bag. After taking a bite of the greasy burger, she dialed the number to the man she loved.

"Why are you calling, Mary?" His voice sent her stomach fluttering. "I thought we discussed you moving on now."

"I have the grandest plans, too. Oh, Draco, you'll be so proud of me."

23

Mary entered the nearest pawn shop and leaned over the counter, giving the man a healthy view of her bosom. She needed a few things, had little funds, and would do anything for Draco, even cheapen herself.

She pointed at an assault rifle hanging on the wall. "I want that and several boxes of ammo." She grinned.

"Going hunting?" The man's gaze flickered over her shoulder, then back to her face.

"Something like that." Her smile faded as she glanced back at the television. The local news station was showing the weather. Hot and muggy today. Nothing that compelling or strange enough to warrant the clerk's rapt attention.

The clerk set the rifle and ammo on the counter. "I'll need you to fill out some paperwork."

"Sure." She lifted the rifle and quickly loaded it as he turned to get the forms. When his hand hovered under the counter, she fired. "I wish you wouldn't have done that."

She glance at the television again and saw her face plastered on the screen. She cursed, grabbed the rest of the ammo and darted outside. Seconds later she sped away from the pawn shop.

~

As had become her norm, Cassidy stood in front of the caseboard in her basement, cup of coffee in hand, and tried to reconstruct the board she'd set up at the cabin and make sense out of the seemingly random clues. Photos and red lines connecting them filled the space. She needed the other board back asap.

"Let's go." Colin came half way down the stairs. "Ingram called. Got an alert from a pawn shop seconds after Mary Jones's photo was shown on the local news station."

Cassidy bounded up the stairs and set her mug in the sink before grabbing her weapon and following Colin out the door. They sped toward the pawn shop, arriving before Ingram was out of his car.

"First responders report a body inside," he said. "My guess is…she caught him pressing the alarm, shot, and fled."

They'd lost her again. Cassidy scanned the area. The same rundown part of town they'd been in yesterday with the same crowd of onlookers. "I'll question the crowd. See if anyone saw anything."

A homeless man got to his feet as Cassidy passed. "I saw what happened." His words slurred and he breathed a wave of whiskey fumes across her face. "Woman went in, I heard a gunshot, and she ran back out with a rifle and got into a rusty Impala."

Cassidy pulled Mary's photo from her bag. "Was it this woman?"

"Yep." He held out his hand and wiggled his fingers. "Don't leave me hanging."

She sighed and fished a twenty dollar bill from her pocket. "Thank you for the information. Which direction did she flee?"

"That way." He pointed the way she and Colin had come.

They'd passed her. She'd be long gone by now.

"We missed her," she said standing next to Colin. "Probably passed her on the highway, but I have an affirmative ID."

A muscle ticked in his jaw. "One step ahead, again, and we have absolutely nothing to go on other than the fact it was definitely her."

"There's also been no sign of the Dragon." Ingram shook his head. "We viewed the store's video footage. Mary Jones entered alone and left alone. The clerk was dead when we arrived."

"Do you think she's acting alone now?" Cassidy glanced between the two men. "Stealing a gun doesn't seem to be Blake Russell's style. What if, now that she's murdered her sisters, she feels she needs to do something more?"

"That's a big what if," Ingram said.

"Remember, these people are mentally unstable. Just because it doesn't mean anything to us, it could make perfect sense to them."

"What warrants this assumption?"

She glanced at Colin and smiled. "I've learned a bit about trusting my instincts from Colin."

"No better person to learn from. This man is the best." Ingram clapped him on the shoulder. "We're going to finish up here. You two head back to the house and study that board. Find what we're missing."

"What we're missing is the killer and my caseboard," Cassidy mumbled. "I stare at that board every morning and every evening. I left it at the cabin."

"We'll get it so you can stare some more." Ingram marched away.

"Bossy man." She exhaled sharply through her nose and fished her cell phone from her pocket. She pressed redial on the last number Blake called her from, not expecting him to answer. When he did, she waved Colin over and mouthed who was on the other end of the line.

"Hello, dear. Now, I need to get a new phone."

"I didn't really expect you to answer." Her eyes widened. "I have a question for you."

"I might have an answer, but make it quick. I don't want you trying to pinpoint my location. I'll hang up in twenty-five seconds."

"Why did Mary steal a gun and shoot a pawnstore clerk? Were you behind that?"

"Definitely not. I have more finesse. Beware of her." Click.

~

"What did he say?" Colin snapped his fingers to get Ingram's attention.

"That he isn't behind Mary's actions this morning and for me to beware."

"She's coming after you." Colin yanked open the door to the jeep and shoved her inside. A crazy woman after Cassidy and a maniac after him. Things were on a downhill slide for sure.

"What are you doing?"

"Saving you." He turned to Ingram. "We'll call if we find out anything." He got into the driver's seat and sped away.

"Don't manhandle me, Colin." Cassidy crossed her arms. "Weren't you the one who said we were aware of the dangers when we took this job? I don't need to be shuffled off home like a wayward teenager."

He cut her a sideways glance. "Have you forgotten one of my duties is to protect you? I wish you hadn't left the dog behind. You don't make it easy, and I can use all the help I can get."

"We'll get her back when this is all over." She lifted her chin and turned away. "I can protect myself."

"Have you forgot who we're dealing with?"

"Nope." She still wouldn't look at him.

"Are you mad at me?" He frowned.

"No, maybe, yes. A little."

"Why?"

She turned and glared. "Everything is going to come to a boil. One of us, or both, may not make it out alive. If Blake wants me to join his so-called murder group, you're in the way. He'll eliminate anything that keeps me from fulfilling his diabolical plan."

"I've told you not to worry about me." Why couldn't she understand he wasn't going anywhere? That sticking close to her was all the plan he had? "I'm good at my job, Cassidy."

"So am I." High spots of color appeared in her cheeks.

"Then, let's work together. This has nothing to do with whether me, or Ingram, think you incapable. It's time for you to get the chip off your shoulder and accept the fact you are no longer a lone wolf."

Her eyes glittered. She started to say something, then clamped her lips together and turned away.

So be it. Angry and alive was better than happy and dead. The only problem he could see was in her attempts to keep him from harm, she might put hers in the bullseye. He couldn't let that happen.

He reached over to take her hand, but she pulled away, clasping her hands in her lap. He sighed and pulled into her driveway. For the first time since meeting her, he didn't open the door for her. Instead, he marched up the steps and onto the porch to punch in the code for the alarm. No blinking red light told him the alarm was set. Had they left in such a hurry that morning they'd forgotten? Possible, but he wasn't taking any chances.

"What's wrong?" Cassidy stepped to his side.

"The alarm isn't set."

"That's my fault. I left behind you this morning. I must have forgotten."

He shot her a sharp look and pulled his weapon from his holster. "Irresponsible."

"I'm not used to being a prisoner in my own home. I'll go in first."

He blocked her path. "No."

Pushing the door open, he peered inside. Everything appeared normal. Cassidy's OCD nature of everything in its place didn't look disturbed. He waved her in. "You've got to be more careful. Follow me as we check each room, even the basement."

She nodded. "I'm sorry."

They checked each room and found nothing out of place. With each search, Colin's frustration grew. He understood how they forgot to set the alarm, but that mistake could have been disastrous.

"Are you hungry?" Cassidy set her gun on the kitchen table. "I could order a pizza."

"Not mad anymore?"

She sighed. "We all make mistakes. I apologize for my rudeness. You're right. I have a chip on my shoulder the size of Mount Everest. It's grown over the years as I've fought to prove my worth in law enforcement." She met his gaze. "I know I'm a good detective. The human side of me wants kudos, I guess."

"I'll give you all the praise you need." He grinned. "A pizza sounds great. Meat lovers, please." He pulled out a kitchen chair and stared toward the kitchen window. The curtains were open a little, moving in a soft breeze. "Did you leave that open?"

"No, I wouldn't have." She moved to close the window and draw the curtains. "Maybe I'm losing my mind." After closing the curtains, she pulled a bottle of red wine from the cupboard. "Want a glass?"

"After what almost happened the last time we drank? No, thanks." Not to mention the fact a killer wanted Cassidy and had warned her about one of his minions. "We need to stay alert."

She put the bottle back on the shelf. "Do you think she'll come tonight?"

"I do." He folded his hands on the table. "The alarm should give us warning, though. I know it's dangerous, but we're sleeping together tonight." Not that he had any intentions of closing his eyes. He didn't need the nightmares or to lose his focus. "I'll take the floor next to the bed. Ingram said all the repairs were made to the wall."

"I'll gather some blankets and pillows." She placed a call for pizza and headed down the hall.

Colin placed his chair to where he could see her. "Don't take those upstairs without me."

"The alarm is set. I'm perfectly safe."

"You don't leave my sight, understand?"

She dropped the bedding on the bottom step. "Am I allowed to use the restroom?"

"The powder room downstairs." Irritable or not, he wasn't going to relent on her staying in sight. Blake Russell had shown he possessed skills far surpassing most of the criminals Colin had dealt with in his career. He wasn't taking any chances. Not only was it his job, but he had come to care for her more than he'd thought possible.

The fiery red-headed detective had wormed her way into his heart and set up roots. He wouldn't survive if he failed to keep her safe. If he'd known leaving Scotland would result in him falling in love, he wasn't sure he would have left. Romance brought entanglements into a law enforcement partnership that muddied the waters and increased risk.

"If not wine, then coffee," Cassidy said exiting the powder room and entering the kitchen. "It's going to be a long sleepless night."

The doorbell rang.

Colin pushed to his feet. "I'll get it."

"There's money in the jar on the table."

"My treat." He turned off the alarm and, after verifying the pizza delivery boy stood there, opened the door.

Stepping into sight, gun pointed at the center of his forehead, was Mary Jones.

24

"Hello, handsome." Mary stepped forward, keeping the gun aimed at his head. "Pizza boy, sit in the corner and be good. Sorry you dropped your joint when I walked up. Smoking that weed is bad for you anyway.

"Now, Handsome, step back nice and slow." When he did, she kicked the door closed. "So nice of you to answer the door."

"I was only expecting pizza." Colin gave her the crooked grin that always worked for him with women.

"Oh, you're a charmer, for sure. It won't work, though." Not returning his smile, she cocked her head to the side. "A shame you'll be dead soon. You and the woman, probably the boy, too."

Cassidy lunged through the doorway her gun aimed at Mary. "Put it down."

"Follow your advice or pretty boy dies right now. Nice and slow. I'll do it. First one leg, then the other. Maybe a graze along one gorgeous cheek." A slow smile spread across her face. "Drop the gun and kick it to me, that's a good girl."

Cassidy's features hardened as she followed the woman's directions.

"All three of you into the living room and strip to your undies. Remove your socks and shoes." Mary watched as they stripped, then laughed. "For a beauty, your lingerie leaves something to be desired."

Colin cut a sideways glance at Cassidy's simple white bra and panties. She was beautiful in her simplicity, and he hoped he'd have a chance to tell her so and elicit a blush from her again.

He glanced around for a weapon. The woman was smart in making him and Cassidy as vulnerable as possible. Cassidy's sparcely decorated home left little for him to use. The floor lamp would be too unwieldy. He'd have to watch for an opportunity to take her down by brute force.

As the delivery boy's baggy jeans dropped to the floor, Colin spotted the corner of a cell phone peeking from the pocket. If he could get to it—

"Handsome, sit in that chair where I can see you. Detective Monroe and Pizza Boy sit on the sofa." Mary leaned against the doorjamb. "Is everyone comfy?"

"My name is Danny." The delivery boy scowled. "If this is a robbery, I only carry twenty dollars on me."

"Aren't you cute." Mary slapped his pimpled cheek. "No more talking. I only have questions for one person in this room and that's the red-headed beauty." She squatted in front of Cassidy. "I don't understand something. Draco hates beautiful people. Why the fixation on you?"

Cassidy laughed. "Didn't he tell you? He's my father."

Mary paled. "Impossible. He would have told me something that important."

"It seems Bla...Draco has a few secrets."

Mary pushed to her feet and paced, keeping the gun trained on those sitting. "This muddles things."

If Colin could distract her a bit more, get her to lower the gun... He shifted, drawing her attention.

"Huh-uh, pretty boy. Stay still. I can see the thoughts in your mind."

If she really could read his mind, she'd drop dead from the violence of his thoughts. Colin glanced at Cassidy. Rather than fear, he saw determination on her face. *That's my girl.* The poor boy didn't know whether to exist in a pot-induced haze or wet himself.

Mary resumed her pacing. "It makes sense, really. Draco's almost protective attitude toward you." She leaned close enough to Cassidy to force her to lean back. "I came here to kill you. I guess I can't do that to the woman who will one day be my stepdaughter. Now, how to get you to Draco. He'll be so pleased, he's bound to give me anything I want. The desire of my heart will soon be mine."

While she was focused on Cassidy, Colin dove for the cell

phone. He managed to punch in Ingram's number and hit speaker before the bullet slammed into his side. The second shot took him high in the thigh.

~

"Stop!" Cassidy scrambled toward him, grabbing their discarded clothes to help staunch the bleeding. "Stay with me, Colin."

"Get up, Detective." Mary rapped her on the shoulder with the revolver. "He's going to bleed to death before help can get here." She cursed as the delivery boy raced through the kitchen.

The slamming of the backdoor told Cassidy the boy made it out. "I won't leave him. You'll have to shoot me, too." Tears burned her throat as Colin's blood soaked into her carpet. Mary knew she couldn't shoot Cassidy. Not unless she wanted to incur Blake's wrath.

The other woman peered through the curtains. "Cops will be here any minute. You might die in a hail of bullets. Are you afraid, Detective?"

Only of Colin dying. "No."

"So brave. Just like your father." Mary pulled out her cell phone. "Draco, I have a dilemma...well, I told you I was going to do something for you...I'm here with your daughter. I didn't know she was your daughter, of course, is she? Really? What a pity. I've shot the Scot. The cops are coming. How do I get out of here with her?" Tears pooled in Mary's eyes, and then ran down her round cheeks. "That's really what you want me to do? I love you...all right, Draco. See you on the other side. Please don't keep me waiting too long."

Mary sighed, the sound as lonely and mournful as anything Cassidy had ever heard. Then, the woman turned the gun on herself and pulled the trigger. Blood and brain matter sprayed the wall behind her. Her eyes widened, then she toppled over. Still.

Shocked, Cassidy couldn't move for a moment. Then, realizing the severity of Colin's wounds, and the fact the danger for her had passed, she darted for the front door and yanked it open as Ingram and an ambulance roared onto her driveway. "Hurry!"

Ingram gave Cassidy a wide-eyed look at her in her underwear as he rushed past her. The paramedics were a bit more professional. They didn't spare her so much as a peek. While they worked on Colin, she donned her sweat pants and tee shirt then slid her feet into flip-flops.

"Can you save him? Please save him." She stepped close as they lifted him onto a gurney. "Colin, can you hear me?" She trotted after the medics, determined to ride in the ambulance. She hoisted herself inside before anyone could say no and took Colin's hand in hers.

This was her fault. For years, she'd managed to not have a partner because of the small size of Clear Springs's population. Now, after being forced into having her second one, she was close to losing him. Not only that he was her partner, but she loved him. Something she'd vowed never to do.

The drive to the hospital seemed to take hours when in actuality it took ten minutes. Cassidy stepped aside as the paramedics rushed Colin inside. A receptionist told her to wait in the waiting room and the doctor would notify her when he had something to report.

Cassidy had never felt more alone in her life. She plopped into a vinyl chair and stared at the ceiling, counting the tiles. She quit when she got to 307. What was taking so long?

A man in blue scrubs walked toward her. She leaped to her feet only to watch as he passed her and approached an older woman. Cassidy sighed and fell back into her chair.

"No news?" Ingram sat next to her.

"None. It's only been an hour." She stared at the ceiling again.

"Tell me what happened at your place."

"We ordered pizza. She was hiding around the corner, using the delivery boy as a shield. When Colin answered the doorbell, she forced the delivery boy inside, made us strip, and had every intention of killing all three of us until she found out I was Blake Russell's daughter. Then, she called him and shot herself. I think he told her to."

"Hmm." Ingram jotted notes on a small notebook. "The delivery boy is fine. He's home with his folks. Mary died immediately. Your house is…smelly." He gave her a wry grin. "I'll send someone over to clean it. Keep your chin up. It'll take more than a crazy woman to kill MacKenzie."

She nodded. It would be her that killed him. Whether by accident or through someone else, she would be at blame. "I hope so."

Two hours later, the doctor came down the long hallway. "Detective Monroe? I'm Doctor Savalli."

Cassidy jumped to her feet. "Is he all right?"

"He's going to be fine. A few months of physical therapy due to the shot to the leg, but he's going to be as good as new."

Relief flooded through her so strongly, her knees weakened. She grabbed the doctor's arm for support. "May I see him?"

"He's unconscious, but yes, you may go in." He directed her to Colin's room.

She hurried to his room and stared down at a stranger. The strong, vibrant man was hidden by tubes and pale skin. "I'm so sorry, Colin." She let the tears she'd been holding in fall down her cheeks. She leaned forward and placed a kiss on his lips. "I can't do this. I love you. Goodbye, sweetheart."

She straightened, and taking a deep breath, left Colin and any hopes for a future with him behind.

PART TWO

Six months later

1

W e need you back. The Dragon is at work again."
Cassidy Monroe closed her eyes. The last thing she wanted was to return to Clear Springs…and Colin MacKenzie. Especially after leaving while he lay in the hospital. She hadn't bothered to wait until he woke to say goodbye. "I'll be there by this evening." She hung up and started packing.

The job in Oklahoma City, while fraught with its own problems and dangers, did not bring her face-to-face with her biological father who wanted all the pretty people dead and had the followers to help make that happen. Blake Russell, Draco, as he called himself, was the proverbial thorn in her side.

She packed three suits, a couple pair of jeans, comfies to sleep in, and several tee shirts, plus toiletries into a large suitcase. After she placed her laptop and chargers safely between the clothes, she zipped the suitcase closed. She dialed the number to a cheap motel in Clear Springs that allowed dogs, booked a room, and headed to her jeep, her best friend and protector, Rosie at her side. Unable to live without her friend, she had retrieved her from the family who had watched over her for a few weeks.

How would Colin react when she walked through the doors of the precinct? He had to be hurt and angry at her leaving the way she did. She'd missed his cocky smile every day of the last six months. Would he say the same about her? Not likely.

She made it to Clear Springs and her motel in a little over five hours. After grabbing a burger from what used to be her favorite burger joint, she headed to the small police station to face the music, as it were.

She parked in front of the small red brick building, then,

taking a deep breath, opened the double doors and stepped inside. Conversation stopped as heads turned. FBI agents Ingram and Smith, plus one she didn't know, headed for the conference room.

Ingram held the door open for her. "It's nice to have you back." He bent down and scratched Rosie's ears. "You, too, girl."

Cassidy raised her eyebrows, knowing it was anything but nice considering the circumstances. "Who's the new agent?"

"Miller. He's a rookie, but shows promise." He paused for a moment. "Just a heads up before you go in. MacKenzie is the new chief. He isn't happy to have you return."

"The feeling is mutual." She squared her shoulders and entered the room, setting her laptop at one end of the table.

Colin fixed a void look on her. "Agents, this is Detective Monroe, and Rosie. I've filled you in on her work the last time we had a run-in with Draco. Detective, we have a body, this one dressed in pink with the same words as last time." He clicked on the overhead projector revealing a pretty girl with her throat slit. "I've located the snuff film and determined the perp is a male around six feet tall and left handed." Another click of the remote in his hand and a poor quality video filled the screen.

Displayed in all its gory glory was a poor girl around the age of eighteen being chased through the woods by a man with a long gait and a hump on his back. Cassidy grimaced as the man grabbed the girl's long dark hair and threw her to the ground. The kill was over in seconds.

She knew the answer before asking, but asked anyway, "Any idea who the man is?"

Colin shook his head, avoiding her gaze. "Not a clue, but we have people checking hospitals for records for males in their thirties with back deformities."

"Why has he waited six months to surface again?"

This time he speared her with a glance. "Anything new going on in your life? You're his trigger."

"If that's the case, then why not start killing in Little Rock?" She would not be the first to look away. "For some reason, he wanted me back here. We need to find out why."

"We're working on it." He turned away. His body language clearly said they were doing fine without her and it wasn't his idea to have her return.

Or maybe that was Cassidy's perception. Either way, he wasn't happy to see her, as she'd suspected.

~

Why did Ingram have to call Cassidy back? Colin organized his files into a pile. They didn't need her. Eventually, Russell slash Draco would mess up and they'd catch him. He sighed. But, more young women would die in the process.

"MacKenzie, Monroe, you're back to working together, please," Ingram said. "You know this killer better than anyone. Try to keep the claws in until we catch him."

Colin and Cassidy groaned out loud. Face red, Colin turned away. They weren't in high school. He could do this and keep things on a strict professional basis. After all, she'd made her feelings perfectly clear when she left him lying on a hospital bed, didn't say goodbye, and broke his heart. That's what he got for stepping over the professional line. It wouldn't happen again.

"What's first?" Cassidy stepped to his side.

"We try to find Quasimoto. Just as Mary Jones did, he'll lead us to Russell." He grabbed his jacket from the back of his chair. "You should probably take a look at the crime scene."

She nodded and followed him outside. "You got a new truck."

He patted the hood of his new Ford 150. "Getting the title of chief came with a raise."

"I thought you wanted to work tech for the FBI."

"I was, until they offered me this. I like Clear Springs. Except for Draco, things are pretty calm." He unlocked the doors and climbed into the driver's seat. Normally, good manner dictated, he open the door for her, but if he wanted to keep things professional, then he needed to treat her like one of the guys and not the beautiful woman she was. "No more sweats?"

"No, I've taken to wearing suits. The Little Rock PD frowned on my casual wardrobe."

That wasn't the only thing that had changed. She'd cut her red hair into a long bob that swung around her face. No more ponytails. She'd also taken to wearing a small amount of makeup. Her new appearance wasn't going to make it easy for him.

They drove down a little-traveled dirt road to where yellow crime scene tape fluttered in the breeze. He cut the ignition and stared at the spot where a young woman lost her life. So many deaths at the hands of Draco and his friends. He shoved the door open, then held up the tape for Cassidy to go under.

She stopped next to the marker where Emma Larson had taken her last breath. Then, she turned in a slow circle, her green eyes taking everything in. She stopped scanning at the words carved into the trunk of a tree. "The pretty must die". Her back stiffened.

"I won't let him get away this time, Colin."

"It wasn't your fault the last time. It was his follower, Mary." He approached her as one might approach a wild deer. With caution.

Her eyes were as hard as emeralds when she glanced at him. "It's me he wants. Why hasn't he come for me?"

"My best guess is that he doesn't think you're worthy yet. He wants you to catch him. He doesn't want to come after you." Colin was a different matter. He constantly expected a bullet in his back from the crazy psycho killer.

"The scene is the same as all the others. Clean." Cassidy snapped a few photos with the camera around her neck, then headed back to the truck.

"Are you hungry?" He asked, climbing back into the driver's seat.

"I ate before arriving at the station. I think I'll head to my hotel."

"Why not your house?"

"I thought it might be harder for my father to bug the place." She fixed a serious look on him. "We don't have to pretend to be friends, Colin. I know I hurt you."

"I think both of us staying at your house is still the best bet. I can't protect you if you're in a hotel room, and I won't share a room with you. Besides, the case board on your mother's murder is still set up in your basement."

"Won't it be hard to live under the same roof with the woman you professed love to?"

"It's going to remain strictly professional."

"So, you've stop sleeping in the nude?"

He shook his head. "I will now."

~

She was back. His precious was back. Draco grinned and rubbed his hands together. Let the fun begin. He'd waited six long months for her to improve her skills and couldn't wait to see whether she was worthy yet to join him.

Glancing around the group of nine men and women fixing rapt faces in his direction, he raised his hands for silence. "Homer did wonderful with his first kill." All heads turned to the tall man with a skeletal face and humpback. "His taxidermist skills have served him well. Let's up the game, shall we?"

He proceeded to lay out the task for Homer. "Your sweet cousin was easy, my friend, but can you succeed when the person pleading with you is your mother?"

"I can." The man's deep voice boomed through the room. "She's the cause of my distress. If not for the abuse heaped on me as a child, I wouldn't have this disfigurement."

"Is she an attractive woman?"

"Very. That's the cause of the abuse."

"Then, we proceed." Draco smiled. He had chosen his followers well. Full of hate, every one of them, and willing to do his bidding. After the fiasco with Mary falling in love with him, despite his own disfigurement, he had thought that, perhaps, he wouldn't be able to achieve his life's calling.

After receiving the knife wound to the face and killing the woman who gave birth to his child, he realized his purpose was to help others gain vengeance on all those who considered themselves better than the rest. It was a worthy calling. One he was proud to pursue.

He handed out leather jackets bearing an embroidered dragon on the back, frowning as Homer tried to fit his over his hump. "We'll have to have yours special made, I'm afraid."

Perhaps he should be pickier about those he chose to follow him. No. If anyone deserved justice, it was this man.

"That concludes our meeting for today. Remember, to put those you want to call out on their crimes in the jar beside the door. You never know when I'll choose someone else to act on their vengeance."

2

With a strange sense of de ja vu, Cassidy carried her things into her house and into the master bedroom. After putting her things away, she headed to the basement and stared at the case board she'd given up on. She knew who her mother's killer was. It was the same man who was sending the faithfully blind to do his dirty work. The problem was...he was like a vapor of smoke. Always vanishing before they could catch him.

She lifted a photo of her mother from a nearby table, looking into a face so much like her own. "I will get him, Mom. I promise."

Replacing the photo, she turned and spotted Colin hovering on the stairs. Her heart hitched. While she knew ending their beginning relationship had been the wisest thing to do, she ached to see him smile at her with the warmth he used to. But, until her father was behind bars, it was too dangerous to love anyone. Loving someone put them at a risk she wasn't willing to do. Someday, maybe, Colin would understand.

"I've checked the house for bugs and cameras. Rosie did a scope of the grounds. Looks clean."

"That's good." She squeezed past him and headed for the kitchen. Since she hadn't anticipated coming back to the house, the refrigerator and cupboards were bare. "I'm going to the grocery store."

"Let me get my keys."

"You don't have to come."

"You know I do. You can't go anywhere alone." He grabbed his keys from the foyer table. "I'll drive."

She sighed. He knew she preferred driving.

Without complaining, willing to give him his moment of surliness, she climbed into the passenger seat. "Nice."

"I got it after…you left and they offered me the promotion. A man needs a truck when a woman dumps him." He started the truck, then squealed tires from the driveway.

"You sound like a country song."

"I felt like one." He cut her a sideways glance. "We'll have to talk about this at some point."

She turned her head and stared out the window. "We don't. You wouldn't understand."

"Try me and give me a little credit."

"Please, don't do this, Colin. Why dig up old hearts and old arguments? Let's focus on the case and forget the past." Hard to do when they were working and living together, but she was determined.

They made the drive to the grocery in silence so thick, Cassidy could hardly breathe. Once Colin parked, she couldn't escape the vehicle fast enough. She grabbed a shopping cart and barreled through the supermarket door.

She made it to the bread aisle before spotting the first dragon jacket. Increasing her speed to follow the man, she turned the corner and spotted another. Not given to coincidence, she knew they had followed her.

'Hey!" She ditched the cart and sprinted.

The two men ducked around a corner. They were gone by the time she turned down the aisle. She dashed to the next aisle, careening into Colin.

His hands wrapped around her waist, steadying her. "What's the rush?"

"Did you see them?" She tried to peer around him. "Two men wearing dragon jackets were here."

"I didn't see anyone."

She glared. "I didn't imagine them." She stepped back and headed to the front of the store. "They have to be here somewhere. Guard the back door."

"I don't want to leave—"

"I have my weapon, go!" She shook her head and stood next to the front door. The men couldn't have disappeared. If Colin wanted her help in catching Russell, aka Draco, then he was going to have to stop shadowing her every single second of the day. She'd feel smothered very soon, not to mention the risk to her heart having him breathing down her neck.

She watched as the two leather wearing men approached her, hands out to show non-aggression. The one man, older with deep acne scars, took a step forward.

"Draco has a message for you."

"I'm listening." She spotted Colin approaching from behind the men.

"He says things are going to get exciting and he looks forward to you joining him."

"When hell freezes over." She smiled. "But, tell him I look forward to speaking with him face to face."

They stared stonily at her, then as one, turned and left the store. Everything in her wanted to arrest them, but neither one of them matched the man on the video. She'd have a better chance of catching Draco if she let these two men go and he came to see her.

She grabbed another cart and set off to finish what she'd started, leaving Colin to follow, or not. She grabbed a couple boxes of cereal, some soup, steaks, vegetables and bread, along with other items, then moved to the cash registers.

Colin followed like a silent specter. Disapproval rolled off like thunder during a monsoon storm.

"Just say it." She stopped and turned.

"Say what?" He barely blinked.

"You think I should have arrested those men."

"Yeah." When he was angry, his Scottish brogue deepened, sending her stomach into flips. "We could have forced them to talk."

"How? Water boarding? Splinters under the fingernails? I want Russell to come to me." She moved up in line. "I gave them a message."

"Him coming to you is too dangerous."

She poked him in the chest with her forefinger. "I don't want any more talk about danger. Girls are dying." She stepped to the counter and began setting her purchases onto the conveyor belt.

"I'll get this." Colin pulled out his wallet.

"No, you won't. I'd have to eat whether you were here or not."

She hated the bickering between them. But, the days of flirtation, kisses, and comradery were things of the past. Once this case was solved, she'd sell her house, move back to Little Rock, and leave the pain of Clear Springs behind her.

Colin tossed his debit card at the cashier, paying despite her saying no, then proceeded to bag their groceries. Fine. Let him play the big man. She crossed her arms and headed for his truck.

Lying on the hood was a yellow rose. "Well, this is new." She read the little card attached. "To the other part of me. Draco." She snapped the flower in half, tossed the pieces to the ground, and got in the truck.

~

Colin stowed the grocery bags in the back of his truck and hooked a net in place to keep them from rolling around the bed. Then, using the tips of his fingers, he picked up the notecard and slipped it into his pocket.

They already knew that if there were fingerprints, they would belong to Blake Russell. The trick was in catching the guy, not finding out his identity.

"You like yellow roses?" He cut a quick glance at his silent passenger.

"I like most flowers, depending on the sender." She continued staring out the window.

So, she wasn't in the mood for conversation. A person would almost think she'd been the one ditched while recuperating in the hospital from a gunshot wound. A bullet he took for her! He sighed inwardly. He'd take another one if he had to. Angry at her or not, she still held a huge piece of his heart in her hands.

They drove back to the house and put the groceries away, still not talking. Something had to change. They couldn't work together that way. Not efficiently.

Once the groceries were put away, he leaned his back against the counter and watched her flit around the kitchen like a nervous hummingbird. This was ridiculous.

He took two steps forward, pulled her close, and planted a hard, hot kiss on her lips. At first, she accepted, then stiffened and shoved him away.

"Are you crazy?!"

"Just getting rid of the tension between us." He crossed his arms and grinned. She sure was cute with her face all red and her eyes shooting green flames.

"That is not the way to do it."

"Sure it is. Now, there's no more kitty cat tip-toeing around. Despite your leaving me, the physical attraction is still there. I forgive you, and I'm willing to be friends and partners."

She narrowed her eyes. "You felt nothing from the kiss?"

He shrugged. "I'm guessing I didn't feel as much as you did." Which was a big fat lie. The kiss had ignited a fire in his belly. He was nowhere near being over her.

"I...felt...nothing."

"Have it your way, little Miss Liar." He tweaked her nose and headed for the room she used as an office. He'd already moved a kitchen chair and a TV tray to the room and set up a makeshift desk for himself. Now, he browsed the internet for more films of Draco or his followers' work.

An hour later, Cassidy brought him a plate with grilled chicken and asparagus. "Supper." She plopped the plate on her desk and stormed out of the room. At least she was feeding him.

By nine o'clock, it became obvious he wouldn't find a new video that night. He stretched his arms over his head and grunted as his spine crackled and popped. Getting up from the hard chair, he carried his plate to the kitchen, pausing at the door to the living room.

Cassidy slept, the television casting blue shadows on her face. On the floor next to the sofa, Rosie stared up at him, one ear twitching. Everything in him wanted to kneel beside Cassidy, draw her into his arms, and hold her. But a woman who would leave a man when he needed her most, couldn't be trusted with the man's heart.

~

Good. Draco rubbed his hands together. They hadn't discovered the camera in the knob of the television or the one peeking through a magnet on the refrigerator. He'd wanted to plant more, but there hadn't been time.

He knew they'd find them eventually. His daughter and her partner were very smart. Very worthy advisories. But, until they did, he would feast upon her beauty while he could.

Yes, she was beautiful, but she was also kind. Not once had he ever witnessed her mistreating anyone no matter what they looked like. If only the world could be more like her.

He scowled as he watched her sleep. Her mother hadn't been the woman he'd thought she was. She'd led him on, taunted him with her beauty, then cut his face, disfiguring him and turning him into the man he was. He supposed he should thank her for turning him into the dragon. If not for the scar on his face, he'd be one of the pretty people.

It wasn't until he lay in his apartment, the stitches in his face on fire, that he realized he had a bigger purpose than college and chasing the latest whore. He was meant for greater things. Then, he spent years building up his fortune so he could sell out and devote his life to ridding the world of those who made the lives of the ordinary...the ugly...unbearable.

He shut off his computer, confident she wasn't going anywhere that night, and headed for an empty lot on the outskirts of town where he had agreed to meet Homer. Before getting out of his Mercedes, Draco watched as the hunchback paced back and forth in front of a still lovely, middle-aged woman. Rather than look frightened, the woman merely looked pissed off. Draco turned on the camera mounted to his dashboard and exited the car.

"Now, now, Mrs. Leroy," he said, pulling his hood over his face, but not before he made sure she got a good look at him. "You mustn't spout obscenities at your son."

She spit in the dirt at his feet. "It's Miss, and who are you? One of his freak friends?"

Draco clenched his fists at his side. His blood pressure spiked. "I really think you should watch what you say."

She spewed a line of curses that would make a conman blush. "Untie me."

"Remove her tongue, Homer, then peel the flesh from her body, strip by agonizing strip." Draco smiled and moved out of sight of the camera, knowing he'd said and done too much already.

Homer withdrew a knife from inside the trench coat he wore. When he gripped his mother's face, squeezing until her tongue began to protrude, her screams rang through the night.

Pity no one could hear except the crows that would feast on her tongue in the morning.

3

The next morning, Cassidy was still steaming from Colin stepping over the boundary line and kissing her. That one act told her that no matter how much time had passed, she wasn't over him. Probably never would be. She sighed and turned off the shower. When Draco was caught, then, and only then, could she think about a relationship.

She towel dried, and got dressed. The moment she stepped from her room, Colin pounced.

"We have another one."

Cassidy closed her eyes. "Last night?"

"Yeah, it's night in the video, but the lights around what looks like a parking lot lit up the scene." He slipped on his holster. "We'll grab breakfast on the run, if that's all right."

"Crime scene first?"

"If you're up to it." He set the alarm and opened the front door, allowing her to go out first.

Cassidy hurried to her jeep before he could say he was going to drive again. She had the key turned in the ignition before he climbed in.

"Why do you always have to be in control?" He cut her a sideways glance. "I outrank you now."

"So?" She backed from the driveway. "I'm here to help you. That means, I get what I want."

"You have as much invested in this case as anyone." He clicked his seatbelt. "You couldn't have stayed away if you wanted to."

She had wanted to stay away, but he was right. If anyone needed to see this through, she did. Not only for the victims, but for her mother. "Where are we going?"

"An empty strip mall on Highway 64." He gave her the address. "Some skateboarders found the body."

The Medical Examiner was already there when they arrived. Cassidy parked as close to the scene as she dared and approached the sign pole where a woman in a pink dress sat, her head lolling to one side.

"Her tongue was cut out," the ME said. "That's new."

"Did you find it?" Cassidy snapped gloves on her hands, then squatted next to the body.

"Uh…" he pointed to birds sitting on electrical wires above their heads. "It's possible the perp took it, but my guess is he tossed it to them. I've never seen so many crows in one place."

As disgusting as the thought, they came where the food was. "Do we have an identity?"

"Martha Leroy, forty seven." Colin handed her a driver's license. "I've got someone making a few calls to find out where she lived, and whether she was visiting."

"She's older than his usual victims." Planting her palms on her thighs, Cassidy pushed to her feet. "Hunchback's mother?"

"That's my guess." Colin shook his head. "At least it helps us identify him a bit more. We're most likely looking for someone with the last name of Leroy."

Once they had all the information they could gather from the crime scene, they drove to the precinct and joined the FBI agents in the conference room. Cassidy headed straight for the strong coffee she knew was hot and ready in the pot.

The first sip made her grimace, but experience taught her that her palate would adjust to the bitterness. She sat at the oval table and waited for Agent Ingram to speak. Instead, he turned things over to Colin.

"This is the second body discovered in as many days. Blake Russell still doesn't seem to be the one doing the killing, but we believe he is always present at the kill."

Agent Miller raised his hand, speaking when Colin nodded in his direction. "Why? I mean, why is this Russell character not doing the killing himself? Why bother taking the time to find followers? Most serial killers get off on doing the dirty work."

Colin shrugged. "That's the million dollar question. Blake

Russell seems to think of himself as some sort of mentor and distributor of justice. He wants Detective Monroe to join him and, presumably, follow in his footsteps."

"The man is nuts."

Colin smiled. "I think we're all in agreement on that. Detective Monroe, do you have anything to add?"

"Not really. Only that this man is my biological father," she said for Miller's benefit. "I am wondering, though, if perhaps we shouldn't set a trap for the man."

They all straightened in their chairs.

"He wants me worthy of joining him. Rather than doing that, maybe I need to leave a trail of emotionally wounded people. I'll pick out the homely, the downtrodden, anyone who fits the profile of his followers. He watches every move I make. He'll see what I'm doing and come after me."

The thought of being cruel was difficult. The act would be more so. Still, it would work. She could offer those she wronged an apology after the fact.

"I don't think you could pull it off," Colin said.

"Why not?" She frowned.

"That's not who you are."

"I can act as if it is."

He glanced at Ingram, who shrugged. "Let's think on it a bit. The idea does hold merit. We need to put a stop to this man's reign of terror."

"I also think I need to do a press conference. We'll give the public an idea of who we are dealing with, post his picture, etc."

Colin's expression turned grave. "Call him out, you mean."

"Yes." She met his stare. "One of these ideas is bound to work. Plus, he's easily recognizable. It will be harder for him to work if he can't venture out."

~

Those were two of the dumbest ideas he'd ever heard. Colin gathered his things and stormed to his office. If he were honest with himself, which he didn't want to be, the ideas actually held merit. If he could only find a way to implement them without Cassidy being the target.

Speaking of the she-devil. Cassidy stepped into his office.

"Don't you knock?"

"Do you?" She crossed her arms.

"What do you want?" He tried to look busy. A difficult task since all his nerves were on high alert with her in the small office.

"You need to stop pouting like a child and let me do what I know needs to be done. I've set the press conference up for an hour from now." She turned and left him feeling like a young boy scolded by his mother.

An hour later, he joined the news reporters and fixed his gaze on Cassidy standing behind the podium. He wished Ingram hadn't called her. She was safer away from there. Maybe Russell would have moved his killings to Little Rock, and maybe not. Maybe…he would have left her alone. Who was he kidding? Everything was happening exactly like the dragon wanted. He dropped the breadcrumbs, he crooked his finger, and Colin, Cassidy, and the FBI agents pecked their way along like mindless birds.

At Ingram's signal, Cassidy began to speak. "I'm Detective Cassidy Monroe. We are alerting the public to the return of a serial killer who calls himself the dragon. His real name is Blake Russell and you will see his photo on your screen. This was taken many years ago. Today, his face is scarred from a knife wound. He is extremely dangerous. If you see this man, please call the number on your screen below."

She held the podium with both hands. "Mr. Russell, I am here and I am waiting. The Clear Springs PD with the help of the FBI will catch you and put you away for the rest of your life. You and your followers." She straightened. "Any questions?"

"You mentioned followers," one reporter asked. "Can you expand on that?"

"Mr. Russell is out to rid the world of pretty people who he believes have wronged the less attractive or deformed. Rather than do the work himself, he trains his followers to carry out his deeds while fulfilling their own desires." She tilted her chin and gave a coy smile. "Those of us who are beautiful were born this way. We can no more help it than those who were born ugly. Does that mean I deserve to die? If so, then I welcome Mr. Russell to come and try."

Colin closed his eyes and exhaled long and hard. She was going to go through with ridiculing others. The outrage in the room was palpable.

An overweight reporter stood. "So, you do believe you are better than me?"

"I didn't say that." Cassidy continued to smile. "Only that we cannot help who we are. Some were born with the tendency to be fat, while others like myself don't have to work to obtain or maintain our beauty."

"I cannot believe the words coming out of your mouth."

Colin feared the woman would slap the simpering smile off Cassidy's face. He stepped forward to interrupt, but stood down when Ingram shook his head.

"I am only stating what I believe. No more questions. Thank you." She ducked her head to leave, but not before Colin spotted the tears glistening in her eyes.

~

Draco threw his glass across the room. The glass shattered, spilling whiskey down the wall.

Silly girl. Did she really think he would believe her ploy? Still, she gravely wounded the heavy-set reporter with her words, fake or not, and would have to be punished.

He scratched his chin. How could he make her pay for her actions without actually harming her physically? What about her dog? No, he couldn't hurt an animal. They judged people on their hearts, not by their physical attributes. He stood and paced the room.

What to do, what to do. He could focus on the Scot, but he enjoyed watching the two of them pretend they no longer cared about each other. Still, hurting the man was a possibility.

Ah. He knew exactly what to do. He picked up the phone and dialed the perfect person to accomplish the task. Seconds later, he had the promise that it would be done that evening. A small thing, really, but should give a strong warning to stop the bad behavior. If not, he'd step up his game and make her really sorry.

4

Dressed and ready for work the next morning, Cassidy stepped onto the porch with Colin and was blown off her feet. A fireball filled the sky. Flames shot out of the windows of her jeep.

Colin helped her to her feet. "Are you all right?"

"You're bleeding." She pointed to a cut on his forehead, then turned to survey the damage. "I loved my jeep." She grabbed a terracotta pot off the porch railing and hurled it at the inferno. Tears burned her throat.

Things had come to this. She smiled through her tears. Her words had gotten through to the dragon. Let the games begin.

"You have a cut on your arm." Colin lifted her left arm and peered at the underside. "You might need stitches."

"Call it in. The paramedics can stitch me up. I'm not going to the hospital." She wiped her right arm across her eyes, then marched back into the house. Grabbing a clean towel and rag, she returned to the porch, handed Colin the rag for his head, and tied the towel around her arm. Then, she sat on the porch and waited.

Five minutes later, sirens wailed in the distance, growing closer. Cassidy closed her eyes, feeling the heat of what was once her jeep on her face. Rosie snuggled close, and she draped her uninjured arm around the dog.

"I am so thankful we weren't in the vehicle," she murmured against the dog's head. "I couldn't bear it if something happened to you."

Colin sat on her other side, hands dangling between his knees. "Now what?"

"I guess you get to drive all the time."

He grinned. "That's a given. What I mean is…what's our next

step? It's your move."

"I never was good at chess." She stood as the fire truck, paramedics, and black suburban filled with FBI agents pulled into the yard. By now, every neighbor within sight of her house was standing in their yard. It was a miracle they hadn't taken up a petition to run her off by now.

"Looks like your press conference started a fire," Ingram said.

"Ha, ha." Cassidy looked past him to where the paramedics approached. "Stitch me up here. I'm not wasting any more of my day."

They looked at each other and shrugged. One of them moved to Colin, the other to Cassidy.

Rosie immediately got to her feet and growled, not letting the man get close to her.

"Call off the dog," he said, backing up.

Cassidy studied the man's face. "I haven't seen you before." She could almost count the perspiration on his forehead.

"I'm new."

"My dog doesn't like you. Why is that?"

"I don't know." His gaze flicked over her right shoulder. A lie, then.

Cassidy motioned to Ingram. "Cuff this man. He's one of Russell's followers."

"How do you know?"

"Look at the burn down the side of his neck. The way his mouth droops when he speaks. Plus, Rosie doesn't like him."

The man whirled and ran.

Smith and Miller tackled him.

"I swear, I didn't know," the other paramedic said. "This is the first time I've ever worked with him."

"No worries, Larson. I know you." Colin hissed as the man sprayed antiseptic on his cuts, then glanced at Cassidy. "It looks as if we have someone to question."

"It does." She watched as the struggling captive was half-dragged, half-walking on his own accord to a waiting squad car.

"Your turn, Detective." The paramedic, Larson, moved to Cassidy. "I think a couple of butterfly bandages will do the trick, but stitches would be best."

"Wonderful." She hadn't been looking forward to being

stitched up without a shot to numb the skin, but would have endured rather than waste more of the day going to the hospital. She sat while he cleaned and dressed the wound on her arm.

"Keep it in a sling until the skin goes back together. You'll have a scar."

"That doesn't bother me."

The tears welled again when a tow truck arrived and hauled what was left of her jeep away. This case had turned her into a slobbery mess. Before the so-called dragon entered the picture, the only time she cried was at a particularly sappy commercial. Nowadays, the tears seemed to lurk in waiting, ready to spill at any second.

She lunged to her feet. "Let's get to the station. Come, Rosie." With her dog at her side, she grabbed her gun, shoved her driver's license into her pocket, then climbed into Colin's truck.

~

Colin stood on one side of the two-way glass and stared at the man on the other side. He wouldn't have considered the fake paramedic ugly. Maybe not exactly handsome, but definitely not the type to risk everything to follow a maniac.

"What are you thinking?" He glanced at Cassidy.

"He isn't going to tell us where Russell is."

"Probably not." Colin opened the door and allowed her to enter first. "Mr. Collins, this is Detective Monroe and I'm Chief Detective MacKenzie. Would you like water or coffee? A soda, perhaps?"

The man continued staring straight ahead.

"Very well." Colin took one of the empty seats. "I hope you don't mind if we record our conversation. Would you like an attorney?"

Still no response.

"I take that as you refusing counsel. What was your purpose in pretending to be a medic? Were you the one who blew up my jeep?" Cassidy sat in the other empty chair.

The man's eyes flicked in her direction.

"So, you were. Alright, what about the first question? No? Okay. Why are you a follower of Draco? You don't seem to fit the profile of the others."

He stood and ripped open his shirt. Two buttons dropped to

the floor. "Get a good look." His chest was covered with burns. "This is what my model mother did to me when I spilled her expensive face cream. Do you know what it feels like to have hot oil poured on you?"

"I'm sorry," Colin said. "We don't know. We empathize. Why wasn't she reported to child protective services?"

"She was, but no one believed my story. They believed the one she told of me playing by the stove while fake tears ran down her unlined cheeks." He crossed his arms and sat. "My sister is just as bad. Says I ruin her vibe when I'm around."

Colin made a note to find out the sister's address and take her into protective custody. "Is your mother still alive?"

"Dead. Fiery car crash." He grinned.

Cassidy shook her head. "Nice to see you've retained your skills at my expense. Mind telling me why?"

"Draco said you needed to be punished for your comments at the press release. What he says to do, we do."

"How many of you are there?" Colin poised his pencil over the pad of paper on the table.

No response.

"Where can we find your leader?"

No answer.

"Mr. Collins, without your cooperation you'll be put behind bars for a very long time. You won't have Blake Russell to tell you what to do, or even to protect you. You'll be on your own with men much meaner than you could ever be. Cooperate, and we can possibly get your sentence lightened."

Still no response.

Colin stood. "Fine. Have it your way." He motioned with his head for Cassidy to follow him from the room.

"Watch your back, pretty lady. I don't think Draco is finished with you." Collins's laugh followed them.

Cassidy turned and approached the man, putting her face inches from his. "Tell my father that I am not afraid of him. What? You didn't know that he was my father? I guess he has secrets from his followers." Back straight, cocky smile on her face, she left the room, leaving the man staring after her.

Colin lifted his eyebrows at Collins. "Like father like daughter, wouldn't you say? She can be as hard as him. It must run in the blood." He followed Cassidy to his office.

He dropped his notes on the desk. "You like leaving a trail of pissed off people, don't you?"

"It's all part of the plan." She sat and rested her crossed ankles on his desk. "Feel free to remove the scowl from your face. It won't change anything. I remember when you smiled all the time."

Before she broke his heart, maybe.

~

He should have done something with the dog, even if temporary. Now, one of his own was behind bars, probably spilling his guts. Rather than be angry, Draco found himself rather proud of his offspring. She was showing her intelligence.

Drumming his fingers on the top of his diningtable, he pondered his next move. Slowly, he needed to increase the risk to Cassidy, forcing her to join him or lose those she cared about. Which wasn't many. His dear daughter was a loner, surrounding herself with no one until the Scot was forced on her. Her having no attachments made his work difficult indeed.

Not to mention that silly press conference. He grinned. The type of bandanas that bikers wore would solve the problem of him being easily recognized. He rather fancied the one with the skull jaw. She'd made no mention of his dragon jacket. All he needed was a Harley, and he'd fit right in with his disguise.

Oh, she was good for him, challenging him, forcing him to stay young. He rubbed his hands together, then booted up his computer. It was easy enough for a man with money to order a motorcycle on line and have it delivered, along with the helmet and bandanna. Life was so exciting.

5

F or crying out loud!" Cassidy yanked open her front door and stared at the flaming dragon on her lawn. How childish could Russell be? She grabbed the water hose and aimed it at what was once a brightly colored piñata of a dragon. What she really wanted to do was hold the hose over Russell's face until he couldn't breathe.

"At least he didn't blow up my truck." Colin stepped onto the porch. "Do you mind if I start parking in the garage?"

She whirled, the hose wetting his bare feet. "That's what you're worried about?"

Colin jumped back and scowled. "That water is cold, and, yes, I'm worried about my truck."

"You should worry about your head." Not that a burning party favor on the lawn was a big thing, but it was clearly a warning—one she had no intentions of backing down on. Let Russell play his foolish games. Fools get caught.

Once the danger of her lawn catching fire was past, she turned off the hose and smiled as Colin tip-toed through the wet grass on his way to his truck. He then drove it into the garage, emerging with a grin. "That's where she belongs."

If only that were true. If Cassidy hadn't have left, if Russell wasn't trying to kill her, so many ifs, her jeep and Colin's truck might have permanent spots next to each other. Maybe not. If not for the case pushing them together, they might never have been more than partners.

"Let's watch a movie and eat popcorn." Colin motioned his head toward the house. "We could use a night off from all this."

"That doesn't help us catch a killer."

"No, but a clear head does." He took the four steps to the porch two at a time and opened the front door. "Come on. No more working tonight."

A night that most people would call normal sounded good. What was better than a good movie, popcorn, a handsome man, and trusty dog? She grinned. "All right." She bounded after him, then dashed to the kitchen. "Pick out a movie while I get popcorn and wine."

She paused reaching for the wine glasses. The last time they'd drank wine and watched a movie they'd almost crossed a line they couldn't uncross. She shook her head. They were different people now. Colin could barely tolerate her. It would be fine.

She popped two bags of buttered popcorn and with the bottle of wine, two bowls of popped goodness and two wine glasses on a tray, carried it all to the living room. "What did you pick?"

"The new Jurassic Park. Seen it?"

"Not yet. I bought it, but haven't had the time." She'd left town before opening the package.

Minutes later, lights turned low, her on one end of the sofa and Colin on the other, they stared as a man trained velociraptors. It wasn't until well into the movie that Cassidy noticed Rosie's gaze wasn't trained on her as usual. Instead, it seemed to be focused on the mantle.

"What are you looking at, girl?" She set her bowl on the coffee table and searched the few photos there. "No!" She grabbed a photo of her mother, smiling, on a beach in California. One of the fondest memories Cassidy had.

The right eye had been cut from the photo. In its place was a tiny camera. "He's been watching us again." That didn't bother her as much as the mutilation of the photograph. She had so few of them. "Do you hear me, father!" She spit the word. "Stop playing games and come and get me."

Colin yanked the framed picture out of her hands, then removed the camera and smashed it with a heavy vase. "We need to search the rest of the house."

"I wouldn't have noticed this one if Rosie hadn't been staring at it. Could she really see it?"

"It must have moved and she saw it or heard it."

Cassidy wanted to throw something. "So much for a relaxing

evening. Let's check my room first. If they're all this tiny, it's going to take a while."

"I could call in help."

She shook her head. "No, we can do this. I'm not in the mood to watch the movie now anyway."

By midnight, they had discovered one in a door pull of a kitchen cabinet, another in the fringe of a lamp on Cassidy's nightstand, one in a painting in Colin's room, and another in Cassidy's bathroom, the freak. All of the cameras were tiny and top-of-the-line in what they could do.

She dropped them into the garbage disposal and turned it on. The grinding sound brought a sense of satisfaction. "I don't know how to keep him out of my house. How many times do we have to change the alarm code?"

Colin dropped into a kitchen chair. "How many different codes can you come up with that you'll remember?"

"You're saying every day?"

"As often as you can come up with something new." He ran his hands through his hair, making the raven strands stand on end. "In other words, I have no idea."

Usually, he had answers. The fact that he was stumped as her filled her with dread. "What do we do?"

"I'd say move, but you have a good security system. We couldn't get this setup in a motel or mountain cabin. My suggestion is..." he lifted his gaze to hers "...we start living at the station until this is solved."

"Absolutely not. We'll sweep the house every time we come home. We'll get dogs trained to protect and attack."

"Your neighbors will love that when taking their babies for a walk." He spun a salt shaker on the table. "I'm beat. Let's talk about this in the morning."

~

Not having suffered from nightmares in a few months, Colin woke from one at four a.m. the next morning. Drenched in sweat, despite only sleeping in a pair of baggy shorts, he climbed out of bed and parted the curtains.

This nightmare was different than his usual. Instead of accidentally shooting a hostage he didn't know, he shot Cassidy. She'd stared up at him, her blood staining his shoes, and whispered, "Why?" It had seemed so real that if, when waking, he hadn't heard her snores from the other room, he'd have barged into her room to check on her.

Rosie padded into his room and nudged his hand. "What's up, girl?" Colin patted her head. "You don't usually leave Cassidy alone."

The dog leaned on the windowsill and peered out. Colin followed her gaze.

Standing in the yard was a man in leather and wearing a skull bandanna over his face. Blake Russell. Their gazes collided for a second, then the other man turned and melted into the trees.

What kind of game was he playing? This tip-toeing around each other was driving Colin insane. Maybe Cassidy's idea of provoking the man was a good thing after all.

"You're up early."

He turned to see a drowsy, and very sexy Cassidy, despite the large tee shirt and too big shorts, standing in the doorway of his room. "We had company."

That seemed to wake her up. She rushed to the window. "Russell?"

"I'm guessing it was. He wore the leather jacket, but had a bandanna over his face." His gaze caressed her profile. "Did I wake you?"

"I heard Rosie's nails on the floor."

"She's the one who let me know he was out there. Come on. I'll make coffee and omelets."

She smiled. "Sounds like a good way to start the day."

He could come up with a few better ways, starting with a heated kiss, but knew he had to keep his distance for the sake of his heart. If Cassidy felt anything for him other than friendship, or tolerance, she would have to make the first move. He couldn't stand the pain of his heart being shredded again. He forced a smile, clapped her on the shoulder as he would one of his buddies, then headed for the kitchen.

Twenty minutes later, they sat at the small table, sipping coffee, reading the newspaper, and eating as if they'd been married for twenty years...except for the small fact the tension was thicker than the jam on his toast. He peered over the sports section of the paper.

Cassidy wasn't even pretending to read anymore, but stared out the small kitchen window.

"What's wrong?"

She shrugged. "Just a feeling that something very bad is going to happen."

His Mom had told him to never ignore a woman's intuition. "Any more information?"

"No, it's just a feeling. I don't know what's going to happen, where, nothing. Just a stirring inside that leaves me rattled."

"Don't shake it off." He pushed to his feet and cleared the table. "Ingram might think we're nuts, going off on a feeling, but I trust you. Let's get dressed."

Sure enough, Ingram listened to Cassidy's 'feeling' with skepticism. "You *feel* as if something is going to happen. Something big. That doesn't help us much."

"I'm putting the force, small though we may be, on high alert anyway." Colin crossed his arms. "Blake Russell was outside our house this morning, and last night he set a piñata of a dragon on fire in the front yard. Because of these things, I'm not discounting anything."

He glanced around the room at the agents and two police officers. "Everyone stay on alert and wear your vests. Dismissed." In a flurry of papers and murmurings, the room cleared, leaving only him and Cassidy.

"I could be wrong, Colin."

"I don't think so. Something is going down. Russell's presence is more obvious. Six months ago, we weren't seeing him or one of his followers every time we turned around. Now, we bump elbows at every turn."

"Sir." The newest rookie poked his head into the room. "The DMV is being held hostage by two men in leather jackets."

6

After exchanging a sad look with Colin, Cassidy raced out the door, Rosie on her heels, as he yelled for someone to call in the SWAT team. She exited the building along with the FBI agents and was in Colin's truck seconds before he slid into the driver's seat.

"There's a vest in your size behind the seat," he said. "Put it on."

"Where's yours?"

"It's back there." He floored the gas pedal and sent them rocketing down the highway. "I'll put it on when we arrive."

Relief flooded through her. She didn't want him taking any unnecessary risks. Those were for her to take. This fight was personal...between her and a mad man who happened to be her biological father. If something were to happen to Colin—"

"We beat SWAT." Colin parked behind the security barrier and grabbed his vest before exiting the truck. He cast a stern look at Cassidy. "Don't do anything foolish."

"Who, me?" She grinned, stepping to the safety of a squad car between her and the DMV building. "Have you confirmed two suspects are inside?" She asked the officer standing there.

"Yes, and they're armed with semi-automatic rifles. Here." He handed her a pair of binoculars.

More than thirty hostages sat in hard plastic chairs and on the floor. The workers weren't behind the counters as usual, so must be with the others. Two men in leather jackets, portraying the colorfully embroidered dragon on the back, paced, rifles on their shoulders. She handed the binoculars back. "Have they made any demands?"

"They want to talk to you." He pointed to a cell phone on the car's hood. "Just hit dial."

"I'm not a hostage negotiator." Her hand trembled as she reached for the phone. What if she said the wrong thing? What if she got someone killed?

"You can do this." Colin placed his hand on her shoulder, and gave a gentle squeeze. "We have faith in you."

Warmth flooded through her at his touch. She nodded and pressed the dial button. "This is Detective Monroe."

"Step into the middle of the road."

"May I ask who I'm speaking with?"

"You're speaking with the fire of the Dragon! Do as I say, or I'll shoot someone. Watch through your spy glasses if you don't believe me."

Colin, binoculars at his eyes, said, "He's pointing the gun at a woman."

"I'm coming," Cassidy said into the phone. "There's no need to shoot anyone." Hopefully, she wasn't stepping out to meet a bullet.

She put a brave front on and stepped into the open, the phone to his left ear, the other hand out at her side. "Now what?"

"See that chalk drawn square on the pavement?"

"Yes?"

"Stand there."

"Is it a bomb, because I've already been there, done that."

"Do it!"

Taking a deep breath, she stepped into the square. "Okay."

"Now, you wait."

"For what?"

"Further instructions."

"Can I move?"

"Not out of that square. If you do, I shoot someone." Click.

She glanced over her shoulder at Colin and shrugged. Already the day was growing warm, abnormally hot for fall. She swiped a hand across her sweating forehead and watched the two men through the window. One by one, they had the hostages form a line of defense in front of the window until the suspects were no longer able to be seen.

Russell had to be behind the brilliant move. So far, none of his followers seemed intelligent enough to think of such an act. She shook her legs to keep the blood circulating and tried to keep focused on what was happening and not on how hot the sun was beating down on the vest.

Movement on the roof caught her attention. A man aimed a gun, no, one of those things that shot out tee shirts at sporting events. A muffled pop, then a small white package lay at her feet. She bent and opened it, pulling out a sheet of computer paper. "For every hour you can stand in that box, a hostage is released. Let's see what you're made of. Father."

She sighed and stuffed the note in her pocket as her phone rang. Colin. "I have to stand here for every hostage in the building."

"That's physically impossible!"

"I don't have a choice."

"Did he say whether I could bring you water, something to eat?"

She shook her head. "He didn't say. I'll ask the suspects inside." She hung up with Colin, then redialed those inside in the building. "Can I have someone bring me a bottle of water?"

"We're sending out a kid. He does not have to return. You earned his freedom." Click.

A young man around the age of sixteen, probably getting his driver's license, darted from the building. He thrust a water bottle into Cassidy's hand, muttered a thank you, and raced to the safety of the squad cars.

She would have liked to have asked him some questions before he hurried away. Instead, she twisted off the bottle cap and guzzled half of the water before setting it at her feet. The enormity of the situation weakened her knees. How could she possibly stand there for more than thirty hours? Her body would shut down. She glanced back at Colin, relieved to see him watching her. She knew he would stay there with her, the entire time. She wouldn't be alone.

She watched as Rosie broke free of her leash and plodded to Cassidy's side where she promptly sat next to her, as close as was physically possible. Tears sprang to Cassidy's eyes at the faithfulness of her friend. "Do you want what's left of my water?" She poured some into the dog's mouth. "Thank you for coming, girl. It's going to be a long wait."

~

A woman and her dog. Rather than portray the picture of contentment and companionship, it was the loneliness thing Colin had ever seen. He stepped around the security barrier and moved to Cassidy's side, expecting a bullet at any moment. When none arrived, he took her hand in his. He wouldn't let her take the stand alone any longer.

"How long have I been here?" Her eyes glistened with tears.

"Three hours."

"Only." She heaved a sigh. "Thank you."

He gave her hand a squeeze. "I'm at your side until the very end."

The DMV door opened and an old woman with a walker emerged. She shuffled toward them, handed them both a bottle of water, then patted Rosie's head. "I've a treat for you, gorgeous." She fished a dog bone from her cavernous purse and laid it on the ground. Her gaze lifted to Colin's. "Thank you. You two are the bravest people I've ever met."

"You're welcome," Cassidy said softly. "And thank you for the dog treat."

"Stand tall. They are watching." She patted Cassidy's arm. "God is with you." She made her way to the waiting officers.

"At least Russell is a man of his word." Colin grinned.

Cassidy giggled. "Only you can find anything good about this situation." She sobered. "People will die today. You realize that, don't you?"

"I'll stand as long as I can. Obviously, it's okay. I'm not dead yet." He winked.

"That's not something you should joke about." She pulled her hand free, wiped it on her pants, then slipped it back into his. "Sweaty."

"It'll cool off soon."

Rosie whined, ate the bone, then lay down, placing her head on her paws.

"Is the old woman right?" Cassidy glanced up. "About God being with us? If so, what about those inside? What about the ones that will die when I collapse?"

"We'll make it." They had to. "And, yes, God is with us.

Always." Just as he planned to always be there for her. "I can't explain why things happen. Take that up with God when you meet him."

By supper time, five more hostages had been released, each bringing them a bottle of water. One brought them each an apple. So, Russell *wanted* them to succeed, but not without pain. Colin shifted, his feet aching in his cowboy boots. He closed his eyes, and dozed, a trick he learned while hiding from a drunken father when he was a child.

Cassidy leaned against him at the twelve hour mark. Her stomach rumbled. Her body trembled.

He put an arm around her shoulders to steady her. "Almost halfway there."

"Mr. Pollyanna."

"Who's that?"

"Nevermind."

"Close your eyes, sweetheart, and rest. Push away the pain in your feet and legs. Ignore the pounding in your head and the sweat cooling on your body. Drift away to a time when life was good and your mother was with you. Maybe at the beach."

She made a soft sound in her throat, then jerked up as a woman and infant walked from the building. "I'm sorry," the woman said. "They didn't give me anything for you."

"We'll manage," Colin told her. "Go home."

"Do you think they're out of water inside?"

He shrugged. "Or they're keeping what's left for themselves."

"I'm tired, Colin."

"Don't quit. Keep leaning on me."

She nodded, keeping her eyes closed. "I guess I'm not as strong as I thought I was."

"You're the strongest person I've ever met." He breathed deeply of her sweat and the faint scent of dust in her hair. Knowing what it took for her to smell that way made it the sweetest scent in the world.

By two a.m., her knees buckled. Colin scooped her into his arms. "I'll hold you." For as long as he could. He nestled her head under his chin. By the time the sun came up, he was swaying on his feet.

"Put me down," she said. "It's your turn to lean on me. Put

your arms around my neck and lay your head on top of mine. I'll stand as long as I can."

"Look. There's no more people standing at the window." With the light of the dawning sun, he could see the window was clear. "We can do this. Only a few more."

"I don't see anyone moving."

"I don't either. Hand me that phone." Hope gave him a bit more strength. He called the suspects. "How many more?"

"None." Two shots rang out.

Grabbing Cassidy's hand, they sprinted toward the DMV, slamming the doors open against the door stoppers.

On the floor lay the two suspects, blood pooling under them.

Cassidy dropped into a chair. "Why?"

"Orders from Russell most likely." He checked for ID. Two brothers, both with wine port stains on their faces. Ray and Raymond Kensingston. He collapsed into a chair next to Cassidy. "I think my feet are bleeding."

She smiled through her tears. "You did it, Colin. I would have failed without you."

He leaned over and kissed her. "We did it." He'd deal with his heart later. After sleeping for two days.

7

The sun was setting the next day when Cassidy rolled out of bed. She'd given a brief statement, not that Ingram didn't already know how the day had transpired, then Colin had driven her home and they'd both crashed within five minutes.

Now, although fatigue still coated her body, and every muscle ached, she combed her room for hidden cameras or recording devices. Not finding any, she headed to Colin's room. His door was open and the room empty.

She found him crashed on the couch, his bloody feet hanging off the edge. What he had done for her the day before could never be repaid, but she knew what might start at repaying the debt.

After filling a basin with warm water and grabbing a rag, hydrogen peroxide, a towel, and bandages, she knelt beside the sofa and took one of his feet in her hands. She gently washed his wounds, trying to ignore the fact he'd woken and now stared at her with more heat in his eyes than was wise.

"Thank you again," she said, binding his feet with clean bandages. "What you did was truly heroic."

"No more so than what you did." He sat up. "What time is it?"

"Almost eight p.m. I'm going to grab something to eat, then go back to bed. Are you hungry?"

"Yes. Let's order a pizza. I'm sure neither one of us feels like cooking." He took her hands in his and forced her to look at him. "Can we talk about…us?"

"There can't be an us, Colin." She pulled free and lifted the basin of blood tinged water. "It's not possible. It's too dangerous."

"I'm aware of the danger, Cassidy." He ran his hands through his hair, causing the strands to stand on end. Stubble dotted his face, giving him a rakish sexiness that played with Cassidy's heart.

She headed for the kitchen before she forgot her resolve to keep her distance. She dumped the water and leaned heavily on the sink. What had she been thinking? Washing his feet was an intimate act. Still, he'd sacrificed for her. It seemed the least she could do.

"Cassidy."

She turned to see him leaning against the doorjamb, shirtless, jeans riding low on his hips, the bandages on his feet shining like badges. She loved him with everything in her. The fact she couldn't act on that love was like a knife to her gut. "I haven't ordered yet." She reached for the phone.

"Stop." He took mincing steps toward her, pain clouding his eyes.

She knew she should rush away, yet she froze, her gaze glued to his. "Please." The one word conveyed all her yeses and all her nos.

His eyes darkened as he cupped her face and lowered his head. "I know." He claimed her lips with such intensity everything around them disappeared.

If she'd thought herself weak yesterday, her legs not strong enough to support her weight, that was nothing compared to now. She wrapped her arms around his neck and held on. The kiss deepened. She melted into him. His arms slid down her arms, over her ribcage and settled on her waist. He groaned and pulled her closer.

The phone rang several times before it jarred her from their kiss. "I need to answer. It could be important." Her chest heaved, her lips felt swollen.

He nodded, then straddled a kitchen chair, the action so masculine she wanted to ignore the phone and lead him upstairs. No, that would accomplish nothing good past the moment of passion. The kiss had led them too close to the same disaster they'd almost fallen into months ago.

She grabbed her cell phone. "Monroe."

"This is Ingram. The Dragon left a message for you."

She leaned against the wall. "What is it?"

"Someone painted a picture of a fire-breathing dragon with a scar down its face. Standing next to it as it seems about to devour a princess, is a red-haired woman who looks remarkably like you."

"What are you not telling me? You wouldn't have called because of a painting. That could have waited until morning."

"The princess wasn't part of the painting. At one time, she'd been a lovely blond girl in a frilly pink dress."

Her stomach plummeted. "We'll be right there." She hung up and turned to Colin. "No rest for now." After explaining the details of the call, she went to change into work clothes.

Colin waited for her at the front door, gym shoes on his feet rather than his usual boots. He opened the front door, set the alarm, then followed her to the truck. "You okay?" He asked, getting into the truck.

"I'd like one good night's sleep." She buckled her seatbelt into place.

"I'm talking about the kiss." His lips twitched.

"Let's not, all right?"

"Sure." He backed a bit too fast from the drive and roared down the highway to the address Ingram had texted to Cassidy.

The address was to a vacant building in the next town. The burned carcass of a woman, tied to a stake at one end of an elaborate painting on the cement wall was surrounded by law enforcement.

"This has to stop." Cassidy shoved open her door. The main problem was...she had no idea how to stop the mad man.

"Sorry to drag you out after the day you had yesterday. I know the two of you are, literally, dead on your feet." Ingram led them to the scene. "The painting isn't the actual message. There's writing on a scroll hanging on the dragon's saddle."

Cassidy made her way closer to the wall and read, "To the real princess. Until the day we ride together, I will be there in the shadows, in the fire, in your mind." Why wouldn't he face her and end all this?

~

Colin did his best not to hobble and to ignore the pain in his feet as he examined the crime scene. "Do we have an ID on the girl?" He asked Ingram.

"He left her purse. She's the sister to one of the dead men who held the hostages yesterday."

"Was she dead before then?"

"Hard to tell, but most likely. The ME will be able to tell us more later."

"Any family?"

"No, not anymore."

Colin glanced to where Cassidy studied the life-size painting. "This had to take a while to do. How did no one notice?"

"Vacant building, no one comes here other than druggies." Ingram shrugged. "They wouldn't have cared. Probably thought it was cool."

"Have you put out feelers for wall artists capable of this type of talent?"

"Yep."

Colin doubted it would lead them anywhere. The artist was probably contacted by a third person if not over the phone. Still, the work was amazing, down to the scorch marks on the painted princess.

By now, the body was removed from the stake and zipped into a body bag. Two medics with masks loaded it onto a gurney. This was the type of scene that caused nightmares.

Cassidy backed away from the wall and glanced from one end to the other before turning and heading around the corner. Colin glanced at Ingram, then followed.

The painting hadn't ended on the main wall. The second wall showed a large nest with many eggs.

"His followers," she said, continuing around the building. "There are ten eggs. I have no idea whether that is his current number or what he started with. Oh, and the painting actually starts here. See, the dragon has no scar." The dragon fought a beautiful red-haired woman. The next picture showed the dragon bleeding. The artist had portrayed the history of Russell and Cassidy's mother in great detail. Cassidy grinned. "We'll face him soon. Look at the corner…there." She pointed.

A much smaller painting showed Cassidy and Colin. Only Cassidy stood next to the dragon and Colin stood alone facing them. Chills skittered up his spine. Russell would be coming for him next.

"Now what?"

She rubbed the side of her nose, thinking a moment, before

speaking. "I'm going to have to join him."

"Absolutely not."

She faced him. "He'll kill you if I don't."

"He'll try. He had the opportunity yesterday and didn't. Maybe he thinks I'm worthy of living." A long shot, but one he chose to hold on to. "He obviously didn't believe your attempt to be one of the ugly pretty people."

"I sent the reporter an apology," she said softly. "I explained to her, in confidence, why I said what I did. She understands."

"Yet, it still bothers you."

"It isn't who I am." She sighed. "Let's go. I can't think without more sleep."

She seemed to be doing just fine. No one else had noticed that the painting continued. "This artist had to be busy for months."

Cassidy stopped. "That's why we didn't hear anything from Russell for six months. He wanted the painting finished before he continued."

"You're a genius!" He gave her a quick one-armed hug. "Maybe you should be chief."

"I'm leaving when this case is solved." She stepped away.

And, just like that, the moon disappeared and he was again in darkness. How could she hold him at arm's length after the kiss and what they'd endured together yesterday? It made no sense. He knew she cared for him. They would catch Russell, they would win. They could be together. He wanted to shake some sense into her.

Once the scene was secured and they were cleared to return home, it was almost midnight. They could get a good six hours of sleep before work, if he could shut off his brain, and emotions, long enough.

Nothing worked. He lay on the sofa, staring at the dark ceiling, while his feet throbbed. He'd chosen to sleep downstairs, not only because climbing them seemed like unnecessary torture to his feet, but anyone entering the house had to pass him to get to Cassidy. Add in how his pulse still raced after her response to his kiss, and there'd be no sleep at all.

He sat up and turned on the television. The local station had picked up the story and plastered the giant dragon photo across the screen. Thankfully, the body had been removed before photos taken.

Something he hadn't noticed earlier at the crime scene was the man in a leather jacket standing on the fringe of the curious onlookers. Too far away to tell if the man was Russell or not. He pounded the pillow next to him. They should know by now that either Russell or one of his cronies was always at the scene when Cassidy showed up. Next time, they'd set a trap.

~

Smart woman. Just like her mother.

Draco rubbed his chin. He knew she'd discover the full painting and the story it told.

When she'd stood there so bravely yesterday, not moving from the square drawn on the pavement, his heart had soared. Then, the Scot had held her when she could stand no more, proving himself as worthy as Draco's daughter.

Unfortunately, there was no room for him in Draco's plans. He was there to protect Cassidy, nothing more. Just in case Draco's followers got over zealous. When the man had served his purpose, he would be eliminated. There was no room for more than one beauty at his side, and that spot was reserved for his daughter. Unless…his mind began to concoct a plan.

8

Bright and early the next morning, Cassidy sat at the conference room table with Colin and the agents as they tried to come up with a plan that would put them one step ahead of Russell, instead of two steps behind. So far, all they'd done was stare at each other.

"I noticed in the late night news that one of Russell's followers, or Russell himself, was there at the crime scene last night," Colin said. "Unfortunately, we know it is only a matter of time before someone else is killed. We need to have agents in the crowd, pretending to be onlookers and catch this guy."

"We should have done this already." Cassidy reached for her coffee. "Six months ago we knew Russell was wherever I was. I'm sorry for forgetting that." They could have caught the man by now. She was off her game, and it was costing them.

"It's a good plan," Ingram spoke up, "but doesn't prevent another death."

That seemed to be the big problem. "I'm going to have to join him."

They all stared at her.

"No." Colin set his lips into a firm line.

"It's the only way." She returned his stare over the rim of her cup.

"What happens when he wants you to attend a killing with him, uh?" His eyes flashed. "How are you going to prove yourself to him?"

"I'll figure it out."

"It's suicide and certain death for me." He turned away.

"Why do you say that?"

"Right now, I have a purpose. When you join him, I no longer have one. I'll be expendable."

"Go into hiding."

He whirled. "Seriously? Are you listening to the words coming out of your mouth?"

The three agents' heads went from one to the other like kittens chasing a string. If not for the seriousness of the situation, Cassidy would have laughed.

"Part of my agreement would be your safety and no more killings." She set her cup down with a plunk, knowing as soon as she spoke that what she said would not happen. Russell might spare Colin, she'd insist, but he would draw the line on stopping what he considered his quest. "Does anyone have a better idea?"

"I'll think of something," Colin said.

The others shook their heads.

"Unless someone does come up with something better, I'm moving forward."

Colin slapped his palms flat on the table. "As the chief, I forbid it."

"I don't work for you." She did her best not to flinch or look away. "I can fulfill my plan just as well from Little Rock."

He mumbled something under his breath. "We're done here. Get out there and find Russell before Detective Monroe does something stupid."

The agents stood. "The FBI doesn't usually let the local police handle things," Ingram said. "You've been doing a good job so far, but if the two of you don't come to some sort of agreement, we're taking over control. You may not like our decision." They marched out of the room.

"Way to go, Chief." She put as much sarcasm into the word as she could. "Let the suits take over."

"Shut it, Monroe."

So, he'd taken to using her last name. It didn't matter. He'd come around to her way of thinking soon enough. "I'm going to start returning calls on messages left in regards to our plea for spottings of Russell. I'll let you know if I find anything." She left him alone and went to the small office assigned to her during her stay.

Two hours later, she chalked all the calls up to trash. Not one was a viable lead. She leaned back in her chair. How could she get a message to Russell outside of another press conference? How could one man, who stood out with his scar and jacket, manage to remain invisible?

She needed a break. "Colin!"

"You do realize the phone has intercom, right?" He stepped into her office. "No need to call me like you would Rosie. Speaking of—she's wandering around the precinct scaring the drunks."

"Good girl. Do you have a normal call we can go on? Something domestic or a robbery? I need to do something simple to clear my head."

"You consider domestic violence simple?" His brow furrowed.

"No, but it is routine."

He shrugged. "We have a couple of regulars fighting. We don't consider them a priority, but maybe you can put the fear of God in them."

She grinned. "What are we waiting for? I'd love to play bad cop."

They drove to a trailer park where several beer toting men laughed and joked outside of a flamingo pink trailer. Through the open window came screams, curses, and the sounds of glass breaking.

"They's at it again," one big guy said with a toothless grin. "Our daily entertainment."

"Hey, Johnson!" A skinny guy yelled through the window. "The cops are here."

"Tell them they ain't needed!"

"Yes, they are!" A woman's shrill voice answered. "I want you in jail."

"You hit me first!"

Cassidy glanced at Colin, grinned again, and bounded up the metal stairs. The door was open. "Police."

"Come on in." A woman, cigarette dangling from ruby lips, plopped onto a sagging sofa. "Take him away."

"Ma'am, I heard him say you hit him first."

"No crime in a woman slugging her man, is there?" She scowled. "He's been out womanizing again."

"Actually, it's a crime for anyone to hit anyone. Sir, do you want to press charges?"

His eyes widened. "I can do that? Well, now, let me think on it."

"While you're thinking…" Cassidy stepped closer to him, "let me give you something else to hurt your brain. Why any woman would stay with a cheating man is beyond me. If you were mine, I'd cut off that…extension of yourself that men prize so highly."

He gulped and paled, covering his groin with both hands.

"So, I suggest you pack a bag and leave. That is, if the lady wants you to." She turned to the woman. "Ma'am?"

"I'd like nothing more. I'm done with him and his ways. There are plenty of fish in this scummy pond."

Cassidy raised at brows at Mr. Johnson. "Sir?"

"Fine. I'm leaving and going back to Oklahoma." He grabbed a set of keys off the table and barged past Colin.

Cassidy turned back to the woman. "I suggest you clean up this place, and yourself, and make something of your life. Good day." She strolled outside, feeling better than she had in days. "That was fun."

Colin laughed. "Is that how you usually handle things? By threatening to cut off precious body parts?"

"When it warrants." She nodded at the onlookers and headed for the truck.

~

"That was an interesting day," Colin said, parking in front of Cassidy's house. "First the Johnsons, then you handcuff a kid stealing candy, just to scare him, you said."

"Don't forget the little old lady shoplifting." She smiled, opening her door. "You must love your job here."

"You did, too, once."

Her smile faded. "I did, I do."

He shook his head. "Little Rock is different. You crave the small town crime, when Russell isn't involved. There's a job for you here, should you choose to return."

"Thanks." She got out of the truck and headed for the house.

Colin unlocked the door and automatically pressed in the security code before he realized the code wasn't set. "Stay behind me." He drew his weapon and headed for the living room.

"Put your gun away, Mr. MacKenzie. I'm not here to kill anyone." The tableside lamp clicked to life, revealing Russell, one ankle poised on a knee, on the sofa. "I'm merely here to talk."

"I'll keep my gun close, thank you."

"How do you keep getting in my house?" Cassidy asked.

"There are ways, my dear. I hope you don't mind that I helped myself to a glass of wine. I found myself parched waiting for your return. Did you enjoy yourself?"

"Cut the pleasantries and tell us what you want." Colin stayed close to Cassidy.

"I prefer to acknowledge social niceties, but simply put, I want my daughter."

"I'm not your daughter." Cassidy took a step forward. "We may share DNA, but that's all. I had a mother, and you killed her."

His eyes hardened. "She gave me this and spurned me, mocked me." He caressed the scar on his face and grinned, one side of his face pulling up to reveal more teeth and gums than normal. "She also gave me you."

"To the point, Russell." Colin pulled Cassidy back to his side.

"Russell sighed. "I want you out of the picture and my daughter at my side."

"Why?" Cassidy frowned. "Why is that so important? I'm one of the pretty people."

He waved away her comment. "Everyone knows that was just an act, dear. Do you realize what we could do together? With my money and power and your brains and beauty, we can run the world. People will tremble before us. You may keep your beauty and be the face of the operation. People respond better to those who look like you."

"I thought the pretty had to die," she said.

"You'll be the queen of them all. If they don't treat others fairly, they'll be punished." He pushed to his feet. "I'm waiting for your answer."

She glanced at Colin, then back to Russell. "What about Colin? You have to swear to spare him."

"I'm afraid I can't make that promise. We don't need him. Unless…" Russell studied Colin for a moment. "you allow me to mess up that face of his."

"Try it." Colin took a step toward the man.

"No!" She put a hand on his chest to stop him. "Either Colin is spared, in every way, and the killings stop or its war between us, Russell. Those are my terms."

"Think on it and let me know in the morning. Don't make a rash decision." Russell turned off the light, plunging them into darkness.

By the time Colin found the light switch, the back door was slamming closed. "I thought you wanted to go with him."

"You're blaming me for the fact he got away?" Cassidy planted her fists on her hips. "I can't give him an answer right away. He'll know it was planned."

He shook his head and rushed to the back door, knowing it was useless. The yard was empty. "Don't spare me in order to catch this guy. I'm willing to make the sacrifice."

"Maybe I'm not." Her eyes shimmered. "We can't have a relationship, Colin, but that doesn't mean I want you dead."

~

Things were going as planned. Cassidy would come to him in the end, especially when her beloved Scot was threatened. Oh, yes. Draco laughed in the privacy of his apartment. "When it came down to the Scot's life or her joining his forces, she'd make the right decision. The first step toward that happening was waiting in the Scot's room.

9

Oh, look, he's courting me now." Colin plucked a pink rose off his bed. "This one has thorns."

"The ones he gave me didn't." Cassidy lifted a note from the top of the duvet cover. "Let the games begin." Things were heating up. An icy fist squeezed her heart. The danger toward Colin had increased a hundred fold, and she had no idea how to keep him safe.

He cupped her cheek. "Don't worry about me."

"You might as well tell the sun not to rise in the morning." She handed him the note and left the room, not wanting him to see how frightened she really was.

She headed for the shower in preparation of bed. As the hot water sprayed over her, she closed her eyes and lifted her face. What was Russell's next move? A rose seemed harmless enough, but only a fool wouldn't think there had to be a warning, a sinister motive, attached.

After her shower, she changed into the shorts and tee shirt she slept in and climbed into bed, patting the mattress beside her. She didn't usually allow Rosie to sleep on the bed, but companionship sounded wonderful. She fell asleep with one hand on her dog's head.

Rosie woofed deep in her throat.

Cassidy shot from the bed, grabbing the pistol from her nightstand. Standing in the dark, she peeled her ears to listen for anything out of the ordinary. There! A creak from a loose floorboard downstairs.

"Come," she whispered.

Her alarm grew as she passed Colin's empty room. Not

because his room was empty, he spent most nights on the sofa, but because he had slept in the bed as evidenced by the tangle of blankets. Had he had one of his nightmares? "Colin?"

Careful not to make a sound as she headed downstairs, she kept one hand on Rosie, and the other ready to fire the gun. She flicked on the hall light.

Two masked men, an unconscious Colin between them, were moving out the front door. "Angriff! Rosie." She gave the German command to attack.

Rosie bolted forward, latching onto one of the assailants legs. The man howled and aimed a gun toward the dog.

Cassidy fired, hitting him in the shoulder. The gun fell. The other man dropped Colin and took aim. She fired again, this shot taking him in the chest. She whirled to train her gun back on the first guy whose blood-curdling screams from Rosie's attack filled the air. "That's good, Rosie. Good girl." With her free hand, she dialed 911, then Ingram. "Watch him."

Rosie took up a guard stance next to the wounded men while Cassidy knelt next to Colin. His breathing seemed regular, his pulse strong. Had they drugged him? How in the world did Russell and his men get into her house?

Ten minutes later paramedics, and Ingram rushed through her front door. "Is he alive?" Ingram glanced at Colin.

"Yes, but I don't know about one of the perps." Cassidy pushed to her feet.

"This one is dead," a paramedic said. "We'll call the coroner and take the detective and the other guy to the hospital."

Another one bit the dust. If she had to, she'd take out Russell's followers one-by-one.

"I'm fine," Colin muttered. "I'm not going anywhere." He sat up and rubbed his hands briskly over his face.

"What happened?" Cassidy knelt beside him again.

"I woke up with a needle going in my neck. Before I could do anything, the world went black. That's all." Bracing a hand on her shoulder, he pushed to his feet. "I guess the rose meant Russell wants to spend more time with me."

"We can't let that happen, Colin." She accepted his offered hand to pull her up. "He'll kill you."

"Probably torture you first," Ingram said. "What?" He

shrugged as they both stared at him. "It would fit his MO. I'm trying to be the voice of reason here."

"It doesn't help." Colin shuffled to the sofa and flopped down. "I could use something for my stomach."

"Like the hospital?" Cassidy glared.

"Like a tums."

One of the paramedics handed him a small packet, then shined a flashlight in his eyes. "If the dizziness doesn't pass within an hour or you start throwing up, go to the hospital."

Colin nodded. "I'll be fine."

"Stop saying that." Cassidy clenched her fists. "This is serious. If Rosie hadn't woke me—"

"But she did." He peered up at her. "Which is exactly what she's supposed to do."

Of all the stubborn…Cassidy stomped to the kitchen to make coffee while the paramedics and ME removed the dead and wounded. Then, she'd have to call someone to clean up the blood and repair the bullet holes in her house. She slammed the coffee pot on the burner. Maybe these were nothing more than Russell's attempts at a distraction.

No, he wanted Colin, and her, and would stop at nothing to achieve that goal. She measured coffee grounds and pressed start.

"What's going on in that head of yours?" Ingram entered the kitchen.

"Trying to figure out how to join Russell without getting Colin killed in the process."

"That's a tough one. You do realize that MacKenzie will sacrifice himself to save lives, right?"

"That's what I'm afraid of." She planted both hands on the counter and watched the coffee percolate. "Instead of him protecting me, it's the other way around."

"You're up to the task."

"I hope so." She also wished she had the same faith in herself that he had in her.

~

Colin tried to ignore the pounding in his head and the nausea in his stomach. As if she knew he didn't feel well, Rosie rested her head on his knee. "Good girl." He scratched her ears. "You may very well have saved my life."

"She did save your life." Cassidy handed him a cup of coffee. "I added mint for your stomach."

"That actually works?"

"It does for me." She sat on the sofa next to him.

He entwined his fingers with hers, then lifted her hand to his lips and kissed her palm. "Whatever happens is meant to happen, sweetheart. I'm not going to do anything foolish, but the most important thing to me is you."

She raised red-rimmed eyes to his. "Then stay alive."

"I intend to." He chuckled and took a sip of his coffee. "Tastes good."

"You should sleep."

"That time is gone. It's four a.m. already." Although, if he closed his eyes, he felt like he could sleep for two days straight. "Let's plan our day."

"After the house is put to rights, you mean?"

"Sure."

"Ingram will make the calls. All I have to do is be here."

"Then, let's see what we can do from here." He grabbed his laptop from the coffee table. "I'm going to check for more films." And pray he didn't find any. Hopefully, Russell's attention was now on him and not on unsuspecting innocent women.

An hour later, Cassidy snoring softly beside him, he closed his computer. No films. No ideas of further action, either. This case had him more stumped than he'd ever been, and he hated it with a passion. An idea sparked to life and he hacked an email program looking for anyone named Draco. When he found someone he thought might be Russell, he sent a message asking for a meeting. He hit send, and settled back to wait.

Ten minutes later, he had a message requesting he meet the dragon at the fishing shack next to the lake later that night. Now, to find a way to do so without Cassidy following, which would be next to impossible.

Moving slowly so he didn't wake her, he headed for the shower in preparation for the day. Russell would have specials plans for Colin that evening. He needed to find a way to hide a weapon on his person that wouldn't be found.

"Cleaners coming at nine," Ingram said. "You two okay for me to leave?"

"I need a weapon that can be hidden easily. Surely, the FBI has some James Bond type of gadgets."

Ingram laughed. "I know a guy. When do you want them by?"

"Noon?"

"See you then."

Colin continued up the stairs and turned the water as hot as he could stand it. Things were going to get ugly come nightfall. He could only pray that God saw fit to see him through what would come, and that Colin had the strength to endure.

By the time he returned downstairs, Cassidy was whipping up pancakes. "What did you find on the computer?"

"Nothing." He got two plates out of the cabinet, then fished in the fridge for the syrup. "He's focused on us now, it seems."

The doorbell rang. They both froze, then reached for their weapons. "I'll get it," Colin said.

"I'm right behind you."

He shook his head and opened the door to see a bouquet of pink roses on the step. "Ah, my admirer strikes again."

"It isn't funny. Throw them away." She stomped back to the kitchen. "I don't care whether I ever see another rose again in my life."

"They smell pretty." He set them in the center of the table. "It isn't the fault of the flowers. If you'd let me, I'd give you flowers every day."

"You're an incorrigible idiot." She ducked her head to try and hide her smile. "It looks as if Russell is going to do that for you."

"Good. Saves me money." He wrapped his arms around her waist and planted a kiss on the back of her neck, knowing it might be the last day he held her in his arms. He intended to make the most of the time he had left.

She giggled and slipped free. "You're not respecting boundaries."

"I never was one to follow the rules."

"You'd better start. Things are going to get nasty," she said, her smile fading. "You need to tread carefully."

"I like nasty." He wiggled his eyebrows.

"Be serious. Russell is not a man to toy with."

He knew that, and he'd know a whole lot more come nightfall.

~

Russell practically danced around the room. Tonight was the night his plan came to fruition. The world would be in his hands. One-by-one his people would take over the world.

10

Colin met Ingram at the end of the drive while Cassidy was in the shower. Phase one complete.

"Be careful how you hold this little thing in your mouth," Ingram said, holding him a razor designed to fit on the roof of his mouth. "Here's an ink pen with a switchblade, but I'm sure Russell will find it. This credit card also has a sharp edge, and the flashlight is a gun. Only fires one shot, so make it count. This is all I could get on such short notice."

"It'll do." It would have to. "Thank you."

Ingram clapped him on the shoulder. "God go with you. I sincerely hope I see you again."

Colin chuckled, although the sound had no humor. "Me, too." He glanced back toward the house. "Take care of her if I don't come back. She'll blame herself."

"I will do my best."

There was little doubt. Ingram had lost his love six months ago at the hands of Russell. Weston had been a beautiful FBI agent who hadn't been able to successfully cover her aversion to Russell's scar. She'd been killed in the shower of her motel room. One way or another, Colin wanted the killing to end, even if it meant the end of him.

He hid his new 'toys' in the flower bed, then entered the house and heard Cassidy's door open. Now, to find a way to disappear later to meet Russell.

"What are our plans for today?" She asked, coming down the stairs.

"I...thought we'd take it easy. I'm feeling woozy." He dropped into a chair.

"We have a case to investigate." She narrowed her eyes. "Since when has anything stopped you before?"

"I think I was poisoned." He tried his best to look pitiful and, judging by the look on her face, failed.

"What's going on?" She crossed her arms. "I thought I heard a car door slam when I got out of the shower."

"It must have been a neighbor." He kept his face averted, pretending to be engrossed in the morning paper.

"You're lying, and I intend to find out what about."

Hopefully, not until it was too late to stop him. If things went as planned, Russell would be behind bars a few hours after dark. If not, then Cassidy would be none the worse off and could try her ploy of joining the man's ranks. Which. Would. Not. Work. There's no way a serial killer such as Blake Russell would stop getting his jollies by killing off those he considers unworthy. It's a personal quest to him.

Cassidy grabbed her purse. "Stay here and pretend to be sick, Chief. I'm heading to the office to follow up on leads."

His head snapped up. "You have some?"

"No, but I intend to find some." She slammed the front door behind her.

He jumped to his feet and watched her walk to the garage, then storm back to the house.

"I need to borrow your keys."

"I might need them. Let me call Ingram to come pick you up. You shouldn't go anywhere alone."

"You shouldn't stay here alone."

"It seems we're at a stalemate."

"Yes, it does." She plopped her purse on the foyer table and headed for her office.

Good. At least he could keep an eye on her until he left. After that, it wouldn't matter. Russell would be busy with Colin.

~

Colin was up to no good. Cassidy leaned back in her chair. Why did he want to keep her in the house all of a sudden when they had a killer to catch? Was he that worried that Russell would harm her? The harm was to Colin, not her. So…why the lies?

She could hear him in his room next door. First, he'd gone outside, then clomped up the stairs, and now paced the floor.

216

Something had him agitated. Could it really be a side effect of whatever had been in the needle last night? No. She still thought he was up to something.

Maybe Ingram knew. She dialed his number. No answer. She was wasting her time. Russell needed to be caught and sitting at home wasn't going to catch him.

She headed to the basement to study the case boards. Ignoring the one on her mother's murder, since she knew now who had killed her, she focused on the board her and Colin had started six months ago.

Hanging there was a picture of Blake Russell, copied from the college yearbook, one of his dumpy apartment, vacated right after they'd visited him, and photos of his victims, ending with the burned carcass of his latest victim. Colin must have tacked it there.

The first victims wore red, now pink. What was the significance of the colors? She leaned against a table full of boxes. There had to be a clue here, much like the dragon mural on the vacant building. Why couldn't she see it?

She made a mental list of what they did know:

1. Blake Russell was Draco.
2. At one time, he'd had ten followers.
3. He felt ridding the world of pretty people who looked down on the more homely as his personal quest.
4. He always showed up at the crime scene.
5. He was always there during the snuff film.
6. He started out dressing his victims in red, now pink.

Of course. Red, faded to pink, then to white as sin, or faults, were washed out of the fabric. She'd bet Rosie's favorite food that white was the color he intended to dress Cassidy in. Everything that had happened up to this point was to cleanse her; make her ready for whatever future plans Russell had. Now, what to do with the information?

She grinned. Black was as far from white as one could get. She needed to start wearing that color. Maybe it would work, maybe it wouldn't, but she'd try anything at this point.

Back in her office, she booted up her laptop and ordered three black suits with dark sunglasses. They'd be delivered in the morning. She considered dying her hair, but couldn't bear the thought of covering up the one thing she had that matched her mother.

For extra measure, she bought several black dresses and heels. Satisfied she'd done what she could on her end, she shut down her computer. It was up to Russell now.

What would it be like to have found her father and have him turn out to be a nice, upstanding citizen who hadn't known about her? But, no, she had to have a psycho that turned her life upside down and forestalled any hopes of a future with a family of her own. Her blood chilled. What if a bit of his crazy ran in her veins? What if it were only a matter of time before she started to act like her father? She couldn't let that, she *wouldn't* let that, happen.

"Are you crying?" Colin peered into her office.

"No." She averted her face. "Tears are a waste of time."

"You waste a lot of time, then." He grinned. "I'm heading out for a pizza."

"Why not call it in?" She turned and searched his face.

"I need a breath of fresh air, and we're low on groceries. You can come, but I'm perfectly capable."

"It's dangerous for us to separate." Yep, he was up to something. Fine. She'd let him go, and…she couldn't even follow him without a car. "I'll go."

Something flickered across his eyes. "Great." He stepped back and waved her past him.

At the grocery store, Cassidy grabbed a cart. "Produce?"

"Sure." Colin gave a stiff smile. "Then maybe a couple of steaks, instead of pizza?"

"Are you okay?" She cocked her head. "You look pale."

"A little nauseous. Let me duck into the bathroom and meet you by the butcher."

"Don't take too long or I'm coming in to check on you." She watched him push open the men's room door, then headed for the steaks. A couple of filets would do nicely on the grill. Maybe a good meal would give them a clear perspective on what to do next regarding the case.

After five minutes of no Colin, she grew annoyed. After ten minutes, she grew worried and, leaving the cart, barged into the men's room. Luckily it was empty. "Colin?" She checked under the stall doors. Empty.

She raced to the parking lot to discover his truck gone. Why had he—oh! Her heart froze. He went to meet Russell on his own. Didn't he know he most likely wouldn't make it out of that meeting alive?

Digging her cell phone from her pocket, she dialed the number for a rental car service and paced the parking lot until the small sedan arrived. Then, she sped to the police station to confront Ingram. Somebody had to know what Colin's plan was and he was her best bet.

She banged into the conference room where the three agents sat. "Where's Colin?"

"I don't know." Ingram kept his focus on the papers in front of him.

"You're lying."

The man sighed. "He's meeting Russell."

"You let him go alone?"

His eyes hardened. "Of course not. We're giving him a head start and following. He's wired."

"You know Russell will find that right off."

"Which is why we leave the moment we know where they're going."

"I'm coming." She crossed her arms.

"No."

"I'll follow."

"You will only increase the risk, Detective." Ingram stood. "Let's go. Colin is at the meeting place."

Cassidy grabbed his arm. "Please. It's Colin. I can keep my...father from killing him. I know I can."

He took a second before answering, then nodded. "I'm going to regret this."

"No, you won't." She released him and followed them to the black SUVs outside.

"Where is the meeting taking place?" She asked, clicking on her seatbelt.

"A shack by the lake."

She knew exactly where they were going.

11

Colin waited next to the fishing shack and turned on his mic. Not that he expected Ingram to do much more than capture Russell, and Russell would find the wire right off.

The sound of rustling leaves and small animals was the only sound greeting him. "He's not here," he whispered.

"He'll show." Ingram's voice came through loud and clear. "We're waiting for your word to move in. We also have a passenger."

Colin closed his eyes. Darn it, Cassidy. Her appearance changed everything. He turned off the mic, ripped off the wire, and ground it under his boot. If things went bad, which they would, he didn't want Cassidy rushing in to save him and putting herself in more danger.

"Saving me work, Mr. MacKenzie?" Russell stepped from the trees, a gun in his hand. "Trying in vain to save my daughter? She will join me before the night is through."

"No." Colin met the man's cold stare. "Me for her. That's the deal."

"So, what? You're willing to join me? Be my right hand man?" Russell shook his head. "You're much too pretty for such a task. My followers won't like it."

Colin grinned. "Do you have any left? We've been picking them off one-by-one."

"There are always more to be found." He waved the gun. "Inside, please."

Colin stepped inside the shack. Other than a rusty boat and some rope, it was empty.

"There is a trapdoor in the floor. Open it and climb down."

He did as instructed and stepped into a tunnel once meant to transport slaves and supplies to the river, no doubt. The moon shined through the trap door they'd entered. On each side of the tunnel were small cell-like rooms.

"Follow the tunnel to the end and turn right."

With Russell aiming the gun at his back, Colin pulled a flashlight from his pocket and started walking. Doom echoed with each thud of his feet on the packed dirt floor. Once Russell closed the trapdoor, the flashlight was their only light.

In a room at the end of the tunnel was a chair and chains. On a nearby table were an assortment of knives. A small generator sat on one corner. So, he was to be tortured before killed. God, give him strength to endure.

"Have a seat, Mr. MacKenzie."

Once he was seated, Russell clamped his hands behind his back and his feet to the chair rungs. "Perhaps, when I'm finished, you will sufficiently hate the world and the way I've scarred you that I will let you join me." He gave a shark-like grin. "We'll see, not that I want to give you false hope."

"Of course not." Colin tested the security of his hands. Since he had the razorblade secured to the roof of his mouth, he'd hoped for rope. Not that it would help with his hands behind his back.

"My daughter most likely knows of these tunnels. At least, I hope so. When she hears your screams, she'll come to save you. To stop the torture, she'll join me. My plan is rather simple." He set up a walkie talkie on the table. "This is set to the same frequency as the police scanner. They will be able to hear you."

Then, he'd do his best to remain silent. "I understand why you killed Maureen, but why the others? Why take me and force Cassidy's hand? You have the wealth to disappear."

"I'm drunk on power. It's really nothing more than that now. Once, it was all about revenge. As my followers grow, and they will come as they see what I can do for them, I will rule this town, then this state, and eventually this country."

The man was certifiably insane. "I don't think it works like that."

"I'll change how it works." He picked up a scalpel. "Where to begin? Are you familiar with fileting a fish?"

"I've done my share." He swallowed against a throat filled

with cotton.

Russell bent over his arm. "Try not to move, all right? I wouldn't want to go too deep, too soon." He cut into Colin's arm, removing the top layer of skin.

Colin bit his lip and groaned.

~

"He's cutting him!" Cassidy dashed through the trees, the walkie talkie clutched in one hand. She knew what lay under the fishing shack. Early in her career, she'd discovered the meth lab there. Ingram and the others would have to keep up with her or be left behind.

Her heart beat in time with her pounding feet. God, please don't let her be too late to save him.

A thudding sound, a guttural groan, then Colin screamed. Was that a generator? Cassidy increased her pace. Was Russell electrocuting him?

She yanked open the trapdoor and descended as fast as she could. Flicking on a flashlight, she raced down the tunnels, glancing in each room as she passed, following Colin's moans. Tears streamed down her face, blinding her.

This was her fault. She fell in love with him and he could die as a result. Attachments only gave the evil hold over a person.

She leaped into the room. "Stop! Please."

Russell drew a knife across Colin's forehead. "Would you like to see him scalped, my dear?"

"No, stop." She held out a hand containing her gun.

"If you shoot me, he will die." He showed her an attachment connected to his heart. "If my heart stops, the chair will electrocute him and his heart will stop a mere second after mine."

"I'll do whatever you want, just spare him."

Russell held out his hand. "Join me."

She stepped forward.

"No...Cassidy." Colin peered through the blood on his face. "Turn around and go."

"I can't." Sobs overtook her. "Not if it means your death."

"Touching." Russell rolled his eyes. "We will leave you now, Mr. MacKenzie. If you feel you are sufficiently scarred, and you recover from your wounds, then, feel free to look me up." He patted the raw flesh on Colin's arm.

Colin hissed. His blue eyes shot daggers. "Believe me, I'll be looking you up."

"One minute, please." Cassidy knelt in front of him. "I love you," she whispered, "but surely you see why we can't be anything other than what we are." She leaned forward and kissed him. "Live, Colin. Live and forget me."

~

For the second time in his life, Colin watched the most precious person to him walk out of his life. He blinked the blood from his eyes. "Cassidy!"

She never looked back. Instead, her hand was in her father's as if she were a young girl taking a walk with a father who loved her. But, she was a woman trapped by a man obsessed. She should have shot Russell. Colin would have made the sacrifice of losing his life to save her.

He ducked his head and gave into unconsciousness. When he woke, Ingram was unlocking the chains binding him to the chair.

"Can you walk?"

"Yes." Colin stood. "You should have gone after them."

"We couldn't find them. Russell must have another way out of here."

The river. "He must have a boat. Go. I'll make my way out."

"He won't harm her. We need to get you to the hospital. Detective Monroe will contact us." Ingram shoved his shoulder under Colin's arm. "We'll get her back. I promise."

"That's a promise you can't keep." One way or the other, Colin would see Cassidy again. He would find her and save her.

He lost consciousness again on the way to the hospital. He woke alone, just as he had the last time he ended up there. Turning his head to the side, he stared out the single window at the rising sun. Cassidy had been in Russell's hands for hours.

~

The first thing Russell did was lock Cassidy into a room. She didn't care. Colin still breathed. For that, Russell could do anything he wanted with her. "I need things from my house. I have packages arriving."

"Someone will take you to collect your things in the morning." Russell smiled at her through the small barred opening in the door. "Goodnight, dear. We'll talk more in a few hours."

"Where am I?"

"The basement of my mansion. You're safe here." He turned and strolled away.

His mansion? She lay on the single bed, surprised at its plushness, and glanced around her cell. Rather posh for a prison. An open door showed a modern bathroom. The walls were covered with original paintings and, if she were correct, were worth a small fortune. A cherry wood table with two chairs sat against one wall. A dorm sized fridge took up space in a corner. She knew without looking that there would be food and drinks. Russell seemed to have thought of everything.

Well, good for him. Tomorrow, she would collect her packages and begin making his life miserable until she could finish him off herself.

Good night, Colin.

She turned her head and cried herself to sleep.

PART THREE

Six weeks later

1

Cassidy swung her legs over the side of the narrow cot. The concrete floor chilled her bare feet. Enough was enough. For six weeks she'd been locked up, pretending to take the medicine Draco, Russell Blake, her father—she mentally spit the word out—had ordered her to take. It was time to pretend the treatment had worked. It was time to act as if she'd come to "her sense" and would be his right hand.

She sat there, head hanging as if in submission and plotted her revenge against the maniac who had fathered her, killed her mother, and devised a plan to kill all the pretty people who treated those they considered beneath them as if they were dirt. The one thing she hadn't quite figured out yet was how she could say she saw Draco's reasoning and be able to prevent more innocent deaths.

"Good morning, my dear." Draco, the knife wound pulling up on the side of his face, stared through the barred window.

Cassidy forced her face to remain impassive. "Good morning...Father." She said the words quietly and in a monotone voice.

"Good. You are ready." Keys jangled as he opened the door. "Come with me." He held out his hand.

Hiding a grimace, Cassidy slipped her hand in his and allowed him to lead her to an elevator. They were whisked up two floors, stepping out into a room that had to have cost enough to feed a third world country.

Draco led her through another door. "This is your room. Your things have been stored in the closet. I expect to see you at breakfast in thirty minutes."

Cassidy shook her head and headed for the closet, not looking back. She opened the double doors. White. Every stitch of clothing, most of them long dresses, was white. She spotted her suitcase and smiled. Except for the items in there.

She dragged the suitcase from the closet and opened it on the large four poster bed covered with a fluffy white duvet. She opened it and pulled out a pair of black slacks and a long-sleeved black blouse. Her choice of clothing would make Draco angry, but this was one thing she wouldn't cave on. She'd given up everything to join him...Colin, her dog, her life. Black was the color of mourning, and oh, how she mourned the loss of the man she loved.

The last sight of him had been of him tied to a chair, tortured within inches of life. The cost of sparing his life had been her joining Draco's ranks. The color black was far more suitable than white.

After a quick shower, she skipped makeup, preferring the clean face look anyway, and left her red hair hanging loose down her black. She smiled at her reflection in the mirror. Her skin, after not seeing the sun for weeks was paler than normal. Her red hair burned against the black of her clothing. She looked like the angel of death. Good. Because, one way or the other, she would send Draco to meet his maker.

Her father frowned as she entered the dining room. "Those are not the clothes I purchased for you."

Her gaze clashed with his. "This color suits me." She sat across from him. The belligerent attitude might make him suspect she'd pretended to take the drugs. Now that she was free of the cell, she didn't care. "You must give me some leeway...Father." The word gagged her.

"Disobedience is not tolerated here."

She hung her head, hiding her emotions behind her veil of hair. "My apologies. Please let me choose my own clothing until I deem myself worthy to wear white." She bit her bottom lip to keep the nausea at bay. He wouldn't kill her, that she knew, at least not yet. But, he could make her life unbearable in his quest to break her.

"There is a meeting of my followers right after breakfast." Draco spread his napkin in his lap. "I am excited to introduce you to them."

"I am pleased to finally meet them." Every single, misled, murdering one.

"With your beauty, I'm sure there is no one who has wronged you, no one you desire to be punished, but you will be there as support to me. To show the others that we are a united front."

She knew of one who had wronged her, and he sat across from her. "Won't they resent me because of my looks?"

Draco grinned. "They are aware that you are as beautiful inside as out."

If he only knew the darkness that stained her heart. She leaned back as a servant placed a plate of eggs and bacon in front of her. Her stomach rumbled. Dare she eat it? What if the cook had drugged the food? She waved the plate away. "I'll fix my own plates from now on."

"You are trying my patience, Cassidy," Draco said, scowling. "But, I will indulge your fancy. One day, you will trust me."

She doubted that. She followed the servant into the large modern kitchen and dished up her own food. The time for submissiveness was done. The avenger was here. All she needed now was a way to rid the world of a maniac.

~

Colin traced the scar on his forehead with his finger. The doctor had assured him it would fade in time. The area of his forearm where he'd been skinned would not fare as well. It would serve as a constant reminder of the man who took Cassidy.

He splashed water on his face and grabbed a nearby towel. For six weeks they'd seen neither Draco or Cassidy. Ingram, the FBI agent in charge, said there was nothing to worry about. That Cassidy was perfectly safe.

How was that possible? How could anyone be safe with a mad man?

He dressed for work and patted Rosie's head. "Let's go, girl."

After Colin's dismissal from the hospital, he'd retrieved the German Shepherd from the family Cassidy had watching her. The dog was the closest thing he had to Cassidy. And, as she had with her owner, Rosie now went everywhere with Colin.

When they entered the small Clear Springs police department, Colin headed for his office. As chief, he usually had a stack of emails. After a week in the hospital, the messages had piled up. He'd just gotten to the bottom of the things that needed his attention.

He booted up his computer and sat back as Ingram entered. "Hey."

"Hey." Ingram sat in the leather chair on the other side of his desk. "Still nothing on Russell Blake or Detective Monroe. But, they're bound to show themselves eventually."

Colin would be ready. He'd like nothing more than to watch Blake bleed out in the street in full view of his so-called followers. "I take Rosie out to the woods every evening for a run. She hasn't sensed anything either. No bodies, no Cassidy, no killer."

"Agents Smith and Miller have searched the web for snuff videos and come up empty there, too. Blake has gone into hiding with his prize."

Colin nodded, knowing the man would surface. Last time, it had taken him six months. "We'll catch him." They would. Then, Colin would never let Cassidy leave him again. Twice was enough.

"I'll spend the day on the web. I know of places your agents don't." Colin crossed his arms. "Anything else happening?"

Ingram shook his head. "Clear Springs is the quiet little town it's supposed to be. Boring." He grinned. "But that's a very good thing for the citizens." He stood. "I'll let you know if we find anything."

Colin nodded. They wouldn't find a trace. Not until Blake surfaced again. *Please, God, let it be soon.*

Every time he saw a red-haired woman on the street, he ran to her only to find out it wasn't Cassidy. Every dark-haired man in an expensive suit or leather jacket had him reaching for his gun. He needed to find Blake before he lost his mind.

After searching the internet for hours, he concluded that Ingram was right. There'd been no more killings. No spottings of leather jackets embroidered with a dragon. Draco and his minions had vanished.

Inactivity caused his worries to grow to the point he welcomed the call of a domestic dispute in the seedier side of town. "Come, Rosie." He shouldered his weapon and told the receptionist he'd answer the call himself.

"Alone?" She frowned.

"I can handle it." He held the door open, letting Rosie bound out before him.

Seconds later, he'd placed the siren on top of his car and sped toward the other side of town. Neighbors had gathered in front of a rusty mobile home. Shouts drifted through the windows.

Colin ordered Rosie to stay in the car, then loudly announced his presence. The trailer door swung open to reveal a skinny, scantily dressed woman who had clearly imbibed too much beer that early in the morning. "You called about a dispute?"

"No." She propped the door open with her hip. "One of those nosey neighbors did. There's nothing going on here that needs the cops."

"Are you sure? It sounded like quite the argument going on in there." Colin peered around her.

A large man reclined on the sofa. "We're good. That no-good broad won't fix me breakfast."

The woman whirled. "Fix it yourself! I'm not your slave."

Colin rubbed his chin. Nothing here that warranted his attention. "Try to keep it down, would you?"

"What kind of accent is that?" The woman gave him a sloppy grin. "It's sexy."

"Scottish." He jumped from the small stoop and headed back to his car. Seeing that no one was going to be dragged away in handcuffs, the neighbors dispersed. Except for one elderly woman leaning on a cane.

Colin stared at her for a moment, then closed his car door and approached her. "May I help you?"

"I saw you on the news. You're looking for that Dragon fella, right?"

Colin's nerves tingled. "You've seen him?"

"No, but I seen someone wearing one of them jackets you mentioned."

"Where?"

"That drugstore on the corner. Word is…the pharmacist there sells anything a person could want, legal or not. But you didn't hear it from me." She turned and shuffled away.

Grateful for a lead, even a small one, Colin called to Rosie, who leaped through the car's open window and followed him across the street. A bell jingled as he opened the door.

"Don't open for ten more minutes." A young man in a white pharmacist jacket stood behind the counter.

"Police." Colin flashed his badge. "I have a witness who said she saw a man in a jacket with a dragon on the back of it come in here a few days ago."

"Yeah, he was here."

"Buying what?"

"Prescription."

"Really?" Colin raised his eyebrows. "Don't make me arrest you for something I'm not really here for."

"Fine." The man sighed. "He wanted something that would make a person cooperate. He bought Scopolamine."

"For motion sickness?"

"Unless you have a reaction to it." The pharmacist grinned. "Then you can get hallucinations. Great stuff. It's also called Devil's Breath by some. Basically, they're like a zombie, except without the face eating part. You can blow this stuff in a person's face even and they'll do whatever you tell them to."

2

The meeting isn't here at the house?" Cassidy stared at the black Mercedes in the garage.

"Of course not." Draco pressed a button on his car fob to open the doors. "I don't want anyone knowing where I live. Including you. Put this on." He handed her a black cloth bag.

That's what she got for taking her medicine like a good girl. She got into the front passenger seat and pulled the bag over her head, digging her sharp pinkie nail into the fabric. It wasn't much, but maybe she could pinpoint some landmarks through the tiny hole.

They drove down a road lined with thick trees. Having the bag over her head made her nauseous as the road twisted and turned on its way down. Depending on how long it took to get to Clear Springs, she reasoned they were on Chief's Head. The closest mountain to town.

Draco turned onto another road and continued to the Highway. Yes, they were headed toward Clear Springs...the seedier side.

"I was thinking, Russell, that—"

"I've told you to call me Father."

She groaned inwardly. "Father...I was thinking of how to make you more powerful."

"I'm listening."

"You're primary goal is to make those who have wronged others suffer, correct? Killing them ends everything." Oh, God, have him listen to her. "Why not hit them where it most hurts? Their finances?"

Draco sat silent for so long, Cassidy turned her head to peer at him through the tiny hole. He stared straight ahead, jaw clenched.

"I should have known killing would not be something a heart as pure as yours would rejoice in. I agree to try your way."

Relief flooded through her so strong and sweet it brought tears to her eyes. She could watch him, pretend to be with him, and spare lives in the process.

They pulled in front of a warehouse. Several vehicles sat out front.

Draco turned off the engine and whipped the cover from Cassidy's head. "I will introduce you and your idea this morning. You will not speak. You will only stand next to me in a unified front. Understand?"

She nodded.

He led her through a small side door and into a large room where ten people sat. Except for two very large men in black suits. Body guards? They all stood when Draco entered.

Motioning for Cassidy to stand next to him, he took up his place in front of a polished wooden podium. Gripping the sides with both hands, he grinned. "You may be seated. Today, is a special day. My daughter has agreed to join our ranks."

"But, she's beautiful!" One man shouted, his face darkening. "She's the type we try to get rid of."

"She is rare. She is beautiful. She is kind. She is my princess, and you shall address her as such." Draco speared the man with a sharp gaze. "I have also come to the realization that there are other ways, more fitting than death, to make our enemies pay."

"So, your daughter has made you soft."

Cassidy wanted to tell the four hundred pound man to shut up. His pock marked face turned down in a scowl. His words caused a flush to rise up Draco's neck.

"One more outburst, Mr. Ross, and there will be consequences. I understand you are new to our group, but we do things with decorum here."

"She's a cop!"

Draco sighed and motioned to one of the men in black. The man stepped forward and before Cassidy couldn't register what was happening, slit the fat man's throat.

"No!" She reached out as the man toppled from his chair, his hands grabbing at his throat.

"I'm sorry, dear, but I must have control and respect here." He turned his attention to the other nine. "Any other doubters here?"

As if one body, they all shook their head.

"Wonderful! You have all been trusty servants. Today's assignment is to write down the name of your enemy, even if you have already done so, and next to that name, you will list what would make them suffer the most. Remember...no killing."

That was fine for him to say. Cassidy stared at the now still form of Mr. Ross.

The bodyguards took the man by his feet and dragged him away, leaving a trail of blood on their way. It had happened so fast. There'd been no way for her to stop it.

"Don't worry, dear. I understand your feelings, but there are things I must do to keep control."

"I cannot condone or understand killing someone in cold blood," she hissed. "You asked me to join you because of the way I am. So respect that part of me!"

His eyes widened. "Your kindness wounds me. It points out the faults within myself." He bowed. "Thank you."

That simple act left her speechless. Was it possible that her presence could change him or would he tire of her pointing out his faults and kill her?

"All rise and pay homage to your Princess!" Draco raised his arms.

The followers stood and cheered.

They were all insane, and insanity was unpredictable and dangerous.

"Smile, my darling." Draco pinched the tender underside of her arm. "These are your people. We will rule them together."

She smiled and gave a slow nod. Now that she had an idea where Draco lived, she had to get word to Agent Ingram. While she hoped Colin wouldn't get involved, she knew that letting the authorities know where the evil resided would be like waving a red flag in front of a bull.

~

Colin knew of Scopolamine, the dangers of the drug. He left the drugstore holding a napkin over his mouth and nose. If Draco wanted to waylay him on the street, Colin would have no defense.

Once in the safe confines of his truck, he locked the doors and called Ingram to tell him what he'd learned.

"You think he's using the drug to control Detective Monroe?"

Colin started the truck's engine. "Why else haven't we heard from her? She infiltrated his circle so we could bring him down."

"She infiltrated so she could save your sorry rear end." Ingram chuckled.

"It isn't funny." Because of Colin's capture and torture, Cassidy had entered the dragon's lair. She was on her own, all because of him.

"She can handle herself," Ingram said. "She won't eat anything that man gives her."

"The problem is, she doesn't have to eat it. If he wants, he can get her to take it in other ways."

"By threatening her with you?"

"Maybe." Colin had to make sure that didn't happen again. "I'm coming in."

Before he arrived at the station, a call came in about a body found on the outskirts of town. Redirecting his way, Colin parked next to a ditch where a very shook up jogging couple waited.

"We just found him." The woman buried her face in her male companion's chest. "It's awful."

"Thank you. If you wouldn't mind waiting by my truck, I'll take your statements in a moment." He squatted next to the body of a very large man. Rosie sniffed around the area. The man hadn't been dead long.

Scratched into the dirt beside him were the words, "The disobedient must die". What had he done to get his throat slit?

Rosie whined, her ears perking up. She glanced toward the tree line but didn't run as she usually did. If the dead man was the result of Blake's work, he wasn't here watching as he once did. Of course, that was so he could watch Cassidy's reaction to a body, and she wasn't here.

He called Rosie to his side and went to question the joggers. Who, of course, knew nothing. A dead end, just like before. The only thing they did know was that Russell Blake was still around.

Back at the office, he booted up his computer, tossed Rosie a dog bone, and settled back in his chair. After a few seconds of going through his usual routines of checking backdoors, via the internet, he ran across a message that had him sitting up and taking notice.

"The dragon lives on Chief's Head."

Could it possibly be from Cassidy? Further searching revealed nothing. The mountain was huge. It would take days, weeks maybe, for a dozen men, which they didn't have, to search the area. He placed a call to a friend of his who owned a helicopter, then leaving Rosie with the receptionist, raced his truck to a small airstrip an hour away.

Another half an hour and they were airborne and speeding back toward Chief's Head. "Do you know how many homes, mansions, and hidden tunnels there are?" The pilot turned the craft. "You're looking for a needle in a haystack."

"I know, but I can get a better feel for where the buildings are from the air. We'll still have to search on foot."

"Good luck, is all I have to say." They circled the mountain a couple of times and flew back to the airport. "Let me know if you need my help again. I'm always ready to bring a psycho down."

"Thank you." While they'd flown, Colin had drawn a crude map of where the buildings were located on the mountain. The pilot was right. Small homes to garish mountains nestled among the trees. It was going to be quite the manhunt.

After returning to Clear Springs, he picked up cheeseburgers and fries for himself and the agents and met the three agents in the conference room. He explained about the message he'd received. "We need to come up with a plan to find Blake."

"If he knows we're coming he'll likely kill Detective Monroe." Ingram unwrapped a burger. "Possibly himself."

"Then we have to make sure he doesn't know we're coming."

"Are you sure the message is from Monroe?"

He wasn't sure of anything. "Who else could it be?"

"Another little old lady at a trailer park." Ingram eyed him as he bit into his cheeseburger.

"I just know." Colin threw his wadded up wrapper at the agent.

The other two, always silent during the meetings, simply stared at Colin and Ingram as they spoke. Silent wraths, that's what they were. Their unblinking gazes gave Colin the creeps.

"Why don't the two of you go do something other than look at us as if we're bugs under a glass dome?" He tossed a French fry at Smith. "I miss Wesson. At least she was eye candy."

At Ingram's fallen expression, Colin apologized. Since the female agent's death at the hands of Draco, they were all careful not to speak of her.

Ingram motioned his head for the other two to leave. "They're good agents. They spend more time working than talking, unlike you Scots."

Colin shrugged. "At least people know what we're thinking. I'm sorry, man, for my unthoughtful comment."

"No worries. It's time to move past the pain and heal." Ingram squeezed three packets of ketchup onto his hamburger wrapper, then added mustard and mayonnaise.

"That's disgusting. It likes like a crime scene."

"A crime scene in my mouth." Ingram smiled, his teeth flashing against his ebony skin. "We'll start searching the mountain at daylight in the morning. I'll see if I can't get help from Little Rock."

"Sounds good. If Cassidy is anywhere around, Rosie will let us know."

3

You did not have to kill that man." Cassidy slammed her car door after they arrived back at the house and she whipped off the covering over her head. She'd spent the long drive in silence, seething at the casual way Draco had ordered the execution.

"He violated the rules." He twirled a set of keys on his finger as he headed to unlock the double oak doors.

Heart aching, Cassidy followed him, entering the house as a helicopter flew low overhead. She started to step outside, but stopped. Doing so would alert Colin to her presence, thus endangering his life.

"Wise choice, daughter." Draco grinned, the scarred side of his face not moving. "Let's have some lunch."

She wanted to ask what drug he gave his servants to prevent them exposing his location. They did his bidding without hesitation, although they moved slow, trancelike. Most likely they were on the same thing he had tried to give her.

She sat in her seat at the large dining table and stared at her biological father. The man who had raped her mother and received the knife wound to the face as a result. A smile played on her lips.

"What is humorous?" Draco paused in placing his napkin in his lap.

"Nothing. It's a beautiful house is all."

"Thank you. It's all yours." He lifted a crystal goblet of water. "Perhaps you would like to head to the kitchen to supervise the serving of your meal."

"I would."

He nodded for her to go. Knowing that taking too long would

241

only incur his wrath, she made her way to the kitchen quickly, eying the exits of the house. There would come a time when she would no longer pretend to be there of her own accord and would need to escape.

She opened the pantry door. The kitchen staff never glanced her way. At the opposite end of the room large enough to be most people's bedroom was another door. She opened it, discovering a set of stairs that led into darkness. A tunnel. She smiled and closed the door, then filled her plate and a soup bowl from the pots on the stove.

As she headed back to the dining room, one of the female servants followed with a tray, heavy of items for Draco to choose from. "Thank you, Sarah," Draco said, giving her an indulgent grin.

The young woman curtsied, eyes downcast, and shuffled away.

"She's a delight," he said, transferring his attention to Cassidy. "I like my women young and red-headed." He lifted a biscuit from the basket on the table and broke it in half. "I've not found a woman equal in beauty to you or your mother. Sad. But, a man has needs, and Sarah is compliant."

"You no longer purchase sex?" She remembered the young prostitute he'd killed a few months ago.

"On occasion, but that is not a fitting conversation for a father to have with his daughter." His eyes hardened.

She shrugged. "You're right." She grabbed a biscuit and buttered it. "What's on the agenda for this afternoon?"

"We decide which of our follower's request to grant."

After lunch, they sat at a small round table in Draco's study. Bookshelves, full of first edition leather bound books filled the shelves. His wealth impressed her.

"How did a man who doesn't like to be around people accumulate all this?" She waved her arm.

"An inheritance and wise investments." He dumped out the small box his followers, because she couldn't think of them as hers, put their requests in. "While we will, eventually, grant all of these, I try to do the ones that seem the most important. Like this one..." He held up a slip of paper. "Helen Murner, the poor dear with the terrible burns on her arms and up her neck wants those responsible to suffer.

"Now, before your endearing request for me to not kill anyone, I would have burned these people alive. Instead, I will assist Helen in burning down their very fine, expensive home."

"After making sure everyone is out of the house."

"Of course." He rang a bell, signaling a young man Cassidy hadn't seen before. Draco wrote something on a sheet of paper and handed it to the man. "Deliver this to Helen Murner."

The man bowed and walked backwards out of the room.

Draco eyed Cassidy's clothes again. "There will be a dark cloak waiting for you in your room. We will meet Helen precisely at dark."

~

Draco looked on his daughter with appreciation as she stood next to him and Helen. Her regal bearing was befitting a queen.

"Are you sure the house is empty?" Cassidy turned to look at him.

"Positive." Not that Draco cared one way or the other, but he'd do almost anything to appease his daughter. "Helen, splash the accelerant along the base of the house. Roger, turn on the camera."

Helen splashed a liberal amount of gasoline on the house, soaking the hem of her skirt in the process. "Fire terrifies me."

"Fire is cleansing," Draco assured her. "Tonight, you avenge your scars." He handed her a torch.

She lit it and set it against the house. Flames roared to life, catching her skirt on fire. She screamed and batted her hands at the blaze.

Cassidy tackled the woman to the ground, using her cloak to beat out her burning skirt. When Helen's skirt was no longer burning, she helped the woman to her feet. "Are you all right?"

"Scared, but fine, thanks to you." Helen beamed at Draco. "You are correct, master, she is a princess." She took Cassidy's hands in her own. "You've burned herself."

"Nothing major. I'll be fine." Cassidy smiled and patted the woman's face, flinching as her raw hands met the woman's face.

Draco would need someone to tend to her as soon as they returned home. The three stepped back to watch the house burn.

A face appeared in a second story window.

"It isn't empty!" Cassidy threw off her cloak and darted into the house before Draco could stop her.

Foolishness! "After her, Roger."

The young man hurried away. Draco had never brought anyone with him before except for the one who's wish he was granting. Now, he'd brought two extra and chaos ensued. He cursed at his weakness.

If Cassidy didn't make it out unharmed, he would kill the woman standing next to him with his own hands.

~

Colin found the video and watched, his heart in his throat, as Cassidy ran into the burning house. He couldn't breathe until she emerged safely, a young woman leaning on her for support.

It appeared that Draco melted into the shadows before the woman could see him.

Knowing that Cassidy was safe, that she was still the caring woman he loved, gave Colin hope. Hope that all would be well and he would save her.

"This is different from the others," Ingram said, watching over Colin's shoulder.

"No one died." Colin grinned up at the agent. "I think maybe Cassidy has made him promise her something. She's had some influence at least."

"She doesn't appear drugged."

Colin had noticed the same thing, and wondered why she stayed with Draco if she weren't. He needed to trust her judgment and wait for a signal.

She glanced up and stared straight into the camera. "Wait," she mouthed.

He nodded, although she couldn't see him. Knowing she was alive and well…he'd do anything she asked…to a degree. "I will, darling, until you need me." He placed his hand flat on the screen, then saved the video to his hard drive.

"See you bright and early," he told Ingram, standing and motioning for Rosie to follow. "I'll meet you right before going up the mountain. There's a tree that had been split in two by lightning. Meet me there."

"Will do." Ingram clapped him on the shoulder. "That amazing woman is managing to help us even in captivity. The world needs more detectives like her."

Colin agreed. With his hand on Rosie's head, he headed for the truck. He'd no sooner unlocked the door, then a man in a leather jacket with a dragon embroidered on it, approached him.

"Master wants the dog."

"Too bad. She's mine now." Colin unlocked the door.

"She belongs to Her Highness."

"Not anymore." Colin bit his upper lip to keep from grinning. Her Highness? "Cassidy Monroe gave up rights to the dog when she left me in that warehouse." He climbed into the driver's seat, hoping the man would believe his anger toward Cassidy. "Give Her Highness a message for me. Tell her fire is suitable and for her to go straight to...well, you can fill in the blank." He started the engine and roared away, pelting the man with gravel from the side of the road.

Hopefully, the reference to fire would let Cassidy know he'd seen the video. "We'll have our girl back soon." He patted Rosie's head. "Very soon."

He entered Cassidy's home, his now, at least temporarily, and armed the alarm. Sitting on the sofa, he booted up his laptop and pulled up the fire video again. Hopefully, facial recognition would give him the name of the scarred woman who set the fire.

He recognized the area. A wealthy family on the outskirts of town. Further searching revealed the house was a total loss. No lives were lost, thanks to a mysterious woman who rescued the daughter of Banker Fred Morrison, then disappeared before authorities arrived. Still, her description was most likely in every newspaper in Arkansas.

There was nothing more he could do until morning. He leaned back against the sofa and glanced at Rosie. Unless...he could put a tracker on the dog and turn her over to Draco. But, if the man found the tracker, he'd kill the dog. Cassidy would never recover. It was best he pretended to now despise his former partner. Safer for everyone involved.

~

"Removing your cloak and running into that building was irresponsible and foolish." Draco's face darkened. "We are there as impartial observers."

"A young woman was about to be burned alive." Cassidy

clenched her fists hard enough to dig her nails into the palms of her hands. "You know I will not stand back and let that happen."

"Perhaps you have forgotten who is the supreme leader here." He rang a bell. Immediately, two large men grabbed Cassidy by the arms and dragged her away.

Despite kicking and screaming, she was dragged to the basement where her arms were hoisted above her head and her shirt ripped from her body. With one snip of a knife, her bra fell to the floor. The men didn't bat an eyelash.

"This will hurt me more than it will hurt you, I promise." Draco raised a whip.

Cassidy closed her eyes and stifled a scream at the first bite of the whip.

"I would drug you, as I'd tried before, but I want you to feel the pain." Another slash. "That's the only way you are going to learn. Spare the rod, spoil the child."

"You're quoting the Bible at me?" She twisted until she could see him. "You sick, twisted, perverted..."

Another strike and she sagged against her bindings. He would not break her. She was strong enough to endure a whipping. She closed her eyes again and thought of Colin. Instead of a happy place, she had a happy man. One she loved dearly, one she knew would take every lash of the whip on her behalf.

After ten strikes, she was cut loose and handed a white robe. She straightened. "Aren't you afraid the wounds on my back will mar the pureness of the fabric?" She sneered, despite the pain.

"I didn't lash out hard enough to cut the skin." Draco handed the whip to one of his henchmen. "Next time, I may not be as careful." He pulled a vial from his pocket, poured some powder into his hand and before she realized exactly what was happening, blew the powder into her face.

"To your room," he said.

She obeyed.

4

Cassidy rolled over in the soft bed, the movement causing pain across her back. What had...ah, yes, now she remembered. At least, she remembered everything up to the point where Draco blew a powder in her face.

She swung her legs over the side of the bed and willed the pounding in her head to subside. Calling him names, letting the thoughts in her head come out of her mouth, had been a stupid thing to do.

Shrugging out of the white cotton gown, she headed to the closet to change. All of her own clothing had been removed. Stark white stared at her. Sighing, she grabbed a dress that reminded her of something an old woman would wear to bed and headed for the shower.

It would take all of her willpower to pretend as if she were still under the effects of the drug. She hadn't eaten any of the food on her nightstand, and didn't have a clue how she was going to skip eating breakfast. She could go a day or two without eating, but she'd need to figure out something soon.

After she'd dressed, she took a deep breath and reached to open her door. Locked. At least this room was a huge improvement over the first one. She knelt beside the bed and fumbled under the mattress for the cell phone she'd hidden there. Ah! Her fingers wrapped around the rectangle. When she was ready, she could alert Colin to her location. She shoved it back in place and prepared to wait for whatever would come.

An hour later, the door opened. Draco stepped inside, his expression grave. Behind him was the young servant woman carrying a tray.

Draco spotted the uneaten food on the nightstand. "Take the fresh food away. She doesn't eat until this is gone."

Cassidy peered up at him from lowered lashes. "My apologies. I…lost my way."

"Don't patronize me." His tone froze her to the bone. "You've done nothing but pretend with me."

She kept silent. Maybe it was time to call Colin after all.

"Give me the phone under your mattress." He held out his hand.

She should have known there were cameras. She was a detective! She sighed and retrieved the phone. Colin would have to find her another way.

Draco ground the phone under the heel of his boot and left the pieces on the floor. "As a reminder," he said, leaving the room.

The click of the lock being engaged seemed to echo in the room.

Cassidy dashed to the window. Barred. There was no escape from what would soon become her hell.

~

Colin rode a four wheeler over the mountain terrain, following Rosie who dashed ahead, nose to the ground. Instinct told him Draco wouldn't be living in one of the more humble homes on the mountainside, so he concentrated his efforts on the mansions.

The first one he'd visited at daybreak had dragged an elderly couple from their beds. From their clear eyes, he'd decided they weren't drugged and he was at the wrong place.

The morning fog was just lifting, revealing Chief's Head in all his forested splendor. Normally, the view would have inspired him. This time, the heavy woods provided an obstacle for Colin to be Cassidy's knight.

Rosie led him across terrain rough enough to almost unseat him. Keeping a tight grip on the handlebars, he slowed his speed. He'd be no help dead.

The walkie-talkie on his hip squawked letting him know the other agents were coming up empty. *Come on, God. A little help here.*

As the sun rose higher, burning off the fog, Colin cut the engine and stared at a grey monstrosity of a house. If a dragon lived in four walls built by man, this would be it.

Rosie whoofed low in her throat, then whined as a face appeared at an upstairs window. Although the face was too far away to make out her features, the red hair gave her away. He'd found Cassidy. He gave the coordinates to the others and settled back to wait.

He pulled a small mirror from a duffel bag tied to the back of the four wheeler and used morse code to send Cassidy a message. "I'm coming," he signaled.

Minutes later, returning signals said she would be ready and for him and the others to wear gas masks and to look for a tunnel that enters the house's kitchen pantry.

Colin pulled a mask from his bag, told the others, and glanced behind him as Ingram and the other two agents pulled up. After they had all donned their masks and grabbed their weapons, they moved forward.

A quick meeting before starting the search had given them their plan. They'd use stealth as long as possible, trying for a back way in. Now, with Cassidy's help, they might have it.

~

Hope sprang in her chest. Wanting to appease Draco for as long as possible, Cassidy turned her back from the camera and pretended to eat. Hiding the food in the folds of her gown, she headed for the bathroom. She flushed most of the food down the toilet and moved the rest around with her fork. She dumped out two-thirds of the orange juice, and all of the coffee, then took her place once again at the window in case Colin needed to signal again.

The door opened behind her. "What are you doing?"

"Watching the sun come up." She turned, keeping her expression as vacant as possible.

"Sit." Draco perched on the edge of her bed and motioned for her to do the same.

She sat, keeping her expression downcast. If he saw the hope in her eyes all would be lost.

"I regret having to punish you. I will send Sarah in to tend to your back, but first…we must talk."

She waited, breathing as slowly as possible.

"Were you truthful when you came to be at my side?"

"No."

"Explain."

"I came only to save Colin." Best to stick as close to the truth as possible if she wanted him to believe she'd eaten the drug-laden food.

"You do realize I have complete control, correct?"

"Yes."

"I could order you to kill Sarah and you could do nothing about it."

"Please don't," she whispered.

He stood and began pacing. "I will only command you to do something so against your grain if you defy me again. I expect complete obedience. You will eat the food placed in front of you. You will do exactly as I say. Do you understand?"

"Yes."

"You will call me Father."

"Yes, Father." The words soured in her stomach.

"Good. Follow me."

He led her downstairs to his study. "It is time to pick another wrong to avenge. No more nonsense of not killing people. All that accomplished was your face being plastered on the front page of every newspaper in the state." He dumped the box containing the requests on the table. "True fear...true vengeance...is fear. Fear of dying, fear of pain, the fear of facing your wrongs. That is what these people must endure to be washed clean."

She wanted to tell Colin to call off the raid. She needed to be there to stop the coming murder. But, if she stayed, Draco might drug her for real again and order her to commit the deed. There wouldn't be anything she could do about it. They needed to take care of him before that happened.

"Pick one," Draco ordered.

She pretended to study the papers in front of her, then grabbed one. Her heart plummeted as she recognized the name of Colin's receptionist, Sharon Wells.

"A very good choice. This woman refused to patch Josephine through when she needed help." Draco slipped the paper into his pocket. "The women went to school together, you see. Josephine, while still overweight, was much heavier back then and did some things she isn't proud of. Still, her actions did not condone the invitation to a slumber party at Sharon's house. A party where

Josephine was recorded changing in the restroom. That video was played during an assembly at school. Yes, Sharon and her friends were disciplined by the school, but the damage had been done. When Josephine called the station for help, Sharon laughed. She claims the call was disconnected, but Josephine believes not."

Cassidy opened her mouth to speak, then realized she hadn't been asked a question. She sat with her head down, her mind frantically trying to come up with a way to save Sharon.

"Josephine will do the deed, dear. All you have to do is stand and watch."

~

Colin switched on the light on his helmet and entered the tunnel. It had taken two hours to find the entrance hidden behind thick brush half a mile from the house. If not for Rosie's keen nose, they'd still be looking. He could only pray it was the right tunnel.

Ingram was happy to let him take charge. He held up a hand to stop the others and listened. Hearing nothing, he clipped a leash on Rosie's collar and moved forward.

The dirt walls and floor smelled damp, most likely kept that way from a nearby spring. The tunnel didn't appear to have been used in a long time since no footprints showed.

The muffled footsteps behind him proved the others were still with them. They'd managed to get three officers from the Little Rock office. Seven men against a dragon. Sounded like good odds to Colin.

They eventually came to a set of wooden steps leading to a door. He held up his hand to halt the others. "There will be no turning back once I open that door," he said. "Be ready for anything. Masks on, weapons ready. We take down Draco and rescue Detective Monroe. Be careful of civilians."

Colin tried the door knob. Locked. He placed a small charge next to the lock and stepped back. A muffled explosion and the door swung open.

A young woman screamed and fell to the ground. A man in his twenties stared with slack mouth. Two large men in dark suits stormed toward Colin.

Rosie barked and charged, ripping the leash from Colin's hand and dodged the two men. Shots from silencers spit out bullets, dropping the men. Colin waved his hand forward. Rosie would give away their position the moment she found Cassidy. Their element of surprise was gone.

Colin followed the dog to a room.

Draco had Cassidy in front of him, a knife to her throat. "Drop the weapon, Mr MacKenzie."

"Take the shot!" Cassidy yelled.

Draco backed toward the fireplace, dragging Cassidy with him. He pushed against a wall sconce, stepped onto the hearth, and disappeared as Cassidy reared her head back, then slipped from his grasp.

"No." Colin ran toward the fireplace as the opening closed.

"You should have taken the shot," Cassidy spit out.

"I could have hit you."

"It would have been worth the sacrifice." She shook her head, one hand holding firm to Rosie's collar. "You have to warn Sharon. She's the next target."

Colin motioned to Ingram, who pulled out his phone. The other officers and agents continued to search for Draco. Colin stared at Cassidy. "I thought you'd be grateful for the rescue."

"I am." She tilted her head. "I saved the life of one and failed to save another. If I stayed, it was only a matter of time before I was drugged and forced to kill someone." Sadness crossed her features. "I had so hoped this would be the end of Draco."

"We'll keep trying. This is the closest we've gotten." He put his arm around her shoulders, wary that she might reject the offer of his touch.

Her fingers skimmed the scar on his arm. "I'm sorry for all you've suffered because of me."

"Promise to never leave me again and it will have been worth it."

Ingram joined them. "There's no sign of him. This old house has got to be full of hiding places."

Colin glanced down at Cassidy, love for her so strong he could hardly breathe. "We'll get him. We have something he wants."

5

The love shining in Colin's eyes threatened to make Cassidy's heart stop. How could he still love her so much after she'd left him, wounded and dying...twice?

With the FBI agents escorting them, and the other officers questioning Draco's staff, they rode the four wheelers back to the vehicles and sped back to town. She sat in the backseat, her arms around Rosie's neck.

Cassidy had risked everything. Her life, Colin's love, her career, for nothing. Draco had escaped again. There would be no more bargaining. He would come for her with a vengeance.

She met Colin's gaze in the rearview mirror. All her efforts to protect him and been in vain.

"Has Sharon been placed in protective custody?" she asked.

"She isn't answering the phone," Ingram replied. "Do you mind if we stop there before heading to your house?"

"I insist. Time is of the essence." Draco would up his quest for revenge to pull Cassidy out of hiding.

They screeched to a halt in front of the police station. Colin was the first through the front doors, followed closely by the agents and Cassidy.

Sharon glanced up from her desk. "What's going on?"

Smith and Miller took her by the arms. Cassidy grabbed her purse.

"We're placing you in protective custody," Ingram said. "Effective immediately."

"But the phones are ringing off the hook." She tried to yank free. "I can't just leave my job. It's like a full moon or something. Fights, robberies...you name it, we have it this morning."

Cassidy glanced at Colin. "Draco."

"He's keeping us busy so you won't go into hiding."

"Agents Smith and Miller will stay at Detective Monroe's with Sharon. Cassidy, change out of that grandma dress and let's hit the streets." Ingram barked orders.

"I've a change of clothes in my locker." Cassidy headed to the locker room and donned the sweat pants and tee shirt she kept there for days she headed to the gym straight from work. She tossed the offending dress in the nearest trashcan and joined the others.

Sharon was still protesting as the agents put her in the back of a squad car. A rookie officer took her place at the reception desk.

"As soon as you can, call for a temp for Sharon," Colin said. "We'll take care of the problems on the street." He glanced at a handful of messages. "First, we'll break up a gang fight downtown. Everyone wears a vest, no exceptions."

The three of them trooped out to Colin's truck. Three against two rival gangs. Cassidy sighed. They'd be lucky to make it out alive.

They drove to a vacant strip mall. Ten gang members of African and Mexican American heritage stood facing each other, yelling taunts and waving guns. It didn't look as if any shots were fired, but things could escalate within seconds.

"Stay in the car, Rosie." Cassidy shoved open her door, along with Colin and Ingram. Side-by-side they made their way to the standoff.

"What's up, gentlemen?" Colin stepped forward.

"These guys are on our turf," a young black man said. "We got word they were taking over."

"We got word they wanted to fight!" A young Hispanic said.

"You were both lied to." Colin kept his gun held at his side. "A few of you have seen the dragon. This is nothing more than a ploy to keep the police occupied."

"We've been had?" The black man shook his head. "I left my supper for this."

"Everyone head home. There's nothing to do here." Colin kept his face impassive. "Agreed?"

The moment the two groups turned to walk away, a pipe bomb was thrown into the street. Colin whirled, covering Cassidy's body with his. Screams filled the air. Shots were fired.

"The rooftop!" Colin motioned to Ingram, who limped in the direction he'd pointed.

"I'm fine." Cassidy shoved Colin off her. "We have to see to them." The radio on her belt squawked. "We have a stabbing on Fourth street."

~

"Call an ambulance." Colin knelt next to a young man with shrapnel in his gut. He cut a strip off the man's tee shirt and pressed against the wound. "Then, come help me!"

"What about the knife?"

"We can't be there and here. We know we're needed here." He glanced at the buildings towering over them. A sniper could pick them off one at a time and there was nothing he could do to save her.

The ambulance arrived and the EMT workers set to work caring for the victims that littered the pavement. Colin grabbed Cassidy's arm and ushered her to the truck. Within minutes of the ambulance's arrival, the two of them headed to pick up Ingram at the end of the street.

Blood soaked the tie he'd tied around his leg. "Don't mind me. It's only a cut. On to the next call."

"You should stay and get checked out." Colin glanced in the rearview mirror.

"Later. Go. There will be enough blood spilled today to worry about me." Ingram closed his eyes and rested his head against the seat.

Colin shook his head and sped toward the next disaster. "I want you to stay in the car, Cassidy. Draco could have finished you off back there."

"It isn't only me he wants." Her eyes flashed. "I have a job to do. I'm not letting him stop me any more than you or Ingram will."

"Amen to that," Ingram muttered.

"I'm surrounded by stubborn idiots." Colin yanked the wheel to the right. Although, if he were truthful, he admired their spunk. He'd be the same, was in fact. Draco wanted him dead, and was working hard to accomplish that goal. Problem was...the man didn't care how many people he took down with them. Including his daughter.

They stopped at a trailer park where an elderly man sat propped against a tree, blood spreading across his stomach. A paramedic knelt next to him.

"We've got him stable. He'll be fine," the paramedic said.

"What happened?" Colin kneeled in the grass.

"A masked man came running toward me, pulled a knife, and here I lie." The old man opened his eyes. "I did nothing to provoke him."

"Which way did he go?"

The man pointed in the direction Colin had come. They hadn't seen anyone wearing a mask or the tell-tale jacket of Draco's followers.

"He isn't following his MO," Cassidy said. "The gang members, this man…they aren't the pretty people he wants dead."

Colin pushed to his feet. "I don't know what his game is, but we'll figure it out. What's next?"

She checked the laptop in the truck. "Robbery at a drugstore. Something called Scopolamine. The robber took all the safe held."

Colin's knees weekend. He explained how the drug worked to Cassidy. "We may not be dealing with just Draco's followers. If he uses this drug, any stranger on the street will do his bidding and have no recollection after it's done."

"This is an FDA approved drug?"

"Yes." Once back in the truck, he studied the laptop. "Hostage situation at the diner. The day is getting better and better."

"We can't shoot if the person isn't in control of their actions."

"I'm aware of that."

"We can shoot to disarm," Ingram said. "The life of one over the lives of many."

Cassidy turned in her seat. "Even if the one holding the gun is innocent?"

"Sometimes tough decisions have to be made."

Colin placed his hand over Cassidy's. "We'll do our best."

"We're doing exactly what Draco wants us to. I know our job requires tough, sometimes split decision, but if these people are under the effect of a drug, they have no choice in what they do."

They stopped a few yards from the diner. Across the street a crowd had gathered. Two squad cars from a neighboring city sat as a barricade.

"One armed man," a middle-aged officer by the name of Schultz, said. "We counted over twenty hostages, some children."

"Has the perp stated any demands?"

"He wants Detective Monroe inside with him."

"Absolutely not."

Cassidy put a hand on his arm. "I'll go. Colin..." she shook her head as he started to protest. "One for the greater good, right? Besides, the drug doesn't last forever. If I can stall the man long enough, the effects will wear off."

"We'll have to put a wire on you."

She nodded. "Make it quick. I'm sure Draco is watching." She motioned her head to a camera on a post.

"The man will follow any orders given him. I'm sure he's wearing a wire from Draco. It might not hurt, though, for you to try and take control." He gazed into the face he loved. So many things had happened since rescuing her from the dragon's lair. There'd been no time for them to talk about a future, if one were possible. "What if you don't come back?"

"I will." She smiled and caressed his face. "Wait for me." She placed a tender kiss on his lips and marched toward the diner.

~

Draco glanced at his computer monitor and rubbed his hands. Having hacked into the security cameras around town, and strategically causing havoc in locations accessible by camera, he was able to watch every time Cassidy responded to a call.

He'd ordered his followers not to make a direct hit against her or the Scot, but if they died in the process, he would have the satisfaction of watching. If not, he'd take care of them himself later.

Leaning forward, he watched as Cassidy, hands in the air, approached the diner. While the man inside had been drugged and ordered to hold the others hostage, and one of Draco's loyal followers was inside to give him further instruction, anything could happen.

The diner door swung open and the zombie-like man ushered Cassidy inside. She could easily overtake him in his stupor, but now that she knew his condition, Draco had full confidence she wouldn't make an aggressive move.

Not her. Not the woman who had a soft spot for every living

being except her biological father. He'd given her every chance to see reason. Now, he'd make her pay, slowly and painfully. She would be his ultimate act of revenge.

6

Detective Monroe asking permission to enter." Cassidy slowly pushed open the door to the diner. She didn't know much about the drug the man had been affected with, but would do all in her power to save the lives of the hostages. Him, too, if possible.

The man stared at her, his eyes vacant, then nodded.

"What is your name?"

"Horace Wells."

"It's nice to meet you, Horace." She glanced at the hostages, lined up on the floor, backs against the breakfast counter. "Is everyone all right?"

They nodded. One little boy around the age of three hid his face in his mother's chest.

"I'll make sure it stays that way. Horace?"

"Yes." His wooden voice sent chills down her.

"Have these people had anything to eat or drink since they became your...guests?"

He looked befuddled.

"Perhaps they could go one by one to the bathroom?"

Horace tilted his head as if listening. "No. There is a back door. They'll escape."

Which had been her plan. She sighed. "Tell the man talking in your ear that I'm the one he wants and to let the others go."

Horace repeated her command verbatim. She did have a semblance of control over him. Of course, so did Draco. It would be a matter of who spoke last before the drug wore off. She would have to make every word count.

She slowly lowered herself onto a chair, turning it to face

Horace. She'd planned on overtaking him, until she saw the bomb strapped to his chest. A little detail it would have been nice to know before she'd entered the building. "Who has the power to ignite the bomb you're wearing?"

"Draco."

Cassidy nodded. Hostage negotiations weren't her strong suit. In fact, she preferred action. She could charge the man, but if Draco were watching, and listening, he'd ignite the bomb before she could save the hostages.

"Let everyone else go and we'll talk. Just the three of us."

Horace stood still for a moment. "Just the children can go. Draco said they are innocent."

"I'm sure the parents are innocent, too. Their names are not in Draco's box."

Cassidy scribbled bomb on a napkin, and handed it to a preteen girl. "Give this to Officer MacKenzie," she whispered in the girl's ear. "Come on, little ones. Let's go." She pushed open the door and ushered out five children. The two who remained behind were nursing infants. "Please allow the mothers of the infants to go. Surely Draco, in all his power and wisdom, wouldn't send the infants out alone."

Horace nodded. "They can go."

Cassidy heaved a sigh. Nine saved, almost twenty to go, counting staff. She could do this. She sat, head lowered, and watched Horace from beneath lowered lashes. Zombie was an apt description. No emotion crossed his features as the children and nursing mothers had left. He really didn't seem as if he knew where he was or what he was doing.

He coughed, the action jiggling the stomach that protruding over the top of his jeans. He smacked fat lips.

With a sigh, Cassidy stood and grabbed a pitcher of ice water. Pouring him a glass, she ordered, "drink this."

He downed it without pausing and set the glass on a table near him.

Cassidy refilled the glass. "For when you need it."

A flicker of something crossed his face. He blinked and glanced at the bomb strapped to his chest. "Where am I? What is this?!" He yanked at the vest he wore.

"Don't!" Cassidy held out her hand. "Are you one of Draco's

followers?"

He nodded, then stilled. "Yes, sir. Your command, sir." Sweat poured down his face as he sat across from Cassidy. "We are to sit and wait further instructions."

So, the drug had worn off.

"What about the hostages?"

Tears trickled down his face. "They stay." He put his hands over his bald head. "Please tell me I didn't kill anyone. I don't have anything against these people."

"You didn't." Cassidy reached across to touch his arm, pulling back when he recoiled. "You have no need to fear me."

"Master says you're a witch."

Well, that was new. "I assure you, I'm not. Where is he watching us from?"

Horace pointed to a camera near the front door.

Cassidy approached the device and looked into the lens. "Your beef is with me. Let Horace and these people go."

"He says no. That you haven't been punished yet."

The words sent ice water through her veins. The only thing that could punish Cassidy was the loss of innocent lives or the life of Colin. She was going to die in that diner, along with the hostages.

No, she wasn't. There had to be a way out. "Are you prepared to die today, Horace?"

He shook his head. "Master holds the trigger."

"You can stop this. These people, you, do not have to die."

His eyes widened. He blinked, once, slowly.

Good. The man was thinking on his own. "Master says for you to stop talking. That your words are poison."

"Very well." She motioned her eyes toward the small hall that led to the restrooms.

The charge on his vest didn't look large. The damage could be confined to the diner. Perhaps, the hostages could take cover if Horace moved fast enough.

Cassidy eyed his bulk. Doubtful he was swift on his feet, but fear could light a fire under anyone.

His gaze flicked to the hall. "Okay," he mouthed. He pushed to his feet, wiping perspiration from his forehead. The man knew he would die, but most of the others might survive. Despite his following the orders of a madman, he would be a true hero that day.

Cassidy stood and shook his hand. Since she faced the camera, she couldn't speak, but instead, put all her feelings and support into the simple handshake. Then, as Horace headed for the hallway, she sat back down and stared into the camera. She smiled.

"Get down! Take cover!" She dove under the table.

The hostages scrambled under the nearest items of furniture.

The bomb exploded as Horace pushed open the men's room door.

Screams filled the air.

Plaster rained onto those huddled on the diner floor.

When the smoke cleared, groans replaced the screams. Sobs reached Cassidy's ears.

She crawled through the debris in search of survivors.

~

Draco cursed. She'd foiled his plan.

He threw the recording device against the wall. Useless now. With the explosion, he couldn't see a thing. Horace was an idiot to listen to anyone but him.

If the fool would have waited, Cassidy would be the one wearing the explosive vest and the man would still be alive to carry out further orders.

He should have killed the Scot when he had a chance. He picked up the phone to assign a new order. One that would end the life of the man his daughter loved. One-by-one everything and everyone she cared about would be gone.

~

Colin sprinted for the diner before the air cleared. The back half of the building was nothing but rubble. The walls of the front half stood, but the roof sagged. "Cassidy!" He climbed through the shattered front window. "Cassidy!"

"I'm here." She waved from where she pressed napkins against a wound in a woman's thigh. "I need help. There's too much blood. I haven't checked the others."

"The ambulance is on its way. You're bleeding." He pressed a hand to the cut on her head.

"I'm fine. Look out for the others."

He nodded, hating to leave her, but there was work to be done, and her wound didn't look life threatening. He went from one to the other, sending those who could walk out to the waiting officers.

One man didn't make it and another who had thrown himself across the body of his wife was in bad shape. A thick sliver of wood protruded from his side.

"Hold on, sir. Help is coming." He instructed the wife not to pull the wood from her husband's side, and found some dishtowels for her to hold against the bleeding wound. Not too bad, considering what could have happened. One dead, two severely wounded, and the rest suffering minor scrapes and contusions.

He returned to Cassidy's side as an ambulance wailed to a stop outside. "Quick thinking, detective."

She gave a sad smile. "It was all I could think of to do. Poor Horace."

"He turned out to be quite the hero. Draco won't like that at all."

"I don't care what he likes." She sat back as, with fresh towels, Colin took over applying pressure to the woman's leg. "Colin." She stared over his shoulder.

He turned. A man, gun drawn, raced toward them from the vacant lot behind the diner.

Colin drew his weapon and fired as shots rang out from the other officers.

The man fell, never having gotten off a shot.

"Draco is getting sloppy." Colin holstered his gun and returned his attention to the victim in front of him.

"He's after you with a vengeance now." Cassidy sat with her back against the counter and held a rag to her head. "You aren't safe. You need to go into hiding."

"Won't happen." He moved back as paramedics took over.

"He won't stop. He has six followers left. They can do a lot of damage."

"When those six are gone, he'll come after me himself. Then, we'll finish this sick game he plays." He helped her to her feet. "Let's get you some medical attention."

He hated the fact that six more misguided people may suffer at the hands of Draco, but if they could take him down before something like the bombing happened again, those six lives, while tragic, would be collateral damage. The thought sickened him.

The mad man may not value life, but Colin knew every one of God's children were precious. If he could stop the murder and insanity, if he had any say in the manner, things would come to a head soon. Draco was going to lose the battle.

While a paramedic tended to Cassidy, Colin filled Ingram in on what had transpired inside the diner. "Detective Monroe told me what happened while we helped the victims."

"Good thing you spotted the shooter coming across the lot." Ingram shook his head. "It's a darn shame what happened here today."

"I'm wearing my vest." Colin grinned and pounded his chest. "He would have had to be a good shot and get me in the head to kill me."

"Don't laugh. You aren't invincible. None of us are." Ingram glanced to where Cassidy was getting treated. "I've seen a lot of things during my career, but Russell Blake, aka Draco, ranks right up there as one of the worst." He turned a stern gaze back to Colin. "You do realize one, or both of you, may not make it out of this alive."

Colin knew he meant him and Cassidy. "I know." He could only pray that if one of them were to fall, it would be him.

"I need stitches." Cassidy moved to his side. "I'm not going in the ambulance, so you'll have to take me."

"Why not the ambulance?"

She smiled. "I'm not leaving your side. Draco wants you dead. Having me close might be the only chance you've got."

He laughed and put an arm around her shoulders. "He wants you dead, too."

"But he wants me to watch while you die."

"True."

Ingram made a face. "You two love birds have the worst skill at romantic talk I've ever heard."

"We'll work on that." Colin cupped Cassidy's face. "Let's get you stitched up. We have some kissing to do."

"We have been rather busy, haven't we?" Her eyes sparkled.

The Emergency Room doctors stitched Cassidy up, and within two hours, they were reclining on the couch, with her knocked out from pain meds. So much for a kissing session.

Colin repositioned himself and laid her head in his lap. He

didn't plan on ever leaving her side either. He smoothed the hair away from her face, careful to avoid the bandage over seven stitches.

His heart ached with love for her and fear of losing her. Twice he'd watched her go. That would not happen again. Not while he had breath left in his body.

"No." She twitched, mumbling in her sleep.

Nightmares, no doubt. Similar to the ones that used to plague him. But, not more. As long as he had Cassidy to care for, the night terrors stayed at bay.

"Shh. I'm right here. No one can hurt you now." He pulled an afghan over her legs and rested his head against the back of the sofa. They'd sleep like that tonight with Rosie at their feet to warn them of any intruders.

He closed his eyes, remembering the heat of her passion the night she'd come to his room to comfort him after his nightmares. The night he'd almost stepped over the boundary he put in place with all of his partners. Except…Cassidy was different than the rest. While he may have felt a physical attraction for a partner over the course of his career, he felt much more for the woman lying in his lap.

7

Cassidy woke stiff and sore and rolled off Colin's lap. She fell to her knees and glanced up. His snores ceased as he opened his eyes.

"Good morning," he grinned. "I hope you slept better than I did."

"I can hardly move." She groaned and, using the coffee table for support, pushed to her feet. "But, I slept like a log. Thank you." She held out her hand to help him up.

He pulled her close, stealing a kiss. When she didn't pull away, the kiss deepened. "This is the proper way to begin a day," he murmured.

Chuckling, she straightened, then sobered. "I owe you so much, Colin…everything in fact."

"You would have been fine without me." He stood and pulled her into his arms, resting his chin on the top of her head. "I'm little more than a distraction."

"A welcome one." She pulled back and peered into his face. "I'm sorry for leaving you."

"It was something you felt you had to do."

"I should have been brave enough to stay."

"You were brave enough to leave and enter the dragon's lair." He kissed her, then swatted her behind. "Go get ready for the day. Who knows what Draco has planned?"

"I want to go away and escape all this." She sighed, as she headed for her bedroom.

Russell Blake wouldn't stop until either she, Colin, or himself were dead. A showdown was coming. One she wanted to avoid at all costs. Still, she had a responsibility to the community. There would be no hiding.

After a long hot shower, she dressed in her black suit, put her hair into a ponytail, and dabbed on mascara and lip gloss. She smiled, remembering the days she wore no makeup and baggy pants to work. That was all before Colin. Funny how a man made a woman see herself in a different light.

When she joined Colin in the living room, he had showered, his hair still damp, and wore a navy tee shirt and jeans. He held his cell phone to his ear. "We're on our way." He turned to Cassidy, his expression grave. "He killed the Carson parents. CPS has taken custody of the child."

Cassidy grit her teeth. The family had gone into hiding weeks ago to escape Draco. Little good it did them. "Where are we going?"

"Sarah Robertson's house."

"The reporter?"

He nodded. "She didn't show up for work today and isn't answering her phone. Ingram wants us to stop by her place before coming in."

"Draco is targeting everyone I know, even if they're only acquaintances." She set the alarm on the house, called to Rosie, and followed Colin to his truck.

After he checked for explosives, they climbed in and roared toward a luxury apartment complex in the center of town. Cassidy reached over and clutched Colin's hand. She knew what they would find at Sarah's and wanted his strength to bolster her.

They rode the elevator to the top floor and knocked on door number 307. When no answer came, Colin tried the knob. The door swung open at his touch.

A strong metallic order assaulted Cassidy's nose. She knew that smell. Knew it meant death. She held her arm across her nose. "He turned off the air conditioning."

"This won't be pretty." Colin led the way into Sarah's bedroom.

Stripped naked and tied to the bedpost, she'd been stabbed several times in the form of an X across her abdomen. Nausea rose and Cassidy gagged. An open window allowed flies to be attracted to the body and a huge swarm buzzed around the room when Colin and Cassidy entered.

"I'll call Ingram." Cassidy bolted from the room.

In the hallway, she bent over and took deep breaths, willing her stomach to settle. Once the feeling of throwing up subsided, she straightened and dialed Ingram. "Sarah Robertson is dead."

"I'll be right there." Click.

She did not want to go back in the room. Taking a deep breath through her nose and then breathing through her mouth, she rejoined Colin.

"Look." He pointed to a piece of paper pinned in place by Sarah's arm.

Cassidy bent closer and read, "This is only the beginning." Her heart dropped. The Carson's, Sarah, who was next? Colin? Ingram? They were the only people she associated with. She had no family, no friends. Until Colin, her career had dominated her personal life.

She'd barely known Sarah. Had only spoken with her once. Was he going to strike at everyone she'd ever carried on a conversation with? "Draco has lost his mind. He's gone off the deep end and is more dangerous than ever."

"It isn't about drawing you out anymore. It's about making you pay."

~

Oh, this was fun. Planning ways to torment his daughter, the betrayer, was the highlight of Draco's days. He popped his daily medication, knowing it was too late for him. Feeling sluggish, he'd gone to the doctor months ago, after Cassidy had gone to Little Rock. Cancer. The dragon had cancer. How ironic.

Now that his symptoms were worsening and he knew Cassidy would not take over his empire, he planned on making sure the world would never forget him. He took a gulp of water from the goblet on his desk and leaned back in his chair.

He'd sacrifice his followers, take down as many people from Clear Creek as he could, then go out in a blaze of glory, befitting a dragon. He grinned. Then, he would rule the next world.

He picked up the phone and set the next phase into motion. Oh, this one would get Cassidy running for sure.

~

Colin had had enough. He stepped onto the apartment balcony when Ingram and the other agents arrived and took huge gulps of air. He'd seen a lot in his time as a police officer, but this was the most brutal thing he'd ever seen.

Draco was killing to punish Cassidy. It was no longer a misguided attempt at revenge for his followers. It was brutal killing.

"I found this tacked to the bathroom mirror." Cassidy handed him a sheet of paper. "It looks like a scavenger hunt." Her eyes widened. "We have to beat him to each clue or somebody dies."

Colin read number one. "The sun sparkles like diamonds across the surface." Easy. He had to mean the lake.

"The only time the surface of the lake sparkles is seconds after sunset. It's a big lake, Colin. His next victim could be anywhere."

"We need to tell Ingram. We'll have to spread out." He hated doing so. That put them all at a great risk. Most likely that was Draco's plan. It scared the wits out of him.

Once the crime scene in the reporter's room was secure, they all congregated back at the office along with some borrowed officers from Little Rock. Ingram turned the meeting over to Colin.

He explained the note Cassidy had found and what they believed it meant. "We'll have to spread out around the lake. This will put every one of us in danger. It's likely a suicide mission for one of us, but if we don't do it, a civilian will surely die." He glanced at the faces around the oval table. Ten officers. Cassidy and one other were the only women.

"This is what we signed up for," Officer Bartram said. "We're at war. Casualties will occur. Hopefully it will be this Draco."

Colin prayed so, but doubted it would be that easy. "Everyone wears swat gear, no exceptions. Everyone wears a wire and carries a radio. If you run across each other, identify yourself. We don't want any friendly fire."

"Lunch." Sharon carried in a tray piled with hamburgers and fries. "Don't look at me that way," she said in response to Colin's glare. "If y'all can risk your life to save this town, then so can I. Besides, I did a bad thing once upon a time."

"That doesn't mean you have to die for it," Cassidy said, relieving her of the tray. "You were a foolish kid."

"I knew right from wrong." Sharon left the room.

"Is she safe?"

"She sleeps in one of the cells at night," Ingram said. "She's safer here than at home. Eat up, folks. Then, we're off to the wilds."

"Stop looking at me like that," Cassidy said.

"Wow. All the women are complaining about the way I look at them today."

"We can do our part. You know I can't stay by your side, even though I said I would. Not this time. We have too much ground to cover." Despair clouded her eyes.

"I know. But you'll be in the section next to me." He pulled down a map of the lake area from a roll on the wall and assigned locations. "We go in quiet. We do not want to start a panic. Approach any civilians cautiously and tell them to clear out as quickly as possible."

With borrowed swat gear and a few more volunteers from Conway, they headed to Clear Springs Lake, five hundred acres of lush wood land. Half took the western trail, Colin, Cassidy and the rest turned east.

A woman hiking with her small children spotted them and screamed.

"Take the children and go. Now. Leave the park," Colin ordered, flashing his badge.

She nodded and took the little ones by the hands and ran. Good. No questions. Things went faster without curiosity.

He left Cassidy next to a group of campsites with instructions to clear the area. He headed down the path, sending any hikers and sightseers he saw home.

~

Cassidy removed her helmet, wanting to look the least formidable possible as she went from tent to tent, telling the campers the police were clearing the area. Her only comment other than that was, "That's classified. Sorry." Then moved on.

The campsites burst into activity as campers dismantled tents and tossed camping gear into trunks and trucks. Cassidy took up position where she could see the entire area. It wasn't enough. If one of Draco's people came from across the grounds, she'd never reach them in time.

So, she walked the perimeter, casting a wary gaze here and there. Every shout from a worried parent or scream from a child made the hair on the back of her neck rise. Time was running out.

The campers had been readying themselves for supper. The sun would set soon and there were way too many people still around.

8

Draco wandered the woods surrounding the lake. Fatigue covered him as effectively as the dark cloak he wore. His time was running out. No more taping of his crimes. The authorities would spot his weakness and act upon it quickly.

The Scot would come, gun blazing. Not a bad thing, but it had to happen in Draco's time...with his daughter lying bleeding at his feet.

There was his target. An FBI agent trying to stay out of sight in the shadows. Draco would make the man scream loud enough to be heard around the lake.

~

Cassidy watched as the last family tossed an ice chest in the back of their truck and roared away. How many were in the woods, unseen? She sighed. She couldn't help them. She could only help those she saw.

She turned toward the lake as the sun set. Diamonds sparkled across the surface. She froze as an unearthly scream carried across the water.

The radio on her hip crackle, then Ingram's voice came through demanding a roll call. Cassidy pushed the button. "Monroe here."

She closed her eyes as Colin responded. The only one not to call out was Miller.

"Miller!" Ingram barked.

"If you hurry, you might save him."

Cassidy froze as Draco's voice came through, followed by another scream. With her gun drawn, Cassidy whirled, trying to

273

determine where the sound came from. She headed for a thin column of smoke rising above the trees at the far end of the lake. Highlighted by the moonlight, the smoke resembled a spirit rising above them all. A foretelling of doom.

"Cassidy," Colin whispered from nearby.

She spun, her gun hand automatically rising. "I could've shot you."

"Sorry. I don't want you alone, is all." He motioned toward the smoke. "Are you headed there?"

"Yes. We have to hurry." With him by her side, she took off at a run. If Draco wanted her and Colin together, he'd just gotten his wish. They'd barge in, guns blazing, to try and save Miller and most likely die in the process.

She glanced over her shoulder at the man she loved. No one else she'd rather die with. However the night ended, a lot of lives had been saved with the clearing of the campsites. Her heart would ache over the loss of Miller, but they all knew the dangers when they left the station earlier that day.

Colin grabbed her arm. "Wait." He parted the branches of the shrubbery in front of them. "Look first."

She nodded. In a small clearing, Miller was tied to a stake. Embers burned at his feet. Draco had cut out his eyes.

"He's still alive! Cover me, Colin." She darted forward. Pulling a small knife from her belt, she sawed at the ropes binding him. "I've got you, Miller."

"Go. Away." The man mumbled through chewed up lips.

"Not until you're down."

Colin grabbed the near-dead man as the ropes cut and laid him on the ground. "Call Ingram. We have to get out of here. We're sitting ducks."

"Get out now. You have three seconds. He made me swallow an explosive. Cutting the ropes set it off."

With a quick glance at Colin, Cassidy dove into the brush. The concussion knocked her flat and removed her helmet. She lay in the leaves and gasped for breath, feeling on the ground for her weapon.

Colin had dove in another direction. She scrambled to her hands and knees, crawling through the brush to find him.

She stopped in front of two shiny black shoes. Colin wore

boots. Her gaze traveled up the dark cloak and into the face of Draco.

"Hello," he said, grabbing her by the hair. His other hand held a knife.

She twisted away as he slashed, the knife catching in her ponytail. She dove for his knees, taking him to the ground with her.

"Let her go!" Colin entered the fray.

"Shoot him," Cassidy ordered.

"You're in the way."

She yanked, leaving most of her ponytail in Draco's hands. He grabbed her around the neck, holding her in front of him and got to his feet. "Put down the gun, Scot, or she loses more than hair."

"Just shoot." Cassidy went limp, sliding through Draco's arm. The knife grazed her neck. Ignoring the burning, she did the only thing she could think of...she sank her teeth into his leg.

Draco howled and pulled free. With a swish of his cloak, he raced into the shadows.

Colin raised his gun and fired.

Draco was gone.

"I told you to shoot him." Cassidy stood and glared.

"I couldn't without hitting you."

"That's a risk we have to take. We can't let him keep getting away." She glanced behind her to where Miller once lay. In the dark, there was no sign of any bit of him. Heart heavy, she stepped into the clearing. "There has to be the next clue in the hunt somewhere around here."

Colin handed her the weapon she'd dropped. "I'm sorry, but I'm not going to kill you, Cassidy. I wouldn't survive it."

Remembering how he'd once had to shoot an innocent woman, and still suffered from the act, she forgave him. "I'm sorry. I know you can't. But if it ever comes down to me or a civilian, you save the civilian, understand?"

~

"Yes." He slowly circled the clearing. Buried next to the fire pit was a small, metal, fireproof box. He knelt next to it and opened it, revealing a slip of paper. "Found it."

Cassidy peered over his shoulder and read out loud, "No food or drink brings out the bite in every living creature." She straightened. "What the heck does that mean? Is he saying we aren't supposed to eat or drink anything?"

An icy fist gripped Colin's heart and squeezed. "I think it means he has Rosie."

"Where? He wouldn't hurt a dog...would he?" Her voice broke.

"To get at you, he might." Colin placed his hands on his thighs and pushed to his feet. "He could also mean the nearby animal shelter." If he meant Rosie, then Sharon was also in danger since they'd left the dog at the station with her. If it was the animal shelter...well, they'd all be splitting up again.

"Did you find him?" Ingram raced to their side. "Miller?"

"Obliterated." Colin handed Ingram the note. "We have to split up again."

"He's picking us off one-by-one." Ingram wadded the clue in his fist. "Take half the men with you to the station, I'll take the rest to the shelter and leave one behind to wait for the crime investigators." He shook his head. "Miller had a wife and two kids. Russell Blake is leaving a path of destruction that is almost erasing this town right off the map. I want him and I want him now."

Colin nodded. Together, he and Cassidy made their way around the lake and back to the truck. Worry over Rosie and Sharon put fuel to his steps. Behind them, he could hear the other group returning to head to their assignment.

Once they reached the truck, Cassidy climbed in and turned to Colin the moment he slid into the driver's seat. "We can't let him hurt my dog."

"I'll do my best to prevent that from happening." He turned the key in the ignition and drove as fast as possible back to town.

They pulled in back of the station and thundered through the door. Sharon, who sat in the conference room feeding Rosie bits of oatmeal cookies, screamed.

Rosie stood, hackles raised, until she spotted Colin and Cassidy. Then her tail wagged hard enough to shake her behind.

"I hope there's enough for all of us." Relief flooded through Colin so strongly at the sight of the dog and woman being all right that he plopped into a chair in lieu of his legs dropping him.

Cassidy hugged Rosie, murmuring words of nonsense. "Should we go to the shelter since this is obviously the wrong place?"

"Rest a few minutes. Ingram will call and let us know if he needs us." Colin grabbed two cookies, eating one in two bites. "Sit and have a cookie, Cassidy. They're good."

"What's going on?" Sharon glanced from one to the other. "You're dressed for war and came barging in here as if you expected to find something."

Colin explained what had transpired the last few hours. "So, yeah, we expected to find something."

She paled. "It's been quiet here. Rosie hasn't even twitched an ear."

"I'm glad to hear it." He finished the second cookie. "When did you have time to bake cookies?"

"They were delivered."

His hand stopped half-way to his mouth. "By whom?"

"The local bakery."

"You didn't order them?"

She shook her head.

"I'll call an ambulance." Cassidy set down the cookie she hadn't eaten. "You need to be checked for poison."

Colin pulled over a trashcan and stuck his finger down his throat, then thrust the can at Sharon. "Your turn."

"But...Rosie? She's only had a few bites."

"Do we have any milk?"

She threw up the cookies, then rushed to the lounge, returning with half a carton. She chugged half of it, then handed it to Colin. After he finished, he poured some in a bowl for the dog. It was the best he could do until the ambulance arrived. So much for a bit of rest.

He got up and waited by the front door for the ambulance. Once it arrived, it took all three of them and Rosie to the hospital where the cookies were checked for poison.

"They're simple oatmeal cookies," the technician said after they'd waited for an hour.

"Just another ploy of Draco's to keep us guessing," Cassidy said.

Colin got an alert on his phone. "Not necessarily. We're out in the open and the station is on fire."

"Where do we go now?"

"I don't want to go to your place. He's too familiar with it. A motel?"

"I have a cabin," Sharon said. "Or, my parents do. It's two hours from here. I doubt he'll know it's there."

Another message came through. "No go. We have to meet up with Ingram. You're staying here at the hospital. I'll be right back."

Colin searched for the hospital chief of staff and explained Sharon's predicament. After being assured she could stay in the nurse's lounge until he returned, he and Cassidy, taking Rosie with them, headed out to meet up with Ingram.

~

Draco hissed as he poured disinfectant on the bullet wound in his side. The Scot was a good shot, but not good enough to bring him down. He held a needle to a cigarette lighter, then threaded it with hospital grade thread. After sewing himself up, thankful the bullet went clean through, he poured a stiff drink of whiskey and downed it in one swallow.

It didn't matter whether the bullet did any internal damage. Draco didn't plan on living long enough.

Once he'd dulled the pain with alcohol, he transferred his attention to his computer monitor and grinned. Every one of his targets were gathered in one place. Showtime!

9

C assidy climbed from the truck, telling Rosie to stay close. After the day they'd had, she wasn't taking any chances with the dog, or Colin, being too far from her side.

Ingram and the rest of law enforcement, including a van that stated bomb squad on the panel, waited outside the animal shelter. "The squad made a sweep of the building. All clear," Ingram said. "I have no idea why we're here."

"I do." Cassidy glanced at the large group. "We're all here, in one place. We need to spread out."

"We can't leave," Smith said. "He'll take us out one by one, just like he did with Miller."

"If we don't spread out," she replied, "he'll take us all out in one full sweep."

Ingram looked deep in thought for a moment, then glanced at Colin. "MacKenzie?"

"I agree with Cassidy. Why make it easy for him?" He studied the rooftop of a nearby building. "We're easy targets for a sniper."

"Spread out!" Ingram waved his arm. "Make it hard on this guy."

"Why stay?" Cassidy put a hand on Rosie's head. If they left, Draco would have to come up with a different plan. If...this was his plan and not a game to divert their attention from something bigger. "Let me see the clue again."

"I wadded it up. Remember?" Ingram looked away.

"It said, 'No food or drink brings out the bite in every living creature.' We must be in the wrong place," Colin said.

"Then what else does it mean?" It didn't make sense to her.

"When was the last time anyone here ate or drank?" Colin

raised his eyebrows. "A while, I'm guessing. And what are we doing? Standing around arguing. Barking. He wants us all here."

Cassidy watched as the group scattered, taking up positions at various outlying buildings. Spotting a small toolshed, she motioned for Rosie to follow and made her way there. It offered a small amount of protection. The others should go where it was safe. She planned on finishing things today.

"Don't run off again." Colin stepped around the shed.

"I thought we weren't supposed to make it easy for him." Her fingers idly ran through Rosie's fur. "The others should go."

"They won't."

Even with his face in shadows, she knew a muscle ticked next to his well-defined lips. Every line of his body was rigid, on alert. She could very well lose him that night. The thought cut through her gut. He seemed as in tune with their surroundings as the well-trained Rosie.

Cassidy was too close to the situation. Her emotions jumbled. The desire to revenge her mother's death had her mind clouded. Sitting around waiting for something to happen was ludicrous. They needed to act before Draco did. She squatted in the shadows, waiting for him to strike.

"No."

She glanced at Colin. "No what?"

"No thinking of tackling this alone. Not now. You've tried that and it didn't work. Have you forgotten you were drugged and held captive for six weeks?"

"I haven't forgotten. You should have left me there."

"You told us where you were."

She sighed. "That was a mistake."

He knelt next to her. "It wasn't. We saved a few people working for him. You're free now."

"I won't be free until he's dead. All I've done was come up with one ridiculous idea after another to catch him. None of them have worked. You've been hospitalized twice because of my poor decisions."

He took her hands in his. "We can discuss all this later. Right now, we have a dragon to slay."

~

Draco pulled up the hood of his cloak. The officers had

scattered, just as he'd thought they would. It wouldn't matter. His plan would still take them all out.

He gazed with fondness at the trigger in his hand and the vest around his chest. One by one.

Stepping out the back door of one of the buildings, he managed to elude the officer turning the corner. Pace along, my friend. It will be the last stroll you take.

He stood in an alcove and glanced into the courtyard, not wanting to miss a single moment of excitement. Fifteen minutes from now, it would all be over and he could move on to dominating the next life.

~

An explosion blew apart a building across the courtyard.

Cassidy lunged to her feet. Law enforcement scattered.

The next building blew, then the next.

"He's herding us." She gripped Rosie's collar. "We need to get to the center of the courtyard."

Colin barked orders into his radio, then grabbed Cassidy's hand. "Stay next to me."

Her heart lurched as they stepped out into the open and met up with the law enforcement still able to move.

The buildings around them blew one by one, creating a ring of fire. Tears sprang to Cassidy's eyes as the shelter blew. "Tell me we got all the animals out."

"We did." Ingram put a hand to his leg. His wound had started bleeding again. "We've lost three men, though."

Another building exploded.

Everyone ducked.

Debris rained on their heads.

Rosie whined and trembled against Cassidy.

When the last building exploded, the group, eight of them left, formed a circle, standing back-to-back like warriors of old. Cassidy clutched her weapon, her eyes scanning the area lit by fire.

From the shadows stepped a cloaked figure. Draco! He approached them like a wraith, his steps leaving no sound.

Rosie barked. Rather than give the command to attack, Cassidy hushed her. To send the dog toward Draco was suicide.

No more chances. No more words. Cassidy lifted her weapon and fired. As she did, the other guns reported next to her.

Draco jerked like a marionette, seconds before he burst into flame.

His plan had been to finish off the rest by getting close enough to take them out with him. Cassidy's knees weakened and she sagged against Colin. "It's finally over." So much death, so much destruction.

A young man's obsession with a beautiful woman had resulted in a life of misery and murder.

~

As four fire trucks roared toward them, followed by two ambulances, Colin pulled Cassidy into his arms. Relief that it was over flooded through him strong enough to bring tears. He'd done it. He'd kept Cassidy alive. The nightmares would end for good.

He rested his chin on her head and glanced at the survivors. None of them had escaped unscathed. All were peppered with at least minor cuts. It wasn't until Cassidy shifted in his embrace that he realized a shard of wood protruded from his leg.

"Limp over to the medic with me," he grinned.

"How can you grin with that thing in your leg?" She returned his smile. "I suppose I could grin with a bullet in every limb of my body, now that it's over."

"I'm sorry that your father turned out to be…crazy."

She chuckled. "He's only the sperm donor. Unfortunately, my mother had no choice in who sired me."

As giddy as they were with relief and lack of rest, Colin knew they'd crash and sleep for hours once they returned home. When they returned home. With a crime scene this large, it would be daybreak by the time they finished.

Cassidy stood next to him while a paramedic dabbed her cuts and removed the wood from his leg. What a pair they were. The last six months had given them more scars then the previous years together. Not only physical ones, but emotional as well.

Brave face or not, Cassidy's smile was fading as she took in the carnage around them.

"It isn't your fault," he said.

"I know. But, I am a factor in all this, whether I want to be or not." Tears filled her eyes as she glanced at him. "I've proven myself worthy, Colin. To be a detective, to be free, to be an avenger. I wish it hadn't taken something so big…so destructive...for me to see it."

He put his arm around her. "You've always been worthy, sweetheart. From the moment you were conceived, your path was laid before you. All you had to do was walk down it."

"My vision was clouded with revenge."

"And mine with regret." He tilted her face toward his and placed a tender kiss on her lips. "We have plans to make, my dear. Plans for the future. After we get some rest."

A soft smile graced her lips. "I'm in total agreement."

The sun was higher in the sky than he'd predicted by the time they got home. Rather than go to their individual beds, the two of them spooned together on the couch and didn't rise until supper time when the ringing telephone disturbed their slumber.

Colin stretched to pull his phone from his pocket. "Yeah?"

"Open the door," Ingram said. "I've something for Cassidy."

"Time to get up, sleeping beauty." He sat, helping Cassidy to a sitting position, then moved to let Ingram in. "Don't you ever sleep?"

"I'll catch up tonight." Ingram handed him a sealed envelope. "Outside the perimeter of the explosions, we found a box. In it was the address to Draco's other house. In his office, we found this."

Cassidy took the letter from him. "I'm afraid to open it. What if this isn't over?"

~

With her finger, Cassidy peeled back the flap on the envelope and pulled out a letter

"Daughter, my time has come to an end. If you're reading this, I've failed to take you with me into the hereafter. Rest assured in the fact that I loved your mother. What she did to me was cruel and unexpected. Her beauty hid an ugliness that the world needed to be rid of." She glanced up.

"What a crock of bull." She continued reading.

"I'm dying of cancer. The doctor gave me six weeks to live. My death by fire was a fitting end for a dragon don't you think? My parting words to you are...keep looking over your shoulder. You never know when another dragon will emerge. Draco."

Cassidy sagged into the nearest chair. "Did we round up his followers?"

Ingram nodded. "Yes, but those that didn't carry out their

threats can't be held."

It might not be over after all. She squared her shoulders. She wouldn't live her life in fear. No more vengeance. She'd act worthy of the badge she carried and the man she loved. "This," she shook the letter, "is nothing more than a last ditch effort to spread fear. I refuse to allow him to have the last word." She ripped the letter into shreds. "Let's order a pizza. I'm starved."

"There's more," Ingram said. "Russell Blake left you his fortune."

"Get rid of it." She didn't want his money.

"Wait a second, sweetheart." Colin sat next to her. "The man was worth millions. Sell his property and do good with the money. Use his evil gain to help others."

She smiled. "Wouldn't that be a thorn in his side? We can rebuild the buildings he's destroyed, give funds to the families of his victims and erect an angel gravestone over my mother's grave. What a great idea. I'll give every cent of it away."

"I'm going to skip the pizza." Ingram rubbed his hands over his eyes. "I'm beat and heading home."

Cassidy watched him limp toward the door, then rushed forward to give him a hug. "Thank you. For everything. I'm terribly sorry for the loss of your friends."

He returned her hug. "They would say their lives were worth it to get rid of such a menace. I'm sure we'll work together again. In fact…the two of you would make great FBI agents."

"No, thanks." She glanced back at Colin. "I think we'll protect Clear Springs together."

Colin shook Ingram's hand, then slipped his arm around Cassidy's waist. "I like that idea. Mr. and Mrs. MacKenzie providing a service to this town."

"Are you proposing?" Her mouth dropped open.

"I guess I am. I'll give you the ring later. So?"

She laughed, throwing her arms around his neck. "You can go now, Ingram. I need to kiss my husband-to-be and we might embarrass you."

He chuckled and closed the door behind him as he left.

10

Three weeks later

Cassidy placed her wedding bouquet on her mother's grave and remained kneeling there. "I did it. I brought Russell down, with the help of a good man. I wish you would have been here to see us, maybe have gotten a little justice of your own."

Refusing to wear white because of the color being associated with Russell, Cassidy smoothed her hand over the blue gown she wore. "The wedding was beautiful. Simple, by the lake, with only close friends." Those who were left, anyway. "The sun sparkled on the water, and a butterfly landed on Colin's hair." As if God himself were placing a blessing on their union.

"You'd like him, Mom. He's kind and handsome, always putting others first." She swiped her hand across her eyes. "I'm finally happy. For so long there had been this huge hole inside of me. Revenge ate at me like the cancer spreading through Russell's body. With his death, I tasted freedom and the ability to open my heart to love. Oh, how I wish you were here."

Footsteps behind her signaled Colin's approach. He held out his hand and pulled her close. "I wish I could have met her."

"The two of you would have gotten along very well." She leaned into him, breathing deep of his musky cologne. "She would have teased you about your tux. Which, you look very handsome in, by the way."

He chuckled. "The others are waiting at the veteran's hall to eat. Are you ready?"

Face heating she said, "I'd rather head straight to the

honeymoon." She tapped a button on his jacket. "You, sir, have been a distraction."

"No more so than you. I'd take you to the hotel now, but I want our first time together to be beautiful. I intend to take my time with you."

She didn't think her face could get any hotter. "Then, we'd best get to the hall and eat before we brush off our guests."

She glanced once more at her mother's grave and smiled. Mom could rest in peace. "I love you, Mom," she whispered.

The End

ABOUT THE AUTHOR

www.cynthiahickey.com

Cynthia Hickey is a multi-published and best-selling author of cozy mysteries and romantic suspense. She has taught writing at many conferences and small writing retreats. She and her husband run the publishing press, Winged Publications. They live in Arizona and Arkansas, becoming snowbirds with three dogs. They have ten grandchildren who keep them busy and tell everyone they know that "Nana is a writer."